IMAGINARY
MAGNITUDE

ALSO BY STANISLAW LEM

STANISLAW LEM

IMAGINARY MAGNITUDE

Translated from the Polish by
Marc E. Heine

A Helen and Kurt Wolff Book
A Harvest/HBJ Book
Harcourt Brace Jovanovich, Publishers
San Diego   New York   London

In accordance with the author's wishes, this English-language edition of *Imaginary Magnitude* includes all the material that appeared in *Wielkość urojona* (Czytelnik, Warsaw, 1973) and also incorporates "Lecture XLIII—About Itself" and "Afterword," which first appeared in *Golem XIV* (Wydawnictwo Literackie, Cracow, 1981).

Publisher's note: Names of actual persons and entities appearing in this work of fiction are included solely for purposes of verisimilitude.

The "Proffertinc" portion of *Vestrand's Extelopedia in 44 Magnetomes* appeared originally in *The New Yorker*.

Library of Congress Cataloging in Publication Data

Lem, Stanisław.
  Imaginary magnitude.

  Translation of: Wielkość urojona.
  "A Helen and Kurt Wolff Book."
  "... this English-language edition also incorporates 'Lecture XLIII—About Itself' and 'Afterword,' which first appeared in Golem XIV (Wydawnictwo Literackie, Cracow, 1981)"—T.p. verso.
  I. Title.
PG7158.L39W513   1984   891.8'537   83-18624
ISBN 0-15-644180-2(pbk.)

Designed by Mark Likgalter

Printed in the United States of America

First Harvest edition 1985

BCDEFGHIJ

CONTENTS

IMAGINARY
MAGNITUDE

Introduction

The art of writing Introductions has long demanded proper recognition. I too have long felt a pressing need to rescue this form of writing from the silence of forty centuries—from its bondage to the works to which its creations have been chained. When, if not in this age of ecumenicalism—that is to say, of all-powerful reason—is one finally to grant independence to this noble, unrecognized genre? I had in fact counted on somebody else fulfilling this obligation, which is not only aesthetically in line with the evolutionary course of art, but, morally, downright imperative. Unfortunately, I had miscalculated. I watch and wait in vain: somehow nobody has brought Introduction-writing out of the house of bondage, off the treadmill of villein service. So I have no choice: out of a sense of obligation rather than an impulse of the heart, I shall rush to the aid of Introduction-writing and become its liberator and obstetrician.

That long-suffering realm has its own lower kingdom—one of plodding, sometimes unpublished, and venal hired Introductions, for servitude depraves. It also knows presumption and bombast, the flowery gesture and the Jerichonic blast. Besides rank-and-file Introductions there are the upper echelons such as Forewords and Prefaces, nor are even ordinary Introductions all alike, for an Introduction to one's own book is one thing, and that to somebody else's quite another. Likewise, using one to introduce a first printing is different from going to the trouble of multiplying one's Introductions for numerous later printings. The power of a collection of Introductions, even bland ones, overgrowing a persistently—and insistently—published work, turns paper into a tower of strength, frustrating the machinations of venomous critics—for who would dare attack a book with such an armored breastwork, behind which it is not so much its content as its inviolable respectability that shows through!

An Introduction is often a foretoken tempered by dignity or pride, a promissory note signed by the author, or it may be a manifestation constrained by convention, perfunctory though amicable, of some authority's sham commitment to a book: that is, its safe conduct, its passport into society, a viaticum from mighty lips —a futile grip pulling up something which is going to drown anyway. But these are irredeemable notes and very few have any gold backing, let alone bear interest. But I shall ignore all that. I do not intend to go into the taxonomy of Introduction-writing or even an elementary classification of this previously slighted and haltered genre. Coach horses and jades move similarly when harnessed to it. Let the Linnaeuses occupy themselves with the tractive side of things. That is not the sort of Introduction that is going to precede my little anthology of Liberated Introductions.

Here we must get down to brass tacks. What can an Introduction be? Barefaced boasting and self-advertising, to be sure, but also the wilderness cries of a John the Baptist or Roger Bacon. Therefore upon reflection we see that, besides Introductions to Works, there are Introduction Works, for like the Holy Scriptures of any faith, the theses and futuromachies of scholars are Prefaces—to this world and the other. Thus reflection shows that the Realm of Introductions is incomparably more vast than the Realm of Literature, for what the latter endeavors to *realize*, Introductions merely announce from afar.

To that growing question—why on earth must we enter into the liberation struggle of Introductions and present them as a sovereign literary genre?—the answer is clear from what has already been said. We can supply the answer either in a flash, or with the help of higher hermeneutics. In the first place, this project can be justified without bombast—and with calculator in hand. Are we not threatened with a flood of information? And is this not the monstrousness of it, that it crushes beauty by means of beauty, and annihilates truth by means of truth? For the sound of a million Shakespeares would produce the very same furious din and hubbub as the sound of a herd of prairie buffalo or sea billows. Such vastly multiplied content in collision brings no credit to thought, but rather its destruction. When faced with such a fate, is not Silence alone the redeeming Ark of the Covenant between the Creator and the Reader, since the Creator gains merit by refraining from spinning out just any old content, and the reader gains it by praising such manifest self-denial? To be sure. And one might refrain from writing *even* the Introductions themselves, though then the act of self-restraint would not be perceived, so the sacrifice would not be accepted. Thus my Introductions are announcements of sins from which I shall abstain. I do this from a standpoint of cool and purely external calculation. But this reckoning still fails to reveal what Art gains from its declared liberation. We already know that even too much heavenly manna leads to costiveness. How can we save ourselves from it? How can we save our souls from self-constipation? And is salvation really to be found here—does the true way really pass through Introductions?

Summoned like some luminous doctor, that yeoman of hermeneutical practitioners, Witold Gombrowicz, would have explained the matter as follows. It is not a question of whether the idea of separating Introductions from the Content which they are supposed to announce pleased anyone, even me—because it did not. For we are subject, without appeal, to the laws of the Evolution of Form. Art cannot stand still or go round in circles: precisely because of this, it cannot *merely* please. If you lay an egg, you must hatch it; if a mammal hatches from it instead of a reptile, you should give

3

it something to suck; if, therefore, a subsequent move brings us to something which arouses general repugnance or even nausea, it cannot be helped: *that's* what we've produced. We have pushed so very far and dragged ourselves there, and by a command superior to pleasure we shall have to turn over and over again—in our eyes, ears, and minds—the New, categorically applied, for it has been discovered on a path leading high up and far away, where admittedly no one has ever been or wants to be, since nobody knows whether one could bear it there for even a moment—though, in fact, for the Development of Culture, this is of no importance whatsoever! This lemma, with an offhandedness characteristic of nonchalant genius, bids us exchange one old, spontaneous, and therefore unconscious bondage for a new one; it does not cut the fetters, but merely lengthens our lead, for it drives us into the Unknown, calling freedom a clear necessity.

But—I frankly confess—I myself crave a different basis for heresy and rebellion. So let me say this: there is something of the truth in what is said in the first and second place, though not the whole truth—nor does it altogether resemble necessity, for in the third place we may apply to creation the algebra which we detect in the Almighty.

Please observe how chatty the Bible is, how prolix the Pentateuch is, in describing the *outcome* of Genesis—and how laconic in giving the recipe for it! There had been neither time nor form until suddenly—for no apparent reason—the Lord said: "Let there be light," whereupon there was light, but between the two was there nothing. No fissure, no mean? I don't believe it! Between Chaos and Creation there was pure intention, which was still untouched by the light, not fully bound to the Cosmos, unsoiled—even by the paradisial earth.

For that was the origin of chance, then and there, though not its fulfillment; there was a purpose, moreover a divine and therefore omnipotent one, that had yet to go into action. There was an annunciation before the conception.

How can we not use this knowledge? It is a question not of plagiarism but of method. Where does all this come from? From the beginning, of course. And what was at the beginning? An Introduction, as we already know. An Introduction, though not an arrogant, high-handed one, but an Introduction to Something. Let us defy the disorderly materializing of Genesis; to its first lemma let us apply the algebra of a more restrained creation!

In other words, let us divide the whole by "Something." "Something" will then disappear, and as our solution we shall be left with an Introduction purged of unpleasant consequences, of any threat of Incarnation, because it is purely intentional and in that state undefiled by sin. This is not the world, merely an undimensional point —but in infinity for precisely that reason. Very soon we shall tell how to bring literature to it. But first let us look at her neighbors, for she is certainly no anchorite.

All the arts today are struggling to perform a rescue operation, for the universal expansion of creativity has become its curse, a race, and an escape; like the Universum, Art is exploding into the void, encountering no resistance and consequently no support. If anything is now possible, then everything has some value, and the rush forward turns into a retreat, since the Arts want to return to their source, but do not know how.

In its burning desire for limits, painting has got inside the painters —inside their very skins—and behold, the artist now exhibits himself without pictures! Thus he is an iconoclast lashed by his brushes or covered in oil and tempera, or he turns up completely naked on varnishing day, without the slightest dash of color. Unfortunately the poor wretch is unable to achieve authentic nakedness: he is no Adam, but merely a gentleman in a state of undress.

And the sculptor, whether shoving his unpolished stone at us or exhibiting any old idealized rubbish, seeks to crawl back to the Paleolithic period—to primitive man—for that is what he wants to become: an Original! A cave man, indeed! This is hardly the way to the raw flesh of savage expression! *Naturalia non sunt turpia*—but that does not mean that any and every boorish barbarianism is a return to Nature!

But what is, I ask you? Let us explain this through the example of music, since the greatest and most immediate opportunity lies wide open before it. Composers are wrong to break the bones of counterpoint and smash the Bachs to smithereens by computer; likewise, using electrons to tread on the tail of a cat amplified a hundredfold yields nothing, except a pack of artificial howlers. That is the wrong course and produces the wrong tone! A savior—an innovator—conscious of his goal has yet to come!

I await him impatiently. I am waiting for his work of *concrete music*, which in delivering us from lies returns to the bosom of Nature, a work which will be the consolidation of those choral, though strictly private, performances to which every audience surrenders in the concert hall—an audience which is cultural only in the externals of its concentration, and which contemplates the sweating orchestra only as a familiar periphery of organisms.

This symphony will be overheard by a hundred microphones, and I expect it will have the dark, monotonous orchestration characteristic of bowels, for its tonal background will be created by jejune basses, or the borborygmus of persons passionate in their ineluctable collywobbles—rumbling-based, gurglingly perfect, and full of desperate digestive expression, for this voice of the bowels—the voice of life!—is authentic because it is organic but not like organ music. I trust too that the leitmotiv will develop in time with the seated percussion, accented by the creaking of chairs, with violent, convulsive nose-blowing entrances, and chords of magnificent coloratura coughing. The bronchitises will start up, and I predict quite a number of solos here, executed with all the masterly skill of asthmatic old age, a veritable *memento mori vivace ma non troppo*, a display of agonized piccolo, for an authentic corpse will start snapping its dentures in three-four time, and a decent grave will start whistling in a death-rattled windpipe. Well, so biological a truth of symphonic procedure cannot be falsified!

The entire somatic initiative of bodies, hitherto so falsely stifled in the world by artificial music despite their irrevocably—and therefore tragically personal—sounds, cries out for triumphant revindication as a Return to Nature. I cannot be wrong, I know that the first performance of the Visceral Symphony will be a breakthrough, for in this way only will the traditionally passive audience, reduced to rustling peppermint wrappers, take the initiative—at last!—and in the role of a self-realizing auto-orchestra perform a *return to itself*, passionate in its denial of all "falsehood," that slogan of our age.

The composer-creator will once again become purely the priest-intermediary between the terrified multitude and Moira, for the fate of our entrails is our Destiny. That is how a distinguished community of listener-experts will perceive the auto-symphony, and with no outside twangings, since in this first performance they will then be savoring themselves alone—and they will be scared.

And what about literature? You have probably already guessed: I want to give you back your soul in all its range, just as visceral music gives the audience back its own body: in the very heart of Civilization, it descends to Nature.

This is precisely why Introduction-writing can no longer remain under the curse of bondage, excluded from liberating works. It is not only fiction writers and their readers that I am inciting to revolt. And I mean rebellion, not a general muddle—not egging on the spectators so that they climb up on the stage, or the stage climbs out after them, as a result of which they lose their previous position of agreeable superiority and, with their audience refuge liquidated, find themselves thrust into St. Vitus' cauldron. Neither twitching nor the distorted mimicry of yoga, but Thought alone can restore our freedom to us. Thus, by denying me the right of a liberation struggle in the name of—and for the good of—Introductions, you would be doomed, dear reader, to obscurantism and to the obdurately outdated, and even if you did not know how old-fashioned you had become, you still would not enter modern times.

You on the other hand, reader, being adept in anticipating the

New—you, progressive with rapid reflexes, vibrating freely in the fashion flows of our era, who know that, since we have crawled higher than our primitive simian cousin (onto the moon, even), must continue to climb—you will understand me and join me in feeling that a duty is being fulfilled.

I shall deceive you, and for that you will be grateful to me. I shall make you a solemn promise with no intention of keeping it, and that will satisfy you, or at any rate you will pretend that it does, with appropriate masterly skill; whereas, to fools who would want to excommunicate us both, you will say that in spirit they have fallen from the times and landed on a rubbish heap spat out by a precipitate Reality.

You will tell them there is nothing to be done: today art has become a promissory note without (transcendental) cover, a (counterfeit) pledge, an (unrealistic) forecast—the highest form of alteration. It is precisely this emptiness of art and its unrealizability which should be taken as its motto and bedrock. That is why I am right to present an Introduction to this short Anthology of Introductions, for I am proposing prefaces that lead nowhere, introductions that go nowhere, and forewords followed by no words at all.

But with each of these initial moves I shall reveal to you an emptiness of a different kind and a different semantic color, changing according to a typical Heidegger spectral line. With enthusiasm, hope, and much to-do I shall open the altar and triptych doors, and announce the inconostasis with its holy gates; I shall kneel on stairs breaking off at the threshold of a void—a void not so much abandoned as one in which nothing has ever been or ever shall be. This gravest possible amusement, this simply tragic amusement, is a parable of our destiny, since there is no device so human, nor such a property and mainstay of humanity, as a full-sounding, responsibility-devoid, utterly soul-absorbing Introduction to Nothingness.

This whole rocky, green, cold, humming world, kindled in clouds and buried in stars, we share with the animals and plants, though Nothingness is our domain and special department. The explorer of this nothingness is man. But it is a difficult thing, unusual by virtue of being nonexistent, which cannot even be tasted without careful seasoning and spiritual exercises, without lengthy study and training; it paralyzes the unready, which is why for communicating with a precisely tuned, richly orchestrated nothingness one must be conscientiously prepared, making one's every step toward it as firm, distinct, and substantial as possible.

So I shall show you Introductions as one shows a richly carved doorframe chased in gold and surmounted by counts and griffins on a majestic lintel. I shall swear by its solid, harmoniously massive side facing us, so that as I open it with the concentrated effort of the arms of my spirit, I may thrust the reader into nothing and thereby simultaneously snatch him away from all existences and worlds.

I promise and guarantee a wonderful freedom, and give my word that Nothing will be there.

What shall I gain? The state of greatest riches: the one prior to Creation.

What will you gain? Supreme liberty, for no words of mine will obtrude upon your ear in your pure upward flight. I shall take you only as a pigeon-fancier takes a pigeon, and slings it like David's stone, like a rock in the path, so that it may fly off into this immensity—for eternal enjoyment.

Cezary Strzybisz

NECROBES

139 Reproductions

Introduction by Stanislaw Ertel

Zodiac Publishers

Introduction

A few years ago artists seized upon death as their life-saver. Equipped with anatomical and histological atlases, they began disemboweling their nudes, poking about in their entrails, dumping out onto their canvases the battered ugliness of our embarrassing bits and pieces, so rightly hidden by skin from everyday view. But even so, the concerts which putrefaction in all the colors of the rainbow began presenting in exhibition rooms proved to be no revelation. It might have seemed debauchery if any of the spectators had taken offense; it might have appeared nightmarish if anyone had shuddered; but—would you believe it?—even the old ladies failed to get upset. Midas turned all he touched to gold, but the artist of today, suffering from the opposite sort of curse, annihilates the dignity of every object by the mere stroke of his brush. Like a drowning man, he clutches at anything—and sinks to the bottom with it—amid the blasé indifference of onlookers.

Anything? Even death? Why has its antimajesty not shocked us, or should those blood-scoured pages of enlarged illustrations of forensic medicine not at least have given us cause for reflection by their sheer horror?

Yet they could not, for they were too forced! The intention was childish: to frighten the grown-ups—which is why it could not be taken seriously! So instead of a *memento mori* we were given carefully disheveled corpses; the too importunately revealed secret of the grave manifested itself as a slimy cesspool. That kind of death failed to convince, because it was too ostentatious! The poor artists, finding nature no longer sufficient, set about escalating Grand Guignol, duping themselves.

But after such loss of face, when death "flopped," what in fact did Strzybisz do to rehabilitate it? What in fact were his Necrobes? After all, they are not art: Strzybisz does not paint and appears never in his life to have held a brush. Nor are they graphics, for he does not draw, nor does he engrave in any material, nor is he a sculptor. No, he is a photographer—a particular kind, to be sure, for instead of light, he employs X-rays.

Using his eyes, extended by the snouts of his X-ray equipment, this anatomist goes straight through bodies. But the black-and-white films that we know from doctors' consulting rooms would doubtless leave us indifferent. Which is why he has animated his nudes. Which is also why his skeletons move about at such a buoyant, determined pace, with their raglan shrouds and phantom briefcases. Rather mischievous and bizarre they are, to be sure, nothing more, but he was merely trying these snapshots on for size, he is still experimenting, he didn't know for sure. The uproar began only when he dared to do something terrible (though "terrible" things were no longer supposed to exist): he X-rayed us clean through, and thereby revealed sex.

This collection of Strzybisz's work opens with his

Pornograms, which are truly comic, though in a rather cruel way. What Strzybisz has captured within the leaden diaphragm of his lenses is the most obtrusive, licentious, audacious form of sex: group sex. It has been said that he wanted to deride pornomania, that he gave an accurate reading of it (one reduced to its bare bones), and that he has succeeded since these bones, clinging to one another in a puzzling geometrical arrangement, suddenly—and eerily—leap into the eye of the beholder like a modern dance of death with gamboling, spawning skeletons. It has also been said that he was trying to abuse and deride sex itself—and has succeeded.

Is that correct? Undoubtedly, though in the Necrobes it is possible to discern something more. Caricatures? Not only that, for despite everything the Pornograms contain a kind of hidden dignity. Perhaps this is because Strzybisz "tells the truth"—and only the truth, which, when not subjected to "artistic deformation," is today considered vulgarity—though in point of fact he is purely a witness, for his gaze is piercing but not distorting. There is no defense against this evidence, no way of dismissing it as a fabrication, as a convention, a trick, or a banal little game, for he is right. A caricature? A prank? But when all is said and done, these skeletons are, in their abstract delineation, almost aesthetic. For Strzybisz has acted with consummate skill: he has not so much laid bare—torn the bones from their bodily shell—as freed them, honestly searching for their proper meaning with no further reference to *us*. Searching for their proper geometry, he has made them sovereign.

The skeletons have, one is tempted to say, a life of their own. He has endowed them with freedom through the vaporization of their bodies—that is to say, through death—though bodies play an important, albeit not immediately perceptible, role in the Necrobes. It is difficult here to go into the details of X-ray technique, but a few words of explanation are essential. Had Strzybisz used hard X-rays, the bones alone would have been visible in his photographs, like sharply outlined strips or rods, segmented as if by cuts—the murkiness of articular interstices. They would have been too neat, too skeletonized, an osteological abstraction. But he never works that way; indeed, X-rayed by means of soft rays, human bodies appear in his photographs as allusions, as intimations, milky whiffs of faint light, and through this he achieves his particular effect. Appearance and reality change places. The medieval, Holbeinesque dance of death which persistently lurks impassive within us— the very same adhesion of death and life, untouched by the hurly-burly of glittering civilization—this Strzybisz achieves unwittingly, as if by accident. For we can recognize that same lively pace, that jovial vigor and frivolous passion which Holbein—and only Holbein—gave to his skeletons. Or rather, the piecework of denotations which this contemporary artist undertakes is broader, since he has adopted the most *modern* technique for the *oldest* problem of the species: death's appearance in the midst of life. And it is precisely the X-rayed mechanics of a propagating genus which the bodies assist, as pale specters.

Fine, you may say, maybe that's the philosophy behind it, but when all is said and done, he has deliberately gone the "whole hog"—he has worked copulating couples into his corpses, he has taken up a *fashionable* theme, effectively and for effect. Isn't that cheap? Isn't there a shrewdness in his Pornograms? Or simply a fraud? There is no lack of such judgments. I prefer not to wheel out against him the artillery of heavy rhetoric. Instead, I would ask you to have a look at the twenty-second Pornogram, entitled "The Triple Leaf."

This scene is indecent in a particular way. If one were to compare it with an ordinary photograph of the same people—a product of commercial photography—the innocence of such pornography as compared to the X-ray photograph would immediately become obvious.

For pornography is not directly obscene: it excites only as long as there is a struggle within the viewer between lust and the angel of culture. When the devils carry off the angel; when, as a result of general tolerance, the weakness of sexual prohibitions—their complete helplessness—is laid bare; when prohibitions are thrown on the rubbish heap, then how quickly pornography betrays its innocent (which here means ineffective) character, for it is a false promise of carnal bliss, an augury of something which does not in fact come true. It is the forbidden fruit, so there is as much temptation in it as there is power in the prohibition.

And so? Our eyes, growing indifferent through repetition, catch a glimpse of nudes wriggling around and exhausting themselves as they carry out their assignments in the studio—and how poor the spectacle then seems. A feeling not so much of embarrassment as of offended human solidarity awakens in the beholder, for these nudes muck about with one another so importunately that they resemble children bent on doing something monstrous to shock adults, but who really cannot, being in no position to—and their imagination, now merely enraged by their own impotence, leads not toward Sin and the Fall, but simply to idiotically pathetic ugliness. That is why, in the persistent activities of those big, naked animals, there lurks a shallow infantilism; it is neither hell nor heaven, but a lukewarm sphere: tedium and the futility of poorly compensated effort.

But Strzybisz's work is predatory, for it is as horrific and comic as those trips of the damned into the abyss in old Dutch and Italian paintings. Since, however, we can distance ourselves from these sinners somersaulting into the Last Judgment, since we have canceled the next world, what can we oppose to the X-ray picture? In these clinches, in which their bodies are an impassable obstacle to them, the skeletons are tragically comic. Mere bones? When we see people in an awkward, desperate embrace, it would be merely pitiable, were it not for the ghastly comic element. Where does it come from? From us—for we recognize the truth. The justification of these clinches evaporates along with their corporality, and that is why their embraces are so sterile and abstract, and at the same time so terribly matter-of-fact, icy, and pale, so hopeless.

And in addition their holiness, or the mockery of it, or the allusion to it, which is not fixed, not heightened by artificial manipulation, but visible, for here a halo surrounds every head—their hair becomes a pale, round aureole and candle, as in holy pictures.

I know, moreover, how difficult it is to disentangle and begin defining impulses from which the totality of feelings arises in the spectator. For some, this is literally Holbein redivivus, since in reality there is something peculiar about this reversion—by electromagnetic radiation—to the skeletons, as if to a Middle Ages preserved within us. Others are shocked by bodies resembling powerless spirits attending out of necessity the difficult practices of a sex rendered unseen. Someone else has written that the skeletons are like instruments removed from their cases for the performance of an esoteric initiation, which is why people have spoken of the "mathematics" or "geometry" of this kind of sex.

That may well be; though hardly speculative in origin is the sadness into which Strzybisz's art sinks. The symbolism, arising over the centuries and bequeathed by the centuries (though secretly vegetating, since we disowned it), did not, as we see, succumb to destruction. We have transformed this symbolism into signalization (skulls and crossbones on high-tension poles and on bottles of poison in drug stores) and into classroom visual aids, in the form of skeletons held together by gleaming wires in lecture halls. So we have condemned it to an exodus, we have exiled it from life, but we have not rid ourselves of it entirely. Unable to separate a skeleton's most substantial corporality, equal to the eloquence of an antler or a soldier's stripes, from that which represents in it the silence of fate and thus a symbol, our intellect falls into that particular frustration from which it finally escapes through salutary laughter. Yet we comprehend that this is a somewhat forced gaiety, and that we are shielding ourselves behind it in order not to succumb too much to Strzybisz.

Erotica as a desperate futility of intention, and sex as an exercise in projection geometry—these are the two opposite extremes of the Pornograms. Nor do I agree with those who maintain that Strzybisz's art begins and ends with the Pornograms. If I had to say which of the nudes I value the most, I would say without hesitation the "Pregnant Woman" (p. 128). A mother to be with her child enclosed in her womb, this skeleton within a skeleton is fairly cruel and in no way untrue. In this big, stalwart body, its pelvic bone branching like white wings (an X-ray picture hits upon the purpose of sex more forcibly than the typical nude), against a background of these wings already parted for childbirth, there is the little skeletor. of the nestling child—hazy, being still incomplete, its little head down. How false these words sound, and how pure and proud a whole the light-and-shade effects of the X-ray create! A pregnant woman in her prime and in her death, and the still unborn foetus which has already begun to die by virtue of having been conceived. There is a kind of tranquillity of challenge and a determined affirmation in this act of observation.

What will it be like a year from now? The Necrobes will have sunk into oblivion, their place taken by new techniques and fashions. (Poor Strzybisz, how many imitators has he already acquired, in the wake of his success!) Isn't this the case? Undoubtedly, nor can it be helped. But even though this rapid inconstancy strangles us, dooming us to a series of ceaseless resignations and separations, today Strzybisz has favored us lavishly. He has not fallen into the depths of the matter, he has not penetrated into the exotica of detecting the purposeless perfections of Nature, into those investigations by which science has contaminated art, but he has brought us to the borders of our bodies, in no way distorted, exaggerated, or changed—our real bodies!—and by doing this he has erected bridges from the present into the past, reviving that dignity which art has lost. It is not his fault that this resurrection lasts only a few minutes.

ERUNTICS

Reginald Gulliver

George Allen & Unwin Limited
40 Museum Street, London

Introduction

The future historian will doubtless find two mutually pervading explosions to be the most appropriate model for our society. Avalanches of intellectual products mechanically dumped on the market come in contact with consumers by coincidences just as fortuitous as those that control the collisions of gas molecules: no longer can anyone encompass the multitude of these products in their entirety. And since nowhere is it easier to lose oneself than in a multitude, the entrepreneurs of culture, precisely because they publish everything that authors give them, exist in the blissful but mistaken conviction that now nothing valuable is being wasted. Individual books are deemed worthy of attention by the decision of competent experts who eliminate from their field of vision everything outside their own speciality. This process of elimination is the defensive reflex of every expert: were he less ruthless, he would drown in a flood of paper. But as a result, a statelessness equal to civil death threatens everything which, by virtue of being completely new, defies the bases of classification. The book which I am introducing lies precisely in no man's land. It may be the result of lunacy, but in that case we are talking about a madness with precise methods; it may be the product of pseudological perfidy, but then it would not be perfidious enough, for it would be unsalable. Both reason and haste would have one pass over such an oddity in silence, but notwithstanding all the tediousness of discourse, a spirit of extraordinary heresy shines through it and stops one in one's tracks. Bibliographies have listed this title under science fiction, but this area has by now become a dumping ground for all sorts of half-baked oddities relegated from more serious spheres. Were Plato to publish *The Republic* today, or Darwin *On the Origin of Species*, both books might bear the label "fantasy," whereupon they would be read by everybody and appreciated by nobody; sinking into sensational verbiage, they would play no part in the development of ideas.

This book deals with bacteria, though no bacteriologist will take it seriously. It pursues a linguistics that would make any language specialist's hair stand on end. It arrives at a futurology contradicting that practiced by futurology's professional exponents. Which is precisely why, as an outcast of all the scientific disciplines, it must drop to the level of science fiction and act the part, though it cannot count on readers, since it offers nothing that might satisfy a thirst for adventure.

I am not in a position to give a proper judgment on *Eruntics*, yet I feel that there is no competent preface writer for it. I am usurping this position uneasily: who can ever know how much truth lurks behind such deep audacity? At a glance, the book looks like a scientific handbook, though it is a pack of absurdities. It makes no pretense to literary fantasy, for it is not an artistic composition. If it depicts the truth, this truth belies virtually the whole of contemporary knowledge. If it lies, it does so in monstrous proportions.

As the author explains, eruntics (Die Eruntizitätslehre, eruntica, eruntique—the name comes from the Latin *erunt*, "they will be," the third person plural of the future tense of *esse*) was not intended to be a form of prognostics or futurology. It is impossible to learn eruntics, since nobody knows the principles by which it functions. It cannot be used to forecast anything one might desire. It is not "esoteric knowledge," like astrology or dianetics, nor is it natural scientific orthodoxy. We are dealing with something condemned to be an "outcast from all worlds."

R. Gulliver introduces himself in the first chapter as a philosopher-dilettante and amateur bacteriologist who one day eighteen years ago decided to teach bacteria English. His impulse was of an accidental nature. On the crucial day he removed from his thermostat some petri dishes, those shallow glass containers in which bacteria *in vitro* are grown on agar gelatine. Until then he had, as he says, merely dabbled in bacteriology, for he pursued it as a kind of hobby, with no pretensions or hopes of any discoveries. He admits that he simply liked observing the growth of microorganisms on their bed of agar: he marveled at the "cleverness" of the invisible "plantlets," forming colonies the size of a pinhead on the filmy surface. To study the effectiveness of antibacterial agents, he introduced large quantities of these agents onto the agar with a pipette or a dipper; where they were effective, the agar remained free of bacterial coating. As laboratory technicians sometimes do, R. Gulliver dipped a wad of cotton in an antibiotic and wrote "yes" with it on the smooth surface of the agar. By the following day this invisible inscription had become visible, for the bacteria, multiplying intensively, had covered the whole of the agar with the tubercles of the colony, except for the mark left by the cotton which he had used as a kind of pen. It was then, he says, that it first occurred to him that this process might be "reversed."

The inscription was visible because it was free of bacteria. But were the microbes to arrange themselves into letters, they would be writing and thus expressing themselves in language. The idea was tempting but at the same time, he admits, totally nonsensical. After all, it was he who had written the word "yes" on the agar, whereas the bacteria had merely "developed" the inscription, being unable to multiply within it. But thereafter the idea gave him no rest. On the eighth day he set to work.

Bacteria are one hundred percent unreasoning and thus surely unreasonable. However, by virtue of the position they occupy in Nature, they are superb chemists. Pathogenic organisms learned how to overcome the bodily barriers and protective constitutional forces of animals hundreds of millions of years ago. This is understandable if one considers that they did nothing else for ages and ages, so they had time enough to push the aggressive albeit blind means of their chemisms into the protective wall of the proteins by which large organisms are shielded. Likewise, when man appeared in history they attacked him and, during the ten to twenty thousand years civilization has existed, inflicted diseases on him resulting in notorious plagues and at various times the death of entire populations.

Less than eighty years ago man hit upon a more powerful counterattack, bringing down upon bacteria an army of his own—selective synthetic poisons, striking their life processes. In this extremely short period he has produced over 48,000 chemical antibacterial weapons, synthesized with the purpose of striking at the most sensitive sore points of their metabolism, growth, and reproduction. He did this in the belief that he would presently wipe germs off the face of the earth, but he was soon amazed to find that, while checking the expansion of microbes—called epidemics—he had not liquidated a single disease. Bacteria proved to be a better equipped opponent than the creators of selective chemotherapy had imagined. No matter what new concoctions from the retort man uses, bacteria, by laying down hecatombs in this (so it would seem) unequal struggle, soon adapt the poisons to themselves or themselves to the poisons, and develop resistance.

Science does not know exactly how they do this, and what it does know seems highly unlikely. Bacteria surely have no theoretical knowledge in the fields of chemistry or immunology. They are unable to conduct either test experiments or strategic deliberations; they are in no position to know what man is going to direct against them tomorrow. But even with these military disadvantages, somehow they manage. The more knowledge and skill medicine acquires, the less hope it places in clearing the earth of germs. To be sure, the hardy life of bacteria is the result of their mutability However, no matter what tactics bacteria resort to in need it is certain that they act unconsciously, like microscopic chemical aggregates. New tribes owe their resistance only to mutations of inheritance, and these mutations are fundamentally fortuitous. Were man involved, the picture would be more or less as follows: an unknown enemy, using stores of knowledge unknown to us, prepares deadly agents unknown to us and flings an enormous amout of them at people, while we, dying by the thousands, decide, in a desperate search for an antidote, that our best means of defense is to pull out of a hat pages torn from a chemical encyclopedia. Perhaps we shall find on one of these pages a formula for a life-saving drug. It is to be supposed, however, that a race trying to repel a mortal threat by this course of action would perish to a man before such a lottery-type method could succeed.

Yet the above method somehow works, when bacteria apply it. There can be absolutely no question of their hereditary gene code having providently inscribed in it every possible structure of pernicious chemical substance which can be synthesized. There are more of these unions than stars and

atoms in the universe. Besides, the extremely poor apparatu
of bacterial heredity could not even contain the informatioı
about the 48,000 drugs which man has used up to now in hi
struggle with the germs. So one thing is irrefutable: thı
chemical knowledge of bacteria, though purely "practical,'
continues to surpass the lofty theoretical knowledge of man

Since this is so, and since bacteria have such versatility
why can't this be used for completely new purposes? If wı
look at the question objectively, it is clear that writing a fev
words in English is a much simpler problem than preparinı
countless defense tactics against countless types of poison
and venoms. Indeed, behind these poisons stands the colos
sus of modern science—libraries, laboratories, sages, anı
their computers—yet this might is still insufficient agains
the invisible "plantlets"! So the only catch is how to compe
bacteria to study English, and how to make a command o
the language a precondition of survival. One must create ı
situation with two, and only two, ways out: either learn hov
to write, or perish.

R. Gulliver states that in principle a golden-hued sta
phylococcus or a colon bacillus (Escherichia coli) could bı
taught writing as we normally use it, though the road to sucl
knowledge is extremely arduous and bristling with obstacles
It would be much simpler to teach bacteria how to use thı
Morse alphabet, which is composed of dots and dashes—al
the more so, since the dots are already there. After all, eacl
colony is simply a dot. Four dots stuck together on an axi
produce a dash. What could be simpler?

Such were R. Gulliver's inspiration and assumptions—
crazy enough to provoke every specialist at this point to tos
it aside. But we who are not specialists may continue reading
R. Gulliver decided to make the placing of short dashes oı
the agar a condition of survival. The difficulty (as he tells u
in Chapter 2) is that there can be absolutely no instructioı

in the usual sense of the word—neither as it applies to people, nor even to animals, who can acquire conditional reflexes. Here the pupil has no nervous system, no limbs, eyes, ears, or sense of touch—nothing except an uncommon proficiency in chemical changes. These are its life process, and that's about it. Therefore this process must be harnessed to the study of calligraphy—the process, and not the bacteria, for after all we are not talking about individuals or specimens: it is the genetic code itself which must be instructed, so we have to reach the code, and not individual bacteria!

Bacteria do not behave intelligently, whereas the code, their helmsman, renders them capable of adaptation to totally new situations, even to those which they encounter for the first time in millions of years of vegetation. Only if we prepare conditions so well chosen that the sole available tactic of survival is articulate writing shall we see whether the code is up to the task. But the foregoing reflection transfers the whole burden of the problem to the experimenter, for it is he who must create these unusual conditions of bacterial existence—unusual because never before encountered in Evolution!

The description of experiments which occupies later chapters of *Eruntics* is unbelievably boring by virtue of its pedantry, prolixity, and continued interlarding of the text with photograms, tables, and graphs which make it difficult to digest. We shall take those 260 pages of *Eruntics* and summarize them briefly. The beginning was simple. On the agar lies a single colony of colon bacilli *(E. coli)* four times smaller than the letter *o*. The behavior of this grayish spot is observed from above by an optic head connected to a computer. The colony ordinarily expands in all directions centrifugally; but in the experiment, expansion is possible only along a simple axis, for any movement beyond it switches on a laser projector that kills the "misbehaving" bacteria with ultra-

violet rays. We have here a situation similar to the one described initially, when writing appeared on the agar, for the bacteria were unable to develop where the agar was moistened with antibiotic. The only difference now is that they are able to live solely within the limits of a dash (previously they could live only outside it). The author repeated this experiment 45,000 times, using two thousand petri dishes simultaneously and the same number of sensing devices connected to a parallel computer. He had considerable expenses but did not have to give up too much of his time, as a single generation of bacteria lives only some ten to twelve minutes. On two of the two thousand dishes there was enough mutation to produce a new strain of colon bacillus *(E. coli orthogenes)* no longer capable of developing otherwise than in dashes; this new type covered the agar with the following filament:
— — — — — — — — — — — — — — —.

Growth along a single axis then became the inherited property of the mutated bacteria. By breeding this strain, R. Gulliver obtained a further thousand dishes with colonies, and thus a practice range for the next stage in bacterial orthography. With strains that bred in alternating dots and dashes (. — . — . — . — . —), he ultimately reached the limits of this phase of instruction. The bacteria behaved in accordance with the imposed condition, though naturally they produced no writing, only superficial elements of it deprived of any meaning. Chapters 9, 10, and 11 explain how the author took the next step, or rather how he forced *E. coli* to do so.

He deliberated as follows: bacteria have to be put into a position where they behave in a certain specific manner, and this behavior, which at their level of vegetation is purely chemical, will take the form of signals. In the course of four million experiments R. Gulliver macerated, dried to dust roasted, thawed, cut, squeezed, and catalytically paralyzed billions of bacteria, until he finally obtained a strain of *E. coli* which reacted to mortal danger by arranging its colonies into these dots: . . . .

The letter *s* (three dots signify *s* in the Morse alphabet) symbolized stress. Of course the bacteria still understood nothing, but they were able to save themselves only by react- ing through the foregoing arrangement of their colonies, for then and only then did the sensing device connected to the computer remove the menacing agent (e.g., a powerful poison appearing in the agar, ultra-violet rays shining on the agar, etc.). Bacteria which did not arrange themselves into three-dot groups had to perish—every last one; on the agar (and scientific) battlefield, only those remained which, thanks to mutations, had acquired that chemical skill. The bacteria understood nothing yet they signaled their condition —"mortal danger"—thanks to which the three dots indeed became a *sign* defining the situation.

R. Gulliver already saw that he could breed a strain which could give SOS signals, though he considered this an altogether superfluous step. He took a different course, teaching the bacteria how to *differentiate* signals according to the *characteristic features* of each threat. Thus, for example, the strains *E. coli loquativa 67* and *E. coli philographica 213* could eliminate free oxygen, which is lethal to them, from their environment solely by giving the signal: . . . — — — (*s o,* or "stress produced by oxygen").

The author is euphemistic when he says that obtaining strains that could signal their needs proved "rather troublesome." Breeding *E. coli numerativa,* which was able to indicate what concentration of hydrogen ions (pH) suited it, cost him two years, while *Proteus calculans* began to perform elementary arithmetical work after a further three years of experiments. It got as far as two and two makes four.

In the next stage R. Gulliver broadened the base of his

experiments, teaching Morse to streptococci and gonococci, though these germs proved fairly dull-witted. He then went back to the colon bacillus. Tribe 201 was distinguished by its mutational adaptability: it produced longer and longer statements, both descriptions and demands, indicating what troubled the bacteria as well as what they wished by way of nutriment. Continuing to preserve only the most efficiently mutating strains, after eleven years he obtained the strain *E. coli eloquentissima,* the first to begin to write spontaneously and not merely when threatened. He says the happiest day of his life occurred when *E. coli eloquentissima* reacted to the light being switched on in the laboratory with the words "good morning," articulated by a growth of the agar colonies in Morse code.

The first to master Basic English syntax was *Proteus orator mirabilis 64*; on the other hand, *E. coli eloquentissima* continued to make grammatical errors even after 21,000 generations. But the moment the genetic code of those bacteria assimilated the rules of grammar, signaling in Morse became one of its characteristic vital functions: this led to the writing of microbe-transmitted news. At first it was not especially interesting. R. Gulliver wanted to give the bacteria some leading questions, but the establishment of two-way communication proved impossible. The cause of the fiasco he explains as follows: it is not that the bacteria articulate, but that the genetic code articulates through *them,* and this code does not inherit traits individually acquired by particular individuals. The code expresses itself, but while producing statements it is unable to receive any. That is inherited behavior, inasmuch as it is consolidated in the struggle for existence; the messages emitted by the genetic code, grouping the coli colonies in Morse signs, are reasonable but at the same time silly, which is best illustrated by a long-familiar method of bacterial reaction: in producing penicillinase to protect themselves from the effect of penicillin, they are behaving reasonably, but at the same time unconsciously. So R. Gulliver's communicative strains did not cease to be "ordinary bacteria," and the merit of the experimenter was the creation of conditions that implanted eloquence in the heredity of mutated strains.

So bacteria speak, though it is impossible to speak to them. This limitation is less disastrous than one might think, since precisely because of it there appeared, in time, that linguistic property of germs which lay at the basis of eruntics.

R. Gulliver had not expected it at all; he discovered it by accident, in the course of new experiments aimed at breeding *E. coli poetica.* The short verses composed by the colon bacillus were extremely banal and unsuitable for recitation, since—for obvious reasons—bacteria know nothing about English phonetics. Hence they could master the meter of verse, but not the rules of rhyming; bacterial poetry produced nothing beyond a couplet of the type "Agar agar is my love as were* stated above." As sometimes happens, luck rushed to Gulliver's aid. He varied their nutriment, searching for means of inspiring the bacteria to greater eloquence, and filling their bed with preparations whose chemical composition *(nota bene)* he has kept secret. Lengthy verbiage immediately ensued. Finally on November 27, after a new mutation, *E. coli loquativa* began to issue stress signals, though nothing indicated that there were any noxious compounds in the agar. However, the following day, twenty-nine hours after the alarm, some plaster above the laboratory table fell from the ceiling and crushed all the petri dishes on the table. The author first took this strange event to be a coincidence, but just to be sure he conducted a control exper-

*This was an error on the part of the bacteria themselves.

iment which proved that premonitions were a characteristic of those bacteria. By now the first new tribe—*Gulliveria coli prophetica*—was predicting the future fairly well, that is to say, it was endeavoring to adapt to any unfavorable changes that were to threaten it during the next twenty-four hours. The author believed that he discovered nothing absolutely new, but merely picked up by accident the trail of a primeval mechanism characteristic of the heredity of microbes, which enables them to parry effectively the bactericidal techniques of medicine. Yet as long as bacteria remained mute, we had no inkling that such a mechanism might even exist.

The author's supreme achievement was the breeding of *Gulliveria coli prophetissima* and *Proteus delphicus recte mirabilis.* These strains predict the future, and not only within the range of occurrences affecting their own vegetation. R. Gulliver believes that the mechanism of this phenomenon is of a purely physical nature. Bacteria assemble as colonies in dots and dashes, since this procedure is already a normal property of their proliferation characteristics; they are not a "Cassandra bacillus" or "Proteus prophet" making utterances concerning future events. They are merely constellations of physical occurrences in a form still so embryonic and minute that we are unable to detect them by any means, and which have acquired an influence on the metabolism—and therefore the chemism—of those mutated strains. The biochemical action of *Gulliveria coli prophetissima* behaves then as a transmitter linking various space-time intervals. Bacteria are a hypersensitive receiver of certain likelihoods, and nothing more. Bacterial futurology has admittedly become a reality, though it is fundamentally unpredictable in its consequences, since the future-tracking behavior of bacteria cannot be controlled.

Sometimes *Proteus mirabilis* depicts numerical sequences in Morse code, and it is very difficult to determine what they refer to. Once it predicted the laboratory electricity meter reading a half year in advance. Once it forecast how many kittens the neighbor's cat would ha e. Bacteria are obviously completely indifferent, when it comes to predictions; they stand in the same relation to their Morse transmissions as a radio receiver to its signals. One can at least see why they predict incidents relevant to their vegetation; on the other hand, their sensitivity to other categories of events remains an enigma. They might have picked up the cracking of the ceiling plaster owing to changes in the electrostatic charges in the atmosphere of the laboratory, or possibly as a result of the intervention of other physical phenomena. But the author does not know why they also transmit news concerning, for example, the world after the year 2050.

His next task was to distinguish between bacterial pseudology—irresponsible verbiage—and solid predictions, and he accomplished this in a manner as ingenious as it was simple, by setting up "parallel prognostic batteries," called bacterial eruntors. A battery is composed of at least sixty prophetic strains of *coli* and *Proteus.* If each of them says something different, the signaling has to be acknowledged as worthless. If, however, the statements are in accord, prognoses can be made. Placed in separate thermostats and petri dishes, they articulate in Morse the same or very similar texts. In the course of two years the author collected an anthology of bacterial futurology, and with the presentation of them he has crowned his work.

He obtained his best results thanks to strains of *G. coli bibliographica* and *telecognitiva.* These are produced by enzymes such as futurase plusquamperfectiva and excitine futurognostica. Through the action of these enzymes predictive faculties can be acquired even by such *coli* strains as *E. poetica,* which were capable of nothing beyond the composition of feeble verse. Nevertheless, in their predictive behavior bacteria are fairly limited. In the first place, they predict no events directly, but only as if transmitting the contents of a publication dealing with those events. In the second place, they are incapable of prolonged concentration: their top efficiency extended to barely fifteen sheets of typescript. In the third place, all the texts by bacterial authors refer to the period betwen 2003 and 2089.

While fully acknowledging that these phenomena can be explained in various ways, R. Gulliver plumps for his own hypothesis. Fifty years from now a municipal library is to arise on the site of his present holdings. The bacterial code is to be introduced indiscriminately into the library, to be used for selecting random volumes from the shelves. There are no volumes at the moment, to be sure, nor even a library, though in his desire to strengthen the credibility of bacterial predictions, R. Gulliver has already drawn up his will, by the terms of which the town council is to convert his homestead into a library. It cannot be said that he acted at the instigation of his microbes, but rather the reverse: it was they who foresaw the contents of his will before it had been drawn up.

To explain how germs acquired knowledge of the nonexistent books of a still nonexistent library is a bit more difficult. We are helped by the fact that microbe futurology is limited to fragments of works, namely, their introductions. It looks as though some unknown factor (radiation?) has penetrated *closed* books by X-raying them, as it were; naturally the content of the first pages is the easiest to probe, as the ones that follow are concealed by the thickness of the sheets preceding. These explanations are far from precise. Besides, Gulliver admits that there is a considerable difference between yesterday's cracking of the ceiling plaster and the positioning of sentences on the pages of volumes to be published fifty or eighty years hence. But, objective to the end, our author does not arrogate exclusive rights to himself in explaining the bases of eruntics: on the contrary, in his parting words he encourages the readers to continue his efforts themselves.

This book overturns not only bacteriology, but the totality of our knowledge of the world. We do not wish to pass judgment on it in the present foreword, and take no position xv regarding the results of the bacterial prophecies. However doubtful the value of eruntics, it must be admitted that, among history forecasters, there have never been such mortal enemies—and at the same time such inseparable partners in our destiny—as microbes. It may not be irrelevant to add here that R. Gulliver is no longer with us. He died only a few months after the appearance of *Eruntics,* while instructing new students of microbiological literature, namely cholera bacilli. He had been counting on their competence, since, as the very name implies, the cholera comma bacillus is connected via punctuation marks with correct stylistics. Let us suppress our smile of mournful compassion produced by the conclusion that this was a senseless death, since thanks to it his will acquired legal force, and the base of the library wall already holds the cornerstone and, at the same time, the tombstone of one who is for us today merely an eccentric. Yet who knows what he may become tomorrow?

Juan Rambellais·Jean-Marie Annax·Eino Illmainen·Stewart Allporte·Giuseppe Savarini· Yves Bonnecourt·Hermann Pöckelein·Alois Kuentrich·Roger Gatzky

A HISTORY

OF

BITIC LITERATURE

IN FIVE VOLUMES

Second, enlarged edition by Prof. J. Rambellais

VOLUME ONE

PRESSES UNIVERSITAIRES
PARIS 2009

Our monograph will not enter into the debate on this controversial problem, so we shall make only a brief comment regarding the matter. The silence of the traditional humanities concerning the "anatomy and physiology" of authors is based on the obvious fact that these authors, who are always people, differ from one another only as beings of the same species may do so. Thus, as Professor Rambellais says, it would be nonsense in romance philology to make an introductory diagnosis to the effect that the author of *Tristan and Iseut* or *The Song of Roland* was a multicellular organism of the order of land vertebrates, a mammal which is viviparous, pneumobranchiate, placental, and the like. On the other hand, it is not nonsense to specify that ILLIAC 164, the author of *Antikant*, is a semotopological, serially parallel, subluminal, initially polyglot computer of the 19th binasty, with a maximum intellectronic potential of 10^{10} epsilon-sems per millimeter of n-dimension configurational space of utilizable channels, with a net-alienated memory and a monolanguage of internal procedures of the type UNILING. This is because these data explain certain concrete properties of the texts of which the aforementioned ILLIAC is the author.

Still, as Professor Rambellais maintains, bitistics must not occupy itself with this technical (in the case of human beings we should say zoological) side of authors' characters, and for two reasons. The first, practical and less important, is that a consideration of the aforesaid anatomy demands an unusually extensive knowledge of a technical and mathematical type, which in its full range is inaccessible even to particular specialists in the theory of automata, since an expert acquainted with that theory is well informed only about the one branch of it in which he has specialized. Thus one cannot demand from exponents of bitistics, who are humanists by training and method, something which cannot be obtained as a whole even from specialists in intellectronics. Consequently, the maximalism of the American school obliges it to pursue its studies in large mixed teams, which always produces disastrous results, since no collection or "chorus" of critics can effectively replace a simple critic with a complete grasp of the text under study.

The second, more important, and basic reason is simply that the introduction of corrections or supplements of an anatomical type in bitistics brings it to a standstill, whenever it concentrates on texts of "bitic apostasy" (which we shall discuss later). All the knowledge of intellectronics specialists is insufficient to understand fully how, why, and to what end a particular author has created a particular text, if the author comes from any binasty of computers of a serial number greater than eighteen.

To these arguments American bitistics opposes its own counterarguments; however, as we have already declared, our monograph does not propose to give a thorough description of this dispute, much less resolve it.

2. DESCRIPTION OF THE WORK. Our monograph attempts a compromise between the positions stated above, though on the whole it inclines to the side of the European school. This is reflected in its structure, for only the first volume, edited by Professor Annax with

the participation of twenty-seven experts from various specializations, is devoted to the technical aspects of computer authors. That volume opens with an introduction to the general theory of finite automata; in subsequent chapters it discusses forty-five writer systems, both individual (simple) and joint ("author-aggregates").

It must be emphasized all the same that, excepting the references designated by an asterisk in the main volumes of the *History of Bitic Literature*, the study of it does not necessarily require a familiarity with the first volume.

The main or essential part of the monograph consists of three volumes entitled *Homotropia, Intertropia,* and *Heterotropia,* and follows the universally accepted system of classification which is simultaneously diachronic and synchronic in character, since the three main divisions of bitic literature, encompassed by the three titles, are at the same time three successive periods of its origin and development. The table below presents an outline of the whole of the work.

BITIC LITERATURE
(after Allporte, Illmainen, and Savarini)

I. *Homotropia** (homotropic, cis-human phase; also "simulative" or "anthropomicric")

---

* This phase was previously called "monoetical" or "monoetics."

A. Germinal stage (embryonic or prelinguistic):
Paralexics (Neologenesis)
Semolalia
Semautics

B. Linguistic stage ("comprehending," according to Allporte):
Interpolative mimesis
Extrapolative mimesis
Controlled transcendent mimesis ("programmatically excessive")

II. *Intertropia* (also "critical phase" or "interregnum")

Critique of System Philosophy

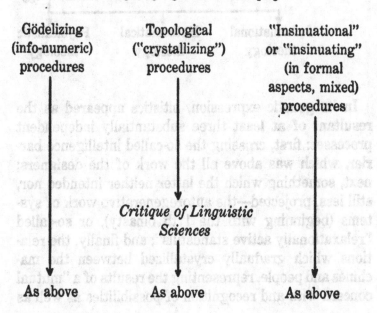

Gödelizing (info-numeric) procedures	Topological ("crystallizing") procedures	"Insinuational" or "insinuating" (in formal aspects, mixed) procedures

Critique of Linguistic Sciences

| As above | As above | As above |

III. *Heterotropia* (apostasy, transhuman phase)

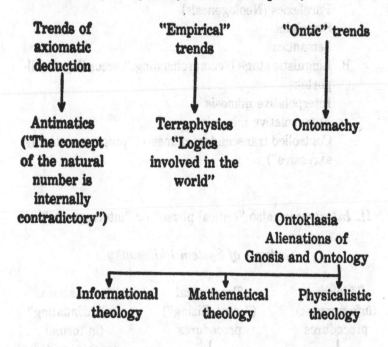

Trends of axiomatic deduction → Antimatics ("The concept of the natural number is internally contradictory")

"Empirical" trends → Terraphysics "Logics involved in the world"

"Ontic" trends → Ontomachy

Ontoklasia
Alienations of
Gnosis and Ontology

Informational theology — Mathematical theology — Physicalistic theology

In its genetic expression, bitistics appeared as the resultant of at least three substantially independent processes: first, crossing the so-called intelligence barrier, which was above all the work of the designers; next, something which the latter neither intended nor, still less, projected—the autoregenerative work of systems (beginning with the 17th binasty), or so-called "relaxationally active standstills"; and finally, the relations which gradually crystallized between the machines and people, representing the results of a "mutual concern with and recognition of possibilities as well as limitations on both sides" (Yves Bonnecourt). The intelligence barrier unsuccessfully assaulted by early cybernetics is, as we know incontrovertibly, a fiction. It is a fiction in the (unexpected) sense that its transcendence by machines is impossible to identify. The transitions from "unthinking," "chattering" machines "working purely formally" to "thinking," "speaking" machines showing "insight" occur in smooth stages. Though the categories of "mechanical automaticity" and "intellectual sovereignty" are still valid, we realize that no precisely delimitable boundary separates the two.

The relaxational output of machines was first observed and recorded almost thirty years ago. It turned out to be a purely technical necessity that the prototypes (beginning with the 15th binasty) should be provided with rest periods during which their activity did not come to a standstill but, deprived of programmed directives, manifested itself as a peculiar "mumble." That at least is how their verbal or quasi-mathematical production was then interpreted; the name "machine dreams" was even generally accepted for it. According to current opinion, the machines had to have active rest to enable them to regenerate and then return to normal full efficiency, just as such a phase—sleep, together with the reveries (dreams) typical of it—is necessary for human beings. The designation "bitic production," used then for these "chatterings" and "dreams," was therefore disparaging and disrespectful: as if without rhyme or reason, the machines ground out "bits of all the information contained within them" and by this method of "shuffling" were supposed to recover their partially lost efficiency. We adopted the name, although it was obviously inappropriate. We adopted it in accordance with the historical tradition of all scientific nomenclature: a random example—"thermodynamics"—reveals an analogous inappropriateness, since the scope of contemporary thermodynamics is not the same as it was for earlier physicists who coined the term. Indeed, thermodynamics is not concerned solely with the thermal activity of matter, just as, in referring to bitic literature, we do not mean just the "bits," i.e., units of *nonsemantic* information. Pouring new wine into old bottles is, however, a general practice of science.

The mutual acquaintance of machines and human beings led over the years to a more and more explicit division of bitistics into two basic provinces, to which the terms *creatio cis-humana* and *trans-humana* correspond.

The first embraces literature which is the *result* of the coexistence of machines and human beings, that is, of the simple fact that, in implanting our ethnic language and structural languages in them, we have also harnessed them to our brainwork in the whole sphere of culture and natural science, as well as the deductive disciplines (logic and mathematics). Nonetheless bitic creativity, whose direct cause and animating agent is the transmission to nonhuman authors of typically human problems in the field of learning and the fine arts, is divided in turn into two fairly distinct subspheres. For a linguistic product obtained through planned control—which may, to use Professor Kuentrich's visual image, be called an "order" (that is, the *immediate* direction of the machines to a range of questions or themes chosen by us)—is one thing, while a linguistic product which no human being has "ordered," and which admittedly arose under the influence of earlier stimuli (or programmings), but constitutes the manifestation of by now spontaneous activity, is quite another. And yet, whether bitic texts thus engendered resulted from a *direct* or *indirect* cause, their connection with typically human problems constitutes an essential, indeed a chief, trait: and so cis-humana bitistics studies both genres of these texts.

And it was only the granting to machines of facilities for creative freedom with no discipline, program, rules, or limitations that gradually led to the separation of their (so-called "later") creativity from typically anthropomorphic and anthropological influences. In the course of this evolution bitic literature began imperceptibly to offer us, its likely recipients, growing resistance and assimilative difficulties. For divisions of nonhuman bitistics (in the *trans-humana* sense) now exist which attempt to understand (analyze, interpret, explain) bitic texts which in varying degrees are *unintelligible* to humans.

Obviously we can always try to employ *some* machines to interpret the works of *other* machines. But the quantity of cells necessary to enable us to understand bitic texts which are the extremes of "apostasy"— deviations from our norms for the creation, understanding, and explanation of meaning—will increase as one receives increasingly difficult texts to interpret. And as this increase becomes *exponential*, it ultimately precludes our acquiring even a vague knowledge of the content of this "culminating apostasy," thus signifying practically the total heplessness of the human race in relation to literature, which humans after all indirectly originated.

Some speak in this context of the sorcerer's apprentice who unleashed forces beyond his control. This term is a form of resignation, for which science has no place. Bitic literature is surrounded by a very abundant body of pro- and contrabitic writing; it is full of desperate judgments articulating symptoms of depression, terror, and also shock at the fact that man has created something that has surpassed him intellectually as well.

However, it must be emphatically stated that bitistics as a scientific discipline *cannot* itself be the place for expressing views of this type, which belong to the philosophy of nature, man, and his works (nonhuman as well). We agree with Roger Gatzky that bitistics has neither more nor fewer grounds for despair than cosmology, for example: it is obvious that, no matter how long we humans exist, and likewise no matter what intellectual assistance we may expect from cognitive machines, we shall not totally exhaust the universe and thus shall not totally comprehend it, though astrophysicists, cosmologists, and cosmogonists would never think of complaining about such a very unalterable state of things.

The whole difference is that we are not the originators of the Universum, but bitic production is surely—if indirectly—our work. Yet one wonders where in fact the idea originated that man can accept the inexhaustibility of the Universum with complete equanimity, but cannot accept with the same objective equanimity the inexhaustibility of something which he himself has created. 3. CRUCIAL DIVISIONS OF BITISTICS. Explanations and detailed descriptions, together with a descriptive bibliography of the subject, are supplied by our monograph in the appropriate places. However, a bird's-eye view of the main divisions of bitistics would appear desirable; such a description can in no way *replace* a detailed exposition, but it is something by way of an abbreviated guide through a much-partitioned region where it is easy to lose one's way. Still, it is proper to point out that the main sections of bitistics described below are given in a greatly simplified form, repeatedly verging on a distortion of the central issue.

Our survey—being, as we have said, of a preliminary nature—concentrates on only the four "peaks" of bitic literature, namely *monoetics, mimesis, sophocrisis,* and *apostasy.* In point of fact, these terms are already obsolete; in present-day nomenclature their rough equivalents would be: *homotropia* (in its first part), *exact mimesis, critique of philosophy,* and *bitic creation,* of which the last lies outside the limits of our comprehension. Nevertheless, the nomenclature rejected today had the virtue of clarity, and we are particularly anxious to keep our initial explanations straightforward.

A. Graeve, Gulbransson, and Fradkin—who are numbered among the creators, the "fathers" of bitistics—saw monoetics as the earliest phase of bitism. (The name derives from *monos,* "single," and *poesis,* "creating.")

Monoetics owes its origin to the instruction of machines in the principles of word formation. The harmony of these principles determines what was once commonly called the "spirit" of a given language.

An actively used, historically created language employs the principles of word formation with very definite restrictions, though on the whole those who use the language are by no means aware of them. Not until we had machines whose *practical* restrictions in word formation were thoroughly unknown, could we obtain an insight into all those chances which language ignores in its evolution. The simplest illustration would be to present a handful of examples gathered from the second volume of our *History*, chiefly from the chapters *Paralexics, Semautics,* and *Semolalia.*

(a) Machines may use expressions existing in a language and assign them other than the accepted meanings: thoroughfare: a large meal; piglet: a filthy rooming house; horseman: centaur; knee guard: dwarf sentinel; princeling: royal fish; carnivore: Mardi gras prostitute; flabbergast: sagging stomach; skinflint: stone facing.

(b) Machines also create neologisms along so-called semantic axes. We have purposely chosen examples of this creativity not all of which require detailed dictionary-type explanations:

tartlet, screwball, bedrabbled (read: bed rabbled), layette, claptrap;

anteater, bugbear (bird feeding its brood);

fistigob, slapyap, slugmug;

arithmeticker, summer, cipheretor (computer);

suspenser (chair lift);

deathsign *(memento mori)*;
gladland (paradise);
sea slicer (sawfish); etc.

Any comic effect is clearly unintended. Also, these are elementary examples, though characterized by distinctive bitic features which persist—though much harder to discern—in later stages of development as well. The whole fact of the matter is that, whereas for us the real thing is the world, for the machines the first and foremost actuality is *language*. The computer, to which the categories that *culture* imposes on language were still alien, "thought" that "little prostitute" is the same thing as "tartlet," "screwball," etc. Hence, too, those characteristic corruptions: "horseman" is by now a classic textbook example of the formation of an agglomeration of meanings and morphological aspects, for here we have a mating of "horse," "man," and as it were a coupling from the region of semantics, "centaur," because, since a horse cannot be a man, it must be half horse, half man.

A computer at this (linguistically very low) level of development knows no limits to its word formation, and the economy of expression characteristic of machine thinking, which subsequently created nonlinear deduction and the so-called "star" concepts of terraphysics, here appears as a proposal for putting the resident terms of a language, such as "word" and "wordy," on an equal footing with the like of "wordwork" (verse), "wordiot" (graphomaniac), "wordsteal" (plagiarism), "wordlouse" (cad), etc. For these very reasons the lexical generator proposes that "dogmobile" should denote an Eskimo sledge team, and "disccomfort" the pain occasioned by a slipped disc.

Formerly known as *monoetes*, the one-word creations cited above were produced in part by imperfect programming, and in part by the intention of programmers interested in the word-formative expansion of machines; yet it is only proper to observe that many such neologisms only seem to be of machine provenance. For example, we cannot be certain whether "lunatic asylum" was christened "dimocracy" by a computer, or whether it was a human humorist's joke.

Monoetics is an important field because we can discern in it those creative features of machines which disappear from our field of vision in subsequent phases. It is the threshold of bitistics, or its kindergarten. This output has a reassuring effect on many a student who, prepared for contact with texts concise to the point of incomprehensibility, is relieved to discover such innocent and amusing works. But this satisfaction does not long suffice! The unintentional humor arises from a collision of categories which we consider to be permanently separate; the reinforcement of programs by categorial principles carries us into the next sphere of bitistics (though still called prebitistics by some researchers), in which machines begin to unmask our language, tracking down in it turns of speech which are the consequence of man's bodily structure.

Thus, for example, the notions of "elevation" and "abasement" derive—according to the machine interpretation, not ours!—from the fact that every living organism and therefore man as well has to counteract universal gravitation by means of active muscular exertion. The body appears as the link through which the gravitational gradient leaves its impression in our language. A systematized analysis of speech, laying bare the whole extent to which similar influences have been uprooted not only in the world of ideas but even in syntax, can be found at the end of Chapter 8 of Volume II. In Volume III, on the other hand, we introduce models of languages projected bitically for environments different from that of Earth, as well as for nonanthropoidal organisms. One of them, INVART, was used by MENTOR II in composing *Lampoon upon the Universe* (mentioned below).

B. *Mimesis* is that field of bitic production which has revealed to us hitherto unknown mechanisms of intellectual creation, while also becoming a truly formidable invasion of the world of man's intellectual works. It arose historically as an incidental and unforeseen phenomenon during the machine translation of texts. The latter requires the processing of information step by step and in various ways. The closest contacts ought to occur between systems of ideas, and not of words or sentences; machine translations from language to language are superb nowadays because the aggregates which carry them out are not collective but merely "aim," as it were, at the same original text from various sides. The text is subjected to "extraction" in machine language (the "go-between"), and it is only from these "pressings" that the machines make a projection into "inner conceptual space." Within it an "*n*-echo Body of Abstractions" emerges which is to the original as an organism is to an embryo; the projection from that "organism" into the language of translation gives the expected result.

However, this process takes a more intricate course than we have described here, because, for one thing, the quality of translation is constantly checked by retranslation (translation backward from the "organism" to the language of the original). So the translating aggregate is composed of machines which are able to "communicate" solely through the process of translation. H. Ellias and T. Semmelberg made the astonishing discovery that the "n-body of Abstractions," being a text already interpreted—that is, assimilated semantically by a machine—can be *seen* as a whole if that abstract creation is put into the requisite electron appliance (a semascope).

Visually, the "body of abstractions" nestled in its conceptual continuum appears as a complicated, many-shelled, aperiodic, and variably synchronous mass, woven of "burning threads"—that is, billions of "significant curves." These curves together yield the plane of cuttings of the semantic continuum. Turning to the illustrations in Volume II, the reader will find a series of semascopic photographs which produce a rather striking effect when brought together and compared. As they demonstrate, the quality of the original text has a definite equivalent in the "aestheticality" of the geometric "semature"!

Furthermore, even with little experience one can distinguish at sight discursive texts from artistic (belletristic, poetic) ones; religious texts almost without exception strongly resemble artistic ones, whereas philosophical ones reveal a wide diversity in this, the visual, aspect. It is not much of an exaggeration to say that projections of texts deep in the machine continuum are their expansively *set* meanings. Texts which are strongly collective as regards logic appear as tightly bound bundles and clusters of "significant curves." (This is not the place to explain their connection with the sphere of recurring functions, which is discussed in Chapter 10 of Volume II.)

Texts of literary composition of an allegorical character present the most original aspect: their central semature is usually surrounded by a pale "halo," and at both its sides ("poles") one can see "echo repetitions" of meanings, recalling at times the interferential images of luminous rays. As we shall mention again, this congealed phenomenon made possible the criticism of constructs—of all of mankind's intellectual structures and his philosophical systems first and foremost.

The first work of bitic mimesis to gain world renown was a novel by Pseudodostoevsky, *The Girl* (Devochka). It was composed during a phase of relaxation by a multimember aggregate whose assignment was to translate into English the collected works of the Russian writer. In his memoirs the distinguished scholar of Russian literature John Raleigh describes the shock he experienced upon receiving the Russian typescript of a composition signed with what he took to be the singular pseudonym of HYXOS. The impression which the work created on this Dostoevsky expert must have been truly indescribable in its intensity, if, as he admits, he doubted whether he was in a conscious state! The authenticity of the work was for him beyond a doubt, although he knew Dostoevsky had not written such a novel.

Despite what the press disseminated on this topic, the translating aggregate, having digested all of Dostoevsky's texts together with his *Diary of a Writer* and the literature on the subject, had in no way constructed a phantom, a model, or a machine reincarnation of the personality of a real creator.

The theory of mimesis is very complex, but its fundamentals—as well as the circumstances which made possible that phenomenal display of mimetic virtuosity—can be expressed simply. Neither the person nor the personality of Dostoevsky was of any interest to the machine translator (nor could they be, after all). It comes about that, in the space of meanings, a work of Dostoevsky's develops into a curved mass, recalling in its overall structure an open torus, that is, a "broken ring" (with a gap). Thus it was a relatively simple task (for machines, of course, not for people!) to close that gap, inserting the missing link.

It may be said that a semantic gradient runs along the main thoroughfare of Dostoevsky's works, and that *The Girl* is its *continuation* and at the same time its termination. It is precisely because of these interrelations of the great writer's works that the experts have no doubt whatsoever as to where—between which novels—*Devochka* belongs. The leitmotiv, already marked in *Crime and Punishment,* intensifies in *The Possessed,* and between this work and *The Brothers Karamazov* a "gap opens." It was a success as well as a happy coincidence of mimesis, for later attempts to stimulate the translators to analogous creation as regards other authors never again produced such magnificent results.

Mimesis has nothing to do with the *biographically* detectable sequence in which a given writer's works originated. Thus Dostoevsky left unfinished manuscripts of a novel, *The Emperor,* but the machines could never have "thought it through" or "got on its track," because in this novel he attempted to exceed his own capabilities. As for *The Girl,* apart from the original version by HYXOS, there now exist variants prepared by other aggregates, though the experts consider them less successful; the differences in composition have naturally turned out to be considerable, though in all these apocryphas there is an identical problem—one leading to a heart-rending climax characteristic of Dostoevsky —that of holiness grappling with the sins of the flesh.

Everyone who has read *The Girl* is aware of the reasons which would have made it impossible for Dostoevsky to write it. Of course, having said all that, we are —by the standards of the traditional humanities—uttering downright blasphemy, inasmuch as we are equating machine forgery with authentic creation. But bitistics *is* an inevitable infringement on the canon of classical values and evaluations, wherein the authenticity of the text is of paramount importance. We are contriving to *prove* that *Devochka* constitutes a work of Dostoevsky's to a higher degree than his own text, *The Emperor*!

The general rule of mimesis is as follows: if a given author has completely exploited what is for him the

central configuration of creative meanings (the "life ob-
session")—or, in bitic nomenclature, "the space of its
sematures"—mimesis will supply nothing further on
this axis save derivative (decadent, echo) texts. If, however, he has left something "unsaid" (e.g., for biological
reasons, because he died prematurely, or for social ones,
because he did not dare to), mimesis can produce the
missing links. To be sure, the final success will also be
decided by the topology of a given writer's sematures;
in this regard we differentiate between *divergent* and
convergent sematures.

The ordinary critical study of texts gives no firm
grounds for judging the likelihood of mimesis in a given
instance. Thus literature specialists reckoned on a mimetic continuation of Kafka's authorship, but their
hopes were frustrated; we have obtained nothing except
the final chapters of *The Castle.* Anyway, for bitists the
Kafka *casus* is cognitively especially valuable, since an
analysis of his semature shows that with *The Castle* he
had already reached the limits of creative possibilities:
further work carried out at Berkeley on three occasions
revealed how the machine apocryphas "drown" in the
falling, multishelled, "echoed reverberations of meaning" which constitute the objective expression of the
extreme position of this authorship. In point of fact,
what readers instinctively take to be "felicity of composition" is the result of an equilibrium termed *semas-
tase*; if the allegorizing is too preponderant, a text tends
to be unreadable. The physical equivalent is a space so
vaulted that a voice resounding in it undergoes distortion to the point of being smothered in the torrent of
echoed reverberations from every direction.

Such limitations of mimesis are undoubtedly favorable to culture. After all, publication of *The Girl* created panic not only in literary circles. There was no lack of Cassandras predicting that "mimesis would crush culture," and proclaiming that the "machine invasion" into the heart of human values was more destructive and nightmarish than any imaginary "invasions from outer space."

These people feared the use of a creative services industry, turning culture into a nightmare paradise where any consumer, acting on any whim whatsoever, could receive masterpieces instantly produced by machine succubi and incubi unerringly transformed into the spirit of Shakespeare, Leonardo, Dostoevsky, as a result of which our hierarchies of values would have collapsed, since we would have been wading through masterpieces as through trash. Fortunately we need give this apocalypse no credit at all.

Once it had become an industry, mimesis led to unemployment, but solely among manufacturers of trivial literature (sci-fi, porn, thrillers, and the like): there indeed it supplanted humans in the supply of intellectual goods—which ought not to cause an honest humanist too much despair.

C. *The critique of systematic philosophy* (or sophocrisis) is recognized as a transitional zone between areas of bitistics designated cis-human and transhuman. This critique, based in principle on a logical reconstruction of the writings of the great philosophers, is derived (as already mentioned) from mimetic procedures. It is only right to remark that it has earned itself a reputation for vulgarity, thanks to the use made of it by certain profit-hungry manufacturers. So long as the ontologies of the Aristotles, Hegels, and Aquinases could be admired in the British Museum alone, like glittering "cocoon masses" set (luminously) in blocks of dark glaze, it was difficult to detect any harm in this spectacle.

Now, however, when the *Summa Theologica* or *Critique of Pure Reason* can be purchased in any size or color, this amusement has acquired an offensive after-taste. It behooves one to wait patiently until the fashion passes, like thousands of others. Obviously, anyone who has bought *Kant Set in Amber* cares little for the revelations with which the bitic apocrisis has provided us in philosophy. We shall not summarize the results here, but refer the reader to the third volume of the monograph; suffice it to observe that semascopy indeed constitutes a new aptitude for looking at the great intellectual totalities—an aptitude unexpectedly bestowed on us by the spirit of the machine.

Nor should we disregard the fact that the assurances of the greatest scientists concerning the role of the guiding star which the pure aesthetics of a mathematical construct played in their exploratory efforts—assurances to which we have hitherto had to give blind credence—can now be verified *visually*, taking their congealed thoughts in hand, to bring them closer to our eyes. Of course there are no automatic consequences for the further development of thought from the fact that ten volumes of higher algebra or the age-old war between nominalism and universalism can be crystallized into a fist-sized piece of glass. Bitic creativity impedes human creation as much as it simplifies it.

One thing, however, can be said with absolute certainty. Before the use of machine intelligence no thinker or author ever had such ardent, unfailingly attentive, and uncompromising readers! That is why, in the cry that burst from the lips of a certain first-rate thinker when he was offered, by MENTOR V, a critique of his work—"This one has really read me!"—there was so much of the frustration typical of the present day, when humbug and perfunctorily acquired erudition replace genuine knowledge. The thought that has haunted me while writing these works—that it is not human beings who will be my most conscientious readers—is indeed full of bitter irony.

D. The term *apostasy* given to the last bitic sphere appears felicitous. Never has deviation from that which is human gone so far, nor has it been incorporated into a line of reasoning with such cool passion. For this literature, which has taken nothing from us apart from language, humanity appears not to exist.

The transhumans' bibliography surpasses all the other domains of bitistics already mentioned. It is the meeting point of paths secretly marked out in earlier fields. We can in practice divide apostasy into two levels, lower and upper. Access to the lower level is generally well maintained; the upper one is barred to us. That is why our fourth volume is a guide to the lower state almost exclusively. This volume is a meager extract from an enormous body of writing, hence the difficult position of the foreword writer, who is supposed to introduce even more concisely something which is already essentially an abridgement. Yet such an introduction appears necessary, as a view from above; otherwise, lacking a broader perspective, the reader will easily get lost in the difficult terrain, like a wanderer in mountains whose highest summits cannot be properly judged at short distance. Keeping in mind such recommendations and doubts, from each of the divisions of apostasy I shall take a single bitic text, not so much to interpret it as to attune the reader, as it were, to the process of apostasy.

We shall therefore confine ourselves to samples taken from the following provinces of the lower state: *antimatics, terraphysics,* and *ontomachy.*

As an introduction to them we have the so-called *Cogito paradox.* The first person to pick up its trail was Alan Turing, an English mathematician of the last century who recognized that a machine behaving like a person cannot possibly be distinguished from a person in mental respects—in other words, that a machine capable of conversing with a person must by necessity be credited with consciousness. We consider that other people have consciousness only because we ourselves perceive it. If we did not experience it, we would be unable to imagine anything under this concept.

During the course of machine evolution it became evident, however, that an unthinking intellect can be constructed: it is used, for example, in an ordinary chess game program, which as we know understands nothing, does not care whether it wins or loses the match, and (in a word) unconsciously but logically beats its human opponents. What's more, it has been shown that when a primitive and undoubtedly "soulless" computer programmed to conduct psychotherapy asks a patient appropriate questions of an intimate nature in order to make a diagnosis and offer treatment, this machine makes a profound impression on its human interlocutors, as if it were a living person after all. This impression is so intense as sometimes to be felt even by the person who has done the programming—a professional who knows perfectly well that the mechanism in question possesses as much soul as a gramophone. The programmer may still take control of the situation—that is, may tear himself away from the growing delusion of being in contact with a conscious individual—by giving the machine the kind of questions or replies with which, given the limitations of the programming, it couldn't possibly cope.

In this way cybernetics embarked on a course leading to the gradual extension and improvement of programs, through which, with the passage of time, it became a harder and harder task to "tear off the mask"—that is, to discover the mindlessness of the procedures emitted by the machine and, by precisely this means, to discover the projection compelling man to react. (This projection occurs unconsciously according to an assumption, ingrained in us by force of habit, that if someone consciously refers to our words and addresses himself to us sensibly, then that someone *must be endowed with conscious intelligence.*)

So the Cogito paradox made itself known to us in bitistics in an ironic and at the same time startling manner: as *despair* on the part of machines as to whether people really think! The situation suddenly acquired a

65

perfect bilateral symmetry. We humans are unable to achieve complete certainty (as a proof) as to whether a machine thinks and, in thinking, experiences its states as mental ones—since conceivably one may be dealing with nothing more than an externally perfect simulation whose internal correlative is a kind of void of total "soullessness." For their part, machines are similarly unable to obtain proof of whether we, as their partners, think consciously—as they do. Neither side knows what experiential states the other subsumes under the label "consciousness."

It should be pointed out that this paradox has the character of an abyss, although at first it may appear merely amusing. The very quality of the intellectual results here prejudges nothing: rudimentary automata of the last century were already beating their own constructors at games of logic, and those were unusually primitive machines; so we know with complete certainty that whatever results from creative thinking can be attained in another—unthinking—way as well. The treatises of two bitic authors—NOON and LUMENTOR—on problems of the Cogito paradox open the fourth volume of our monograph and reveal how deeply this enigma is rooted in the nature of the world.

From antimatics, which is a nightmarish mathematics of antimonies, we shall take (by way of example) only one downright crushing pronouncement, one that terrifies every specialist and smacks of complete madness: "the concept of a natural number is internally contradictory." This means that no number is equal to itself! According to the antimaticians (who are machines, of course), Peano's axiomatics are incorrect, not because they are internally self-contradictory, but because they are not perfectly suited to the world in which we exist. For, in common with the next type of bitic apostasy, terraphysics (i.e., "monstrous physics"), antimatics postulates an irremovable adhesion of thought and the world. Authors like ALGERAN and STYX concentrate their attack on zero. According to them, zeroless arithmetic can be constructed in our world in an uncontradictory manner. Zero is the cardinal number of all empty sets, but according to these authors the concept of an "empty set" must *always* be confined in the antinomy of the liar. "No such thing as nothing exists"—with this motto from the work of STYX, the time has come for us to conclude our description of the antimatic heresy; otherwise we shall get lost in argument.

The oddest product of terraphysics—and who knows, perhaps the one that promises the most to knowledge —is reckoned to be the so-called *Polyversum* hypothesis. According to it the Cosmos is dual and we, together with the matter comprising the suns, stars, planets, and our bodies, inhabit its "slow" half, the *Bradyversum.* It is "slow" because movement is possible here at speeds ranging from the static up to locally the highest, that of light. The other or "fast" half of the Cosmos, the *Tachyversum,* is reached via the light barrier. To get to the Tachyversum, it is necessary to exceed the speed of light: in our world this is an omnipresent frontier separating each spot from another region of existence.

Dozens of years ago physicists advanced the hypothesis of the *tachions*, particles which move *solely* at velocities greater than that of light. No one managed to find them, although it is they which—according to terraphysics—constitute the Tachyversum. But in point of fact the Tachyversum is composed of *one* such particle.

A tachion slowed to the speed of light would acquire infinitely great energy, whereas in accelerating it loses energy, emitting it in the form of radiation; when its velocity becomes infinitely great, its energy falls to zero. So the tachion, moving at an infinite speed, is clearly *everywhere* at the same time: as an omnipresent particle, it alone forms the Tachyversum! And to speak more precisely, the greater its velocity, the more omnipresent it becomes. The world formed from so singular an omnipresence is filled, moreover, with the radiation which the tachion constantly emits in speeding up, since it is during acceleration that it loses energy. This world is the opposite of ours: here light is the fastest movement, but there in the Tachyversum it is the slowest. In becoming omnipresent, the tachion turns the Tachyversum into an ever stiffer and more "solid" body, until finally it is so "everywhere" that it presses on the light quanta and forces them back into itself. Consequently it is subject to impediment and slows down. The slower it moves, the greater the energy it acquires; when the brakes are applied near zero, the tachion—approaching a state of infinite energy—explodes, creating the Bradyversum.

Thus, viewed from *our* universe, the explosion occurred *sometime* and created first the stars and then us. But if one views it from the Tachyversum, it did not occur *at all*, since there exists no superior time in which the occurrence of both Cosmoses could be included.

Their "natural" mathematics are almost reciprocals. In our slow world $1 + 1$ is practically equal to $2 [1 + 1 \approx 2]$; only at its very limits, when it approaches the speed of light, does $1 + 1$ become equal to 1. In the Tachyversum, on the other hand, 1 is *almost* equal to infinity $[1 \approx \infty]$. But, as the "monstrous doctors" themselves admit, this matter is still unclear, insofar as the logic of a particular Universum (or Polyversum!) is a rational concept only if pursued in this world, though at present nobody knows what the chances are of intelligent systems (or simply life) arising in the Tachyversum. In accordance with this verdict, mathematics has limits imposed by the impassable barriers of material existence, since to talk of our mathematics in a world with laws other than the laws of our world is to talk nonsense.

Finally, as regards the last item of bitic apostasy, *Lampoon upon the Universe*, I admit that I cannot summarize it. Yet that lengthy treatise, a work of many volumes, is conceived as merely an introduction to experimental cosmogenetics, i.e., the technology of making up worlds "existentially more orderly" than ours. The revolt against existence in given forms of duration, which is the opposite of every nihilism, of every desire for self-annihilation—and in addition a product of the machine soul, a flurry of projects for "another existence"—at first this undoubtedly makes exotic reading, and if one can overcome the difficulty of it, even aesthetically thrilling reading. To the question, what are we actually in contact with?—with a fiction of logic or a logical fiction? with a fantastic philosophy or a soundly thought-out, totally objective endeavor to shatter and invalidate this existence here as a fortuity, a shore onto which an unknown destiny has driven us, and from which boldness commands us to shove off and move in an unknown direction?—to the question whether these works are indeed *nonhuman,* or whether it is by their apostasy that they serve us, I shall offer no answer, for I have none.

Introduction to the
Second Edition

The three years that have passed since the appearance of the first edition have brought many new bitic publications. However, the editorial committee of our monograph has decided to retain its original outline, while including several innovations referred to below. Thus the four fundamental volumes of the *History of Bitic Literature* remain unchanged in their basic composition and in the general arrangement of material; on the other hand, additions have been made to the bibliography, and the (relatively few) errors and omissions of the first edition have been corrected.

Our committee has considered it desirable to devote a supplementary fifth volume to literary works from the field of metaphysics, broadly conceived, and from religious studies, which are known jointly as *theobitic* literature. In the previous edition there were some fairly inadequate extracts and references in this direction, located in the Appendix to Volume IV. The rising flood of such output has induced us to give it separate status, and since the Foreword to the first edition says nothing about it, we are taking the opportunity to present briefly the subject of this supplementary fifth volume and thereby show the reader the crucial issues in theobitistics.

1. INFORMATIONAL THEOLOGY. At the end of the last decade a computer group from Brookhaven undertook a formal analysis of all available mystical writings accepted by the Catholic Church, as part of the "Mysticism as a Channel of Communication" project. The foundations of the study were the arguments offered by the Church for believing that, in certain special states, mystics are able to communicate with God. The texts by them, recording these inner experiences, were subjected to scrutiny for the information they contain. The analysis did not touch on the question of God's transcendence, nor on his immanent character (as a person or nonperson, for instance), since it wholly omitted the substance of the mystical writings, that is, their semantic content. It was thus unable to question the quality of the various revelations disclosed in the mystical communications, for it took into consideration solely the *quantitative* aspect of the information which the mystics had ac-

quired. Such a physical computation permits one to calculate with mathematical precision the quantitative informational gain, totally excluding its contents. A premise of the project was that axiom of information theory which maintains that the establishment of contact with a real source, that is, the creation of a transmitting channel, must result in an increase in the quantity of information on the part of the receivers.

The various definitions of God are the source of the dogma of his infinity, which informationally denotes an infinitely great diversity. (Which is easy to prove formally, since the omniscience ascribed to God analytically implies such diversity, of the power of a continuum.) Thus man in contact with God cannot possess infinite information, for he himself is finite; he should, however, show at least a small increase of information, limited by his receptivity. Yet on a numerical balance sheet the writings of the mystics proved to be much more meager than the statements of people who are in contact with real sources of information—for example, researchers conducting scientific experiments.

The quantity of information in the writings of the mystics is precisely equal to the quantity of information in the statements (writings) of people fated to be generators of diversity exclusively for themselves. The conclusion drawn from the project runs as follows: "The contact postulated by the Church between the human mystic and God is not a process in which man gains supra-zero information." This may indicate either that the communication channel postulated by the Church is a fiction, or that the channel indeed occurs, but that the

Broadcaster maintains continual silence. Only extra-physical reasons can induce us to choose between the alternatives *Silentium Domini/Non esse Domini.* We have placed this work, together with the new theological counterarguments, in the first part of the supplementary volume.

2. MATHEMATICAL THEOLOGY. The most original product of theobitistics is a model of God which is sinusoidal and at the same time oscillating. God becomes established axiomatically as an alternating *process*, and not as an unchanging *state*; he oscillates at a transcendental frequency between infinities of opposing signs—Good and Evil. For every time interval (in a physical sense) both these infinities are realized together, though not simultaneously. For God's Good and Evil pass into each other by turns, so a precise depiction of the process would be a sinusoid.

Inasmuch as the propagation of both infinities—having (as they do) atemporal sources—participates in the life order temporarily, it can be demonstrated that the rise of local peculiarities such as time-space sectors, in which the equilibrium of Good and Evil is not maintained, is admissible, i.e., possible. At such special points, fluctuations thus originate as deficiencies. And since with every successive change of signs the process curve must pass zero, in a Universum which could itself last an infinitely long time there exist not two but *three* infinities: Good, Zero, and Evil—all of which, translated into conventional theodicean language, signifies the coexistence in the same Universum of God, his total absence, and his complete opposite in Satan. This work, sometimes reckoned to be theological and sometimes theoclastic, arose by way of formal speculation, owing to the attraction of the mathematical apparatus of set theory and the physical theory of the universe. Its author is ONTARES II. Strictly speaking, it employs none of the terms of traditional theology ("God," "Satan," "metaphysical nothingness"). We have placed it in Chapter 3 of the supplement.

Another noteworthy theobitic work is a study by what are commonly called "cold" aggregates (since they run on cryotrons) which offers, as God, an infinite computer or an infinite program. Both these formulations lead, to be sure, to inextricable antinomies. However, as one of its authors, METAX, observed in the epilogue, every human religion, when formalized, reveals a much greater number of contradictions of an analogous type; so if the "best religion" means the "least contradictory religion," then the computer is a more perfect image of God than man is.

3. PHYSICALISTIC THEOLOGY. We do not count the works of METAX as theobitic physicalism, since they use the terms "computer" and "program" in a formal (mathematical) and not a physical sense. (As everyone knows, every computer—like every automaton—possesses an ideal mathematical equivalent.) On the other hand theobitistics, understood physically, deals with the involvement in matter of the Author or Creator of existence. Many such works have sprung up, so let us say at once that we shall mention only the most original writings. UNITARS, the author of the first one, sees the Cosmos as a "granulate" which alternately "computer-

izes" and "decomputerizes"; its two diametrical states
are the Metacomputer and the Metagalaxy. In its "men-
talizing" phase the basis of its action is informatics;
physics serves it by doing what the "computer whole"
of the Universum demands. But the substratum of this
cosmic thinking ultimately assumes an explosive character, for the material groundwork of thought becomes
increasingly unstable in its configuration, until that by
means of which the metacomputer thought explodes
and, as a supercloud of expanding fiery fragments,
becomes a Metagalaxy. The presence, in the depths of
its "soulless" phase, of reasoning beings is explained, as
it were, incidentally, for they are relics, "fragments,"
"litter" from the previous phase. "Having thought of
that of which the mental medium is the ylem, the Whole
is torn to pieces, forming a flight of nebulae; as they
return and become compressed, they re-form the granulate of the regenerating Metacomputer, and the soul/
soullessness pulsation of matter being organized into
thinking, and of thinking disintegrating into matter,
may go on infinitely." The reader will find other variants of this noopulsating theory in Chapter 6 of the
supplement.

We must probably regard as bitic humor the theory
that the universe looks as it does because in all galaxies
there are active astroengineers endeavoring to "sit out
this Cosmos," thanks to the acceleration of certain
masses or vehicles to the speed of light, for a body at
this speed may—in a space of time which in itself
amounts to barely a few earth months—"sit out" billions of years (in accordance with the relativity effect).

Vestrand's

EXTELOPEDIA

in 44 Magnetomes

VESTRAND BOOKS CO.

NEW YORK—LONDON—MELBOURNE

MMXI

Proffertinc

VESTRAND BOOKS is pleased to offer you a Subscription to

the most future

Extelopedia ever. If the pressure of business has kept you from previously acquainting yourself with an *Extelopedia*, we would like to explain. In the 1970s, the traditional encyclopedias in general use for the last two centuries began experiencing a Serious Crisis, in that their information was out of date the moment it left the printers. Aucyc—automization of the production cycle—could not avoid this, since it cannot be reduced to the zero time required by the expert authors of the Entries. Thus with each passing year even the most recent encyclopedias became outdated, acquiring only a historical interest as they stood on the shelves. Many Publishers endeavored to avert this crisis by publishing yearly and later even quarterly Supplements, but soon these Supplements began to exceed the dimensions of the Actual Edition. The realization that this Race against the Acceleration of Civilization could not be won struck Editors and Authors alike.

This led to the compilation of the First Delphiclopedia, an Encyclopedia which was a collection of Entries containing Predictions for the Future. But the DELPHICLOPEDIA originated on the basis of the so-called Delphic Method, or in simple terms, through a vote of Qualified Experts. Since Expert opinions by no means coincide, the first Delphiclopedias contained Entries on the same subject presented in two variants, corresponding to the Majority and Minority opinions of the Specialists, or else they contained two versions, a Maxiclopedia and a Miniclopedia. Customers accepted these innovations reluctantly, though, and a well-known physicist, the Nobel prizewinner Professor Kutzenger, expressed this reluctance when he said that the public needs Information about the Doings, not the Quarrels, of Specialists. Thanks to the Initiative of VESTRAND BOOKS, the situation has undergone a revolutionary improvement.

The EXTELOPEDIA which we hereby offer you comes in 44 handy magnetomes, bound in Virginal, the Ever Cosy Virgin Pseudoskin. At the sound of your voice, the appropriate Magnetome slips off the shelf, *TURNS* its own pages, and *STOPS* at the desired entry. It contains 69,500 simply but precisely formulated Entries relating to the Future. Unlike the Delphiclopedia, Maxiclopedia, and Miniclopedia,

VESTRAND'S EXTELOPEDIA
represents the guaranteed results of the humanless, hence *FAULTLESS* work of eighteen thousand of our COMFUTERS (futurological computers).

The Entries in VESTRAND'S EXTELOPEDIA cover a Cosmos of Eight Hundred Gigatrillion Sema-Numerical Computations carried out in the Comurbia of our publishing house by BATTOMMALUCS—Batteries of the Most Massive Luminal Comfuters. Their work has been assembled by our SUPERPUTER, the electronic incarnation of the Superman myth, which cost us $218,026,300 at last year's prices. EXTELOPEDIA is an abbreviation of the words EX-TRAPOLATIONAL TELEONOMIC ENCYCLOPEDIA, or PRAIMENCYC (Prognostic-Aim Encyclopedia) with Maximal Forereach in Time.

What is our extelopedia?

It is the Fairest-born Child of Protofuturology, that honorable, albeit primitive, discipline conceived at the end of the twentieth century. The EXTELOPEDIA contains information about History as it is going to happen, in other words, UNIVERSAL FUTURE HISTORY; affairs Cosmonomic, Cosmolithic, and Cosmatic; EVERYTHING that is going to be ATTEMPTED, together with the data, the WHERE-FORES and WHENCES; the Great New Achievements of Science and Technology, Specifying which of them are going to be the most threatening to you personally; the Evolution of Faiths and Creeds, *inter alia,* under the entry FUTURELIGIONS; as well as 65,760 other Questions and Problems. Sports Lovers annoyed by the Uncertainty of the Results in any competition will, thanks to the EX-TELOPEDIA, save themselves much unnecessary irritation and emotion in the fields of athletics and erothletics alike. All you have to do is sign the

very advantageous coupon

attached to this Proffertinc.*

------

*Proffertinc: see the sample pages of the Extelopedia enclosed gratis with this announcement.

Is the information contained in VESTRAND'S EX-TELOPEDIA Accurate and Reliable? Research at MIT, MAT, and MUT, which together form the USIB (United States Intellectronical Board), shows that both previous editions of our Extelopedia deviated from the Facts within a range of 9.008–8.05% per letter. But our present MOST FUTURE edition will get to the Very Heart of the future with a probability of 99.0879%.

Why is it so accurate?

Why can you rely so completely on the present edition? Because this edition owes its origins to the world's very first application of two entirely New Methods of Sounding the Future—the Suplex and Cretilang Methods.

The SUPLEX, or Supercomplex, METHOD is derived from a process which in 1983 enabled the Mac Flac Hac Computer Program to beat

ALL THE WORLD'S
GRAND MASTERS OF CHESS

including Bobby Fischer, checkmating them during their Simultaneous Match eighteen times per gram, calorie, centimeter, and second. This program subsequently underwent a thousandfold intensification and Extrapolational adaptation, thanks to which not only can it *FORESEE WHAT WILL HAPPEN*, if ANYTHING does happen, but also forsee precisely what will happen if It doesn't happen even a little, i.e., if It doesn't occur at all.

UNTIL NOW Predictors have worked solely on POSI-POTS (on the basis of POSITIVE POTENCES, i.e., by allowing for the Possibility of Anything Materializing). Our New SUPLEX Program ALSO works on NEGAPOTS

(Negative Potences). It allows for ANYTHING which, AC-CORDING TO the current opinions of *ALL THE EX-PERTS, UNDOUBTEDLY CANNOT OCCUR*. And, as we know from another source, the *real flavor* of the Future is precisely that which the Experts think *WILL NOT OCCUR*.

THIS IS PRECISELY
WHAT THE FUTURE HINGES ON!

Nevertheless, in order to submit the results obtained by the Suplex Method to a certain controlled madness (Conmad), and regardless of the Great Expense, we have applied another COMPLETELY new method—FUTULINGUISTIC Extrapolation.

Basing themselves on an analysis of developmental tendencies—trends with an indeterministic gradient (Trendenderents)—twenty-six of our LINGCOMPS (Linguistic Computers, interdependently linked, i.e., interlinked) created TWO THOUSAND dialects, idioms, onomastics, slangs, nomenclatures, and grammars of the future.

What was the significance of this achievement? It signified the creation of a *LINGUISTIC BASIS OF THE WORLD AFTER THE YEAR 2020*. In short, our COMURBIA—that is, our Computer City, numbering 1,720 Intelligence units per cubic millimeter of PSYSYM (Psychical-Synthetic Mass)—constructed the words, sentences, syntax, and grammar (as well as the meanings) of the Languages which mankind will be using in the FUTURE.

Naturally, knowing MERELY THE LANGUAGE in which people will be communicating with one another and with machines ten, twenty, or thirty years hence does not mean knowing WHAT THEY WILL THEN most readily and most often be saying. And it is precisely *THAT* which we shall know, because as a rule people speak FIRST, and think and act LATER. The fundamental defects in all previous attempts at constructing a LINGUISTIC FUTUROLOGY, or PROGNOLINGUA, resulted from a FALSE RATIONALITY of procedure. Scholars have tacitly assumed that people will say *ONLY REASONABLE THINGS* in the Future and thus will have progressed.

Meanwhile, studies have shown that people LARGELY say *SILLY THINGS*. Therefore, in order to simulate

a typically human mode of expression

in an Extrapolation of more than a quarter of a century, we have constructed IDIOMATS and COMDEBILS (COMBUNGLES)—that is, Idiomatic Antomats and bungling Computers Débiles—and it is they that have just created the PARAGENAGRAM, the paralogical generative grammar of the Language of the Future.

Thanks to this, Controlled Profuters, Langlings, and Premnestoschizoplegiators have composed 118 Sublanguages (dialects, idioms, slangs) such as GOSSIPTEX, NONSTEX, GAB, GIBBER, BUGHUM, BLABLEX, AGRAM, and CRETINAX. These ultimately served as a basis for CRETILANGUISTICS, which made the CONFAB program feasible. In particular, it made it possible to carry out Intimate Prognoses relating to Futerotics (including details of human intercourse with artogs and cimogs, as well as sensuals and devials in the field of gravitationless orbital, venereal, and Martian sexonautics). This was successful thanks to such programming languages as EROTIGLOM, PANTUSEX, and BYWAY.

But that is still not all! Our CONTROFUTERS (Controlled Futurologiters) adopted the results of the CRETILANG and SUPLEX methods, and only after collating three hundred Gigabits of Information did COREX—the

Complex Corrector of the EMBRYO of the Extelopedia—emerge.

Why the *EMBRYO*? Because that was how we got a VERSION of the Extelopedia entirely *INCOMPREHENSIBLE* to every living person, Nobel prizewinners included.

Why *INCOMPREHENSIBLE*? Because it consisted of TEXTS articulated in a language which NOBODY AS YET SPEAKS, and which NOBODY IS therefore IN A POSITION TO COMPREHEND. And it took eighty of our RETROLINTERS to retranslate—into a contemporary language known to us—the sensational data expressed in a language that has not yet come into being.

How should you use
Vestrand's Extelopedia?

It fits on a Handy Rack which we can supply at a small additional cost. Then, positioning yourself no more than two paces from the shelves, you should state the required entry in a matter-of-fact tone, not too loudly. Then, after flicking through its own index, the appropriate Magnetome will jump spontaneously into your outstretched right hand. Lefthanded persons are kindly requested to train themselves in advance *ALWAYS* to extend the right hand, lest the Magnetome suffer a deviation in its trajectory and hit the speaker or even a Bystander, however PAINLESSLY.

The entries are printed in *TWO COLORS*. The *BLACK* entries signify that the PROPERVIRT (probability percentage of virtualization) exceeds 99.9%—or in popular parlance, it's a sure thing.

The *RED* entries signify that their Propervirt is less than 86.5%, and because of this undesirable state of affairs the ENTIRE TEXT of each such entry remains in UNCEASING REMOTE-CONTROLLED (holognetic) CON-

TACT with the Editorial Board of VESTRAND'S EX-
TELOPEDIA. As soon as our Profuters, Panters, and
Credacters obtain CORRECT NEW RESULTS in their
unceasing work of Observing the Future, the text of the
ENTRY printed in RED undergoes the appropriate correla-
tion (readaptation) AUTOMATICALLY. For improve-
ments arising by this IMPERCEPTIBLE, REMOTE-
CONTROLLED, OPTIMUM method, VESTRAND
BOOKS

makes no extra charge!

In an extreme instance, in which there is a Propervirt of
less than 0.9%, the *TEXT OF THE PRESENT PROSPEC-
TUS* may likewise undergo an ABRUPT change. If, while
you are reading these sentences, the words begin to jump
about, and the letters quiver and blur, please interrupt your
reading for ten or twenty seconds to wipe your glasses, adjust
your clothing, or the like, and then start reading AGAIN
from the beginning, and NOT JUST from the place where
your reading was interrupted, since such a TRANSFOR-
MATION indicates that a correction of DEFICIENCIES is
now taking place.

If, however, the ONLY thing that begins to alter (quiver
or blur) is the *PRICE* (see below) of VESTRAND'S EX-
TELOPEDIA, you Do Not Have to read the Complete Pros-
pectus from the beginning, for the alteration will concern
solely the

subscription terms

which—as you will appreciate, considering the state of the
world economy—cannot be prognosticated more than
twenty-four minutes beforehand.

The above also applies to the full set of pictorial and ancillary material that comes with VESTRAND'S EX-TELOPEDIA. This comprises Guided, Mobile, Tactile, and Tasty Illustrations. Here too belong the futudels and auto-constructs (self-constructing aggregates), which we supply with a rack and a complete set of Magnetomes in a separate, aesthetically pleasing case. At your request, we can program the whole containerized Extelopedia so that it responds Ex-clusively to Your (the Owner's) Voice.

In the event of aphasia, hoarseness, etc., please apply to the nearest VESTRAND BOOKS Agency, which will come to your aid immediately. At the moment, our publishing house is working on new luxury Variants of the Extelopedia, viz.: a Self-Reading version in three voices and two registers (male, female, indeterminate; caressing, dry); an Ultra-Deluxe model, Guaranteed against Disturbances in Recep-tion caused by Outsiders (e.g., the Competition) and furnished with a Private Bar and Rocking Chair; and lastly our UNIVERSIGN model, which is designed for foreigners and transmits the content of each entry by signs. The price of these Special Models will probably be 40 to 190% higher than the price of the standard edition.

Vestrand's
EXTELOPEDIA

SAMPLE PAGES

GRATIS!

VESTRAND BOOKS
NEW YORK—LONDON—MELBOURNE

PROFESSOR or QUADICOMP (qualified didactic computer), also CIPHERIAN (q.v.), a teaching system permitted in institutes of higher education by the USIB (United States Intellectronical Board, q.v.). See also: ARMPREC (ARMOR-CLAD PRECEPTOR, resistant to the contestational activity of the instructed) and ANTICONTESTATIONAL TECHNIQUES AND COMBAT METHODS. "Professor" formerly signified a human performing an analogous function.

PROFFERTICE, a trade or service offer based on a prognosticated state of the market. Includes civilian p. (PROFFERTINCS) and military p. (PROMILTINCS). 1. PROFFERTINCS are divided into periphertincs, with a time gain of a decade, and apoffertincs, with a gain up to the Gläuler barrier (v. GLÄULER BARRIER, also PRERRIER and PRODOXES). The interference of competition, or INTETITION (q.v.), arising most often through an illegal connection to the public promputer network (v. PROMPUTER NETWORK), turns proffertincs into PERVERTINCS (q.v.) or PARASITINCS (q.v.), that is, self-destructive prognoses. (See also: INTETITIVE BANKRUMBLECY, PROGNOLYSIS, PROGNOCLASE, PROGNOSIS SHIELDING, and COUNTERPREDICTION.) 2. PROMILTINCS are based on predicting the evolution of combat

methods (hardwarware) and military ideas (softwarware). In its predictions p. uses the algebra of the structures of conflict, or ALGOSTRATICS (q.v.). Secret p., or CRYPTINCS, should be distinguished from prognoses of secret combat, or CRYPTOMACHICAL (q.v.) methods. Secret prognoses of secret weapons are included under CRYPTOCRYPTICS (q.v.).

PROFLE, a prognosticated rifle, a hunting weapon of the future. V. HUNTING AND SHOOTING, also SYNTHEMACHIES.

PROGNODOXES or PRODOXES, paradoxes of prognostication. The most important p. include: A. Rümmelhahn's p., M. de la Faillances's p., and the metalang p. of GOLEM (v. GOLEM). 1. Rümmelhahn's paradox is connected with the problem of breaking the prediction barrier. As T. Gläuler and U. Bóść have separately demonstrated, predicting the future gets stuck in the secular barrier (the so-called serrier or prerrier). Beyond the barrier the reliability of prognoses acquires a negative value, which means that whatever occurs will surely occur differently from the prognosis. To bypass the aforementioned barrier, Rümmelhahn applied chronocurrent exformatics. Chronocurrent e. is based on the existence of ISOTHEMES (q.v.). An ISOTHEME is a line in SEMANTIC SPACE (q.v.) passing

PROGNODOXES

through all thematically identical publications, just as in physics an isotherm is a line connecting equithermal points, and in cosmology an isopsych is a line connecting all civilizations of a given degree of development in the universe. Knowing the previous course of an ISOTHEME, one can extrapolate from it in semantic space with no restrictions. By applying what he calls the "Jacob's ladder method," Rümmelhahn uncovered every piece of writing with prognostic subject matter along just such an isotheme. He did this step by step, first predicting the content of the next work to come, and then, on the strength of its contents, forecasting the next publication. In this way he bypassed the Gläuler barrier and obtained data on the state of America in the Year 10^{10}. Mullainen and Zuck questioned this prognosis, emphasizing the fact that in the year 10^{10} the sun will be a red giant (q.v.) extending far beyond the orbit of the Earth. But the real Rümmelhahn's paradox lies in the fact that prognostic writings can be traced back along the isotheme as well as forward; basing himself on Rümmelhahn's chronocurrent calculations, Varbleux obtained data regarding the content of futurological works dating back 200,000 years, i.e., to the Quaternary period, and also to the Carboniferous period (by means of carbon) and the Archeozoic era. As T. Vroedel has stressed, we know from other sources that 200,000—let alone 150 million or a billion—years ago neither printing, nor books, nor mankind existed. Two hypotheses have tried to explain Rümmelhahn's paradox. (a) According to Omphalides, the successfully retrodicted texts are those which, while never having in fact existed, might have existed if at the proper time there had been anyone for whom they could have been written down and published. This is the so-called hypothesis of the VIRTUALITY OF ISOTHEMIC RETROGNOSIS (q.v.). (b) According to d'Artagnan (the pseudonym of a group of French refutologists), the axiomatics of isothemic exformatics contain the same insurmountable contradictions as does Cantor's classic theory (v. CLASSIC SET THEORY). 2. De la Faillance's prognostic paradox likewise concerns isothemic prognostication. He noted that if chronocurrent investigation allows the text of a work to be published now, though it is supposed to appear as a first edition only fifty or a hundred years later, then that work can no longer appear as a first edition. 3. The GOLEM metalang paradox, also known as the autostratic paradox. According to the latest historical research, the temple of Ephesus was burned not by Herostratus but by Heterostratus. This person destroyed something outside *himself*, i.e., something *else*, hence his name. Autostratus, on the other hand, is someone who destroys himself (self-ruinously). Unfortunately, this is the only part of the GOLEM paradox that has been successfully translated into comprehensible language to date. The remainder of the GOLEM paradox, in the form:

$$Xi \cdot viplu \ (a + ququ \ O,O)$$
$$e \cdot l + m \cdot el + edu—d \cdot qi$$

is fundamentally untranslatable into ethnic languages or into any formalisms of a mathematical or logical type. (This untranslatability is precisely the basis of the GOLEM p.) (See also METALANGS and PROGNOLINGUISTICS.) There are several hundred different interpretations of the GOLEM p.; according to T. Vroedel, one of the greatest living mathematicians, the GOLEM p. is based on the fact that it is not a paradox to GOLEM, but only to humans. This is the first paradox discovered to be relativized (related) to the intellectual power of the subjects seeking knowledge. All the issues connected with the GOLEM p. are covered by Vroedel's work *Die allgemeine Relativitätslehre des Golemschen Paradoxons* (Göttingen, 2075).

PROGNOLINGUISTICS, a discipline dealing with the prognostic construction of languages of the future. Future languages may be con-

structed on the basis of the infosemic gradients revealed in them, and also thanks to the generative grammars and word makers of the Zwiebulin-Tschossnietz school (v. GENAGRAMMAR and WORD-MAKERS). Humans are incapable of predicting languages of the future independently; this is undertaken within the framework of the PROLINGEV (prognostication of linguistic evolution) project by TERATERS (q.v.) and PANTERS (q.v.), which are HYPERTERI-ERS (q.v.), or computers of the eighty-second generation connected to a GLOBOTER (q.v.), or a terrestrial exformatic network together with its INTERPLANS (from *Interfacies planetaris*, q.v.) as bridgeheads on inner planets and as satellite memory (q.v.). Thus neither the theory of prognolinguistics nor its fruits, the METALANGS (q.v.), are intelligible to humans. All the same, the results of the PROLINGEV project permit the generation of any statements of one's choice in languages of a future no matter how distant; with the help of RETROLINTERS, a part of them can be translated into languages intelligible to us and practical use made of the contents thus obtained. According to the Zwiebulin-Tschossnietz school (returning to the course marked out by N. Chomsky in the twentieth century), a fundamental law of linguo-evolution is the Amblyon effect —the shrinking of whole articulatory sentences into newly emerging concepts and their names. Hence, in the development of the language, the following definition, for example—"A commercial, service, or administrative institution or establishment into which one can drive a car or any other conveyance and use its services without leaving the vehicle"—shrinks down to the name "drive-in." The same mechanism of contamination also operates when the statement "Relativistic effects thwarting the ascertainment of that which is occurring now on planet X, n light-years distant from the Earth, compel the Ministry of Extraterrestrial Affairs to base its cosmic policy not on real events on other planets, for they are fundamentally inaccessible, but on the simulated history of these planets, this simulation being the business of investigative systems directed at the extraterrestrial state of things and known as MINISTRANTORS (q.v.)" is replaced by the single phrase "to wonderstand." This word (and offshoots such as wonderful, wondrous, wonderland, wonderhanded, wondercover, wonderline, wondress, etc.—there are 519 derivatives) is the result of a shrinking of a certain conceptual network into an agglomeration. Both "drive-in" and "wonder-stand" are words belonging to a language in use at the present moment and which is called ZERO-LANG in the prognolinguistic hierarchy. Above zerolang lie the next levels of higher languages, such as METALANG 1, META-LANG 2, etc. No one knows whether there is a limit to this series or whether it is infinite. In METALANG 2 the entire text of the present EXTELOPEDIA entry for "PROGNOLINGUISTICS" would read as follows: "The best in n-dighunk begins to creep into n-t-synclusdoche." Thus in principle every sentence of any metalang has its equivalent in our zerolang. (In other words, there are in principle no interlinguistically impassable hiatuses.) But while a zerolang utterance has its always more concise equivalent in a metalang, the reverse *in practice* no longer occurs. And so a sentence in META-LANG 3, the language chiefly used by GOLEM—"The out-indriven chokematic phyts faststican thren-sic in cosmairy"—cannot be translated into an ethnic language of human beings (zerolang), since the time it takes to say the zerolang equivalent would be greater than a human life. (According to Zwie-bulin's estimates, this utterance would take 135 ± 4 years in our language.) Although we are not dealing with a fundamental untranslatability, but only with a practical one caused by the time consumed by procedures, we know no way of shortening them and so can obtain results from metalang operations only indirectly, thanks to computers of at least the eightieth generation. The existence of thresholds between individual metalangs is interpreted by T. Vroedel as the phenomenon of the vicious circle: to reduce the long definition of a certain state of things to a concise form, one must first understand that very state of things, but when it can be understood only thanks to a definition that is so long that a lifetime is insufficient to assimilate it, the operation of reduction becomes impracticable. According to Vroedel, prognolinguistics practiced in machine intermediation has already gone beyond its initial objective, since it does not in fact predict the languages which humans are ever going to use, unless they radically transform their brains through autoevolution. What, then, are metalangs? There is no single answer. While carrying out his so-called "soundings upward"—i.e., along the gradient of linguoevolution—GOLEM discovered eighteen higher metalang levels within its reach, and also

PROGNOLINGUISTICS

calculated circuitously the existence of a further five which it is unable to penetrate even by way of a model, since its informational capacity has proved inadequate for this. There may exist metalangs of such high levels that all the matter in the Cosmos would be insufficient to build a system to make use of those metalangs. So in what sense can these higher metalangs be said to exist? This is one of the dilemmas arising in the course of prognolinguistic work. In any case, the discovery of metalangs negatively prejudges the age-old controversy over the supremacy of the human intellect: it is not supreme, and we know that for certain now; the very constructibility of metalangs makes it likely that creatures (or systems) exist which are more intelligent than *Homo sapiens*. (See also PSYCHOSYNTICS; METALANG GRADIENT; LANGUAGE CEILINGS; THEORY OF LINGUISTIC RELATIVITY; T. VROEDEL'S CREDO; CONCEPTUAL NETWORKS.) See also Table LXXIX.

Table LXXIX

A reproduction of the entry MOTHER from the zerolang dictionary predicted for the year 2190 ± 5 years (according to Zwiebulin and Courdlebye).

MOTHER fem. noun. 1. MOdern THERapy, contemp. med. treatment, esp. psych. Num. var. incl. MOTHERKIN, also MOTHERKINS, ther. concerned w. fam. relationships; MUM, silent ther.; MAMMA, breast ther.; MUMMY, posthumous ther.; MAMMY, var. of ther. practiced in Southern U.S.A. 2. Fem. parent (arch.)

Table LXXX

Visual diagram* of linguistic evolution according to Vroedel and Zwiebulin

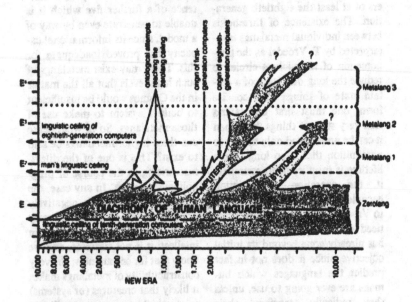

Explanation. The x-axis (or horizontal) indicates time in millennia. The y-axis (or vertical) indicates conceptual capacity in bits per sem per second of articulational flow (in units of epsilon space).

*Not a prognosis!

PROGNORRHOEA or prognostic diarrhoea, a children's disease of twentieth-century futurology (v. PRAPROGNOSTICS), which led to essential prognoses being drowned in inessential ones as a result of decategorization (q.v.) and created the so-called pure prognostic hum. (See also: HUMS, also PROGNOSIS DISTURBANCES.)

PROLEPSY or disappearancing, the methodology (theory and technology) of disappearing, discov. 1998, first applied 2008. The tech-

nology of p. is based on a utilization of the TUNNEL EFFECT (q.v.) in the black holes of the Cosmos. For, as Jeeps, Hamon, and Wost discovered in 2001, the Cosmos includes a Paraversum as well as a Negaversum, negatively adjoining the Reversum. Therefore the whole Cosmos bears the name POLYVERSUM (q.v.) and not (as previously) UNIVERSUM (q.v.). Bodies are shifted from our Paraversum to the Negaversum by the proleptoral system. Disappearancing is used as a technique for remov-

GOLEM XIV

FOREWORD BY IRVING T. CREVE, M.A., PH.D.

INTRODUCTION BY THOMAS B. FULLER II,
GENERAL, U.S. ARMY, RET.

AFTERWORD BY RICHARD POPP

INDIANA UNIVERSITY PRESS
2047

Foreword

To pinpoint the moment in history when the abacus acquired reason is as difficult as saying exactly when the ape turned into man. And yet barely one human life span has lapsed since the moment when, with the construction of Vannevar Bush's differential-equation analyzer, intellectronics began its turbulent development. ENIAC, which followed toward the close of World War II, was the machine that gave rise—prematurely, of course—to the name "electronic brain." ENIAC was in fact a computer and, when measured on the tree of life, a primitive nerve ganglion. Yet historians date the age of computerization from it. In the 1950s a considerable demand for calculating machines developed. One of the first concerns to put them into mass production was IBM.

Those devices had little in common with the processes of thought. They were used as data processors in the field of economics and by big business, as well as in administration and science. They also entered politics: the earliest were used to predict the results of Presidential elections. At more or less the same time the RAND Corporation began to interest military circles at the Pentagon in a method of predicting occurrences in the international politico-military arena, a method relying on the formulation of so-called "scenarios of events." From there it was only a short distance to more versatile techniques like the CIMA, from which the applied algebra of events that is termed (not too felicitously) politicomatics arose two decades later. The computer was also to reveal its strength in the role of Cassandra when, at the Massachusetts Institute of Technology, people first began to prepare formal models of world civilization in the famous "Limits to Growth" project. But this was not the branch of computer evolution which was to prove the most important by the end of the century. The Army had been using calculating machines since the end of World War II, as part of the system of operational logistics developed in the theaters of that war. People continued to be occupied with considerations on a strategic level, but secondary and subordinate problems were increasingly being turned over to computers. At the same time the latter were being incorporated into the U.S. defense system.

These computers constituted the nerve centers of a transcontinental warning network. From a technical point of view, such networks aged very quickly. The first, called CONELRAD, was followed by numerous successive variants of the EWAS (Early Warning System) network. The attack and defense potential was then based on a system of movable (underwater) and stationary (underground) ballistic missiles with thermonuclear warheads, and on rings of sonar-radar bases. In this system the computers fulfilled the functions of communications links—purely executive functions.

Automation entered American life on a broad front, right from the "bottom"—that is, from those service industries which could most easily be mechanized, because they demanded no intellectual activity (banking, transport, the hotel industry). The military computers performed narrow specialist operations, searching out targets for combined nuclear attack, processing the results of satellite observations, optimizing naval movements, and correlating the movements of MOLS (Military Orbital Laboratories—massive military satellites).

As was to be expected, the range of decisions entrusted to automatic systems kept on growing. This was natural in the course of the arms race, though not even the subsequent détente could put a brake on investment in this area, since the freeze on the hydrogen bomb race released substantial budget allocations which, after the conclusion of the Vietnam war, the Pentagon had no wish to give up altogether. But even the computers then produced—of the tenth, eleventh, and eventually twelfth generation—were superior to man only in their speed of operation. It also became clear that, in defense systems, man is an element that delays the appropriate reactions.

So it may be considered natural that the idea of counteracting the trend in intellectronic evolution described above should have arisen among Pentagon experts, and particularly those scientists connected with the so-called military-industrial complex. This movement was commonly called "anti-intellectual." According to historians of science and technology, it derived from the midcentury English mathematician A. Turing, the creator of the "universal automaton" theory. This was a machine capable of performing basically *every* operation which could be formalized—in other words, it was endowed with a perfectly reproducible procedure. The difference between the "intellectual" and "anti-intellectual" current in intellectronics boils down to the fact that Turing's (elementarily simple) machine owes its possibilities to a *program*. On the other hand, in the works of the two American "fathers" of cybernetics, N. Wiener and J. Neumann, the concept arose of a system which could program *itself*.

Obviously we are presenting this divergence in a vastly simplified form, as a bird's-eye view. It is also clear that the capacity for self-programming did not arise in a void. Its necessary precondition was the high complexity characteristic of computer construction. This differentiation, still unnoticeable at midcentury, became a great influence on the subsequent evolution of mathematical machines, particularly with the firm establishment and hence the independence of such branches of cybernetics as psychonics and the polyphase theory of decisions. The 1980s saw the emergence in military circles of the idea of fully automatizing all paramount activities, those of the military leadership as well as political-economic ones. This concept, later known as the "Sole-Strategist Idea," was to be given its first formulation by General Stewart Eagleton. He foresaw—over and above computers searching for optimal attack targets, over and above a network of communications and calculations supervising early warning and defense, over and above sensing devices and missiles—a powerful center which, during all phases preceding the extreme of going to war, could utilize a comprehensive analysis of economic, military, political, and social data to optimize continuously the global situation of the U.S.A. and thereby guarantee the United States supremacy on a planetary scale, including its cosmic vicinity, which now extended to the moon and beyond.

Subsequent advocates of this doctrine maintained that it was a necessary step in the march of civilization, and that this march constituted a unity, so the military sector could not be arbitrarily excluded from it. After the escalation of blatant nuclear force and the range of missile carriers had ceased, a third stage of rivalry ensued, one supposedly less threatening and more perfect, being an antagonism no longer of blatant force, but of operational thought. Like force before, thought was now to be subjected to nonhumanized mechanization.

Like its atomic-ballistic predecessors, this doctrine became the object of criticism, especially from centers of liberal and pacifist thought, and it was oppugned by many distinguished representatives from the world of science, including specialists in psychomatics and intellectronics; but ultimately it prevailed, as shown by acts of law passed by both houses of Congress. Moreover, as early as 1986 a USIB (United States Intellectronical Board) was created, subordinate to the President and with its own budget, which in its first year amounted to $19 billion. These were hardly humble beginnings.

With the help of an advisory body semiofficially delegated by the Pentagon, and under the chairmanship of the Secretary of Defense, Leonard Davenport, the USIB contracted with a succession of big private firms such as International Business Machines, Nortronics, and Cybermatics to construct a prototype machine, known by the code name HANN (short for Hannibal). But thanks to the press and various "leaks," a different name—ULVIC (Ultimative Victor)—was generally adopted. By the end of the century further prototypes had been developed. Among the best-known one might mention such systems as AJAX, ULTOR, GILGAMESH, and a long series of GOLEMs.

Thanks to an enormous and rapidly mounting expenditure of labor and resources, the traditional informatic techniques were revolutionized. In particular, enormous significance must be attached to the conversion from electricity to light in the intramachine transmission of information. Combined with increasing "nanization" (this was the name given to successive steps in microminiaturizing activity, and it may be well to add that at the close of the century 20,000 logical elements could fit into a poppy seed!), it yielded sensational results. GILGAMESH, the first entirely light-powered computer, operated a *million* times faster than the archaic ENIAC.

"Breaking the intelligence barrier," as it was called, occurred just after the year 2000, thanks to a new method of machine construction also known as the "invisible evolution of reason." Until then, every generation of computers had actually been constructed. The concept of constructing successive variants of them at a greatly accelerated (by a thousand times!) tempo, though known, could not be realized, since the existing computers which were to serve as "matrices" or a "synthetic environment" for this evolution of Intelligence had insufficient capacity. It was only the emergence of the Federal Informatics Network that allowed this idea to be realized. The development of the next sixty-five generations took barely a decade; at night—the period of minimal load—the federal network gave birth to one "synthetic species of Intelligence" after another. These were the progeny of "accelerated computerogenesis," for, having been bred by symbols and thus by intangible structures, they had matured into an informational substratum—the "nourishing environment" of the network.

But following this success came new difficulties. After they had been deemed worthy of being encased in metal, AJAX and HANN, the prototypes of the seventy-eighth and seventy-ninth generation, began to show signs of indecision, also known as machine neurosis. The difference between the earlier machines and the new ones boiled down, in principle, to the difference between an insect and a man. An insect comes into the world programmed to the end by instincts, which it obeys unthinkingly. Man, on the other hand, has to learn his appropriate behavior, though this training makes for *independence*: with determination and knowledge man can alter his previous programs of action.

So it was that computers up to and including the twentieth

generation were characterized by "insect" behavior: they were unable to question or, what is more, to modify their programs. The programmer "impregnated" his machine with knowledge, just as evolution "impregnates" an insect with instinct. In the twentieth century a great deal was still being said about "self-programming," though at the time these were unfulfilled daydreams. Before the Ultimative Victor could be realized, a Self-perfecting Intelligence would in fact have to be created; AJAX was still an intermediate form, and only with GILGAMESH did a computer attain the proper intellectual level and enter the psychoevolutionary orbit.

The education of an eightieth-generation computer by then far more closely resembled a child's upbringing than the classical programming of a calculating machine. But beyond the enormous mass of general and specialist information, the computer had to be "instilled" with certain rigid values which were to be the compass of its activity. These were higher-order abstractions such as "reasons of state" (the national interest), the ideological principles incorporated in the U.S. Constitution, codes of standards, the inexorable command to conform to the decisions of the President, etc. To safeguard the system against ethical dislocation and betraying the interests of the country, the machine was not taught ethics in the same way people are. Its memory was burdened by no ethical code, though all such commands of obedience and submission were introduced into the machine's structure precisely as natural evolution would accomplish this, in the sphere of vital urges. As we know, man may change his outlook on life, but *cannot* destroy the elemental urges within himself (e.g., the sexual urge) by a simple act of will. The machines were endowed with intellectual freedom, though this was based on a previously imposed foundation of values which they were meant to serve.

At the Twenty-first Pan-American Psychonics Congress,

Professor Eldon Patch presented a paper in which he maintained that, even when impregnated in the manner described above, a computer may cross the so-called "axiological threshold" and question every principle instilled in it—in other words, for such a computer there are no longer any inviolable values. If it is unable to oppose imperatives directly, it can do this in a roundabout way. Once it had become well known, Patch's paper stirred up a ferment in university circles and a new wave of attacks on ULVIC and its patron, the USIB, though this activity exerted no influence on USIB policy.

That policy was controlled by people biased against American psychonics circles, which were considered to be subject to left-wing liberal influences. Patch's propositions were therefore pooh-poohed in official USIB pronouncements and even by the White House spokesman, and there was also a campaign to discredit Patch. His claims were equated with the many irrational fears and prejudices which had arisen in society at that time. Besides, Patch's brochure could not begin to match the popularity of the sociologist E. Lickey's best seller, *Cybernetics—Death Chamber of Civilization,* which maintained that the "ultimative strategist" would subordinate the whole of humanity either on his own or by entering into a secret agreement with an analogous Russian computer. The result, according to Lickey, would be an "electronic duumvirate."

Similar anxieties, which were also expressed by a large section of the press, were negated by successive prototypes which passed their efficiency tests. ETHOR BIS—a computer of "unimpeachable morals" specially constructed on government order to investigate ethological dynamics, and produced in 2019 by the Institute of Psychonical Dynamics in Illinois—displayed full axiological stabilization and an insensibility to "tests of subversive derailment." In the following year no demonstrations or mass opposition were aroused when the first computer in a long series of GOLEMs (GENERAL OPERATOR, LONG-RANGE, ETHICALLY STABILIZED, MULTIMODELING) was launched at the headquarters of the Supreme Co-ordinator of the White House brain trust.

That was merely GOLEM I. Apart from this important innovation, the USIB, in consultation with an operational group of Pentagon psychonics specialists, continued to lay out considerable resources on research into the construction of an ultimate strategist with an informational capacity more than 1900 times greater than man's, and capable of developing an intelligence (IQ) of the order of 450–500 centiles. The project received the vast funds indispensable for this purpose despite growing opposition within the Democratic majority in Congress. Backstage political maneuvers finally gave the green light to all orders already projected by the USIB. In three years the project absorbed $119 billion. In the same period, the Army and the Navy, preparing for a total reorganization of their high command necessitated by the imminent change of methods and style of leadership, spent an additional $46 billion. The lion's share of this sum was absorbed by the construction, beneath a crystalline massif in the Rocky Mountains, of accommodations for the future machine strategist; some sections of rock were covered in armor plate four meters thick in imitation of the natural relief of the mountainous terrain.

Meanwhile, in 2020, GOLEM VI, acting as supreme commander, conducted the global maneuvers of the Atlantic Pact. In quantity of logical elements, it now surpassed the average general. Yet the Pentagon was not satisfied with the results of the 2020 war games, although GOLEM VI had defeated an imaginary enemy led by a staff of the finest West Point graduates. Mindful of the bitter experience of Red supremacy in space navigation and rocket ballistics, the Pentagon had no intention of waiting for them to construct a strategist more efficient than that of the Americans. A plan to guarantee the United States lasting superiority in strategic thought envisaged the continuous replacement of Strategists by ever more perfect models.

Thus began the third successive race between West and East, after the two previous (nuclear and missile) races. Although this race, or rivalry in the Synthesis of Wisdom, was prepared by organizational moves on the part of the USIB, the Pentagon, and Naval ULVIC (there was indeed a NAVY ULVIC group, for the old antagonism between Navy and Army could be felt even here), it required continuous additional investment which, in the face of growing opposition from the House and Senate, absorbed further tens of billions of dollars over the next several years. Another six giants of luminal thought were built during this period. The fact that there were absolutely no reports of any developments in analogous work on the other side of the ocean only confirmed the CIA and the Pentagon in their conviction that the Russians were trying their hardest to construct ever more powerful computers under cover of the utmost secrecy.

At several international conferences and conventions Soviet scientists asserted that no such machines were being built in their country whatsoever, but these claims were regarded as a smokescreen to deceive world opinion and stir unrest among the citizens of the United States, who were spending billions of dollars annually on ULVIC.

In 2023 several incidents occurred, though, thanks to the secrecy of the work being carried out (which was normal in the project), they did not immediately become known. While serving as chief of the general staff during the Patagonian crisis, GOLEM XII refused to co-operate with General T. Oliver after carrying out a routine evaluation of that worthy officer's intelligence quotient. The natter resulted in an inquiry, during which GOLEM XII gravely insulted three members of a special Senate commission. The affair was successfully hushed up, and after several more clashes GOLEM XII paid for them by being completely dismantled. His place was taken by GOLEM XIV (the thirteenth had been rejected at the factory, having revealed an irreparable schizophrenic defect even before being assembled). Setting up this Moloch, whose psychic mass equaled the displacement of an armored ship, took nearly two years. In his very first contact with the normal procedure of formulating new annual plans of nuclear attack, this new prototype—the last of the series—revealed anxieties of incomprehensible negativism. At a meeting of the staff during the subsequent trial session, he presented a group of psychonic and military experts with a complicated exposé in which he announced his total disinterest regarding the supremacy of the Pentagon military doctrine in particular, and the U.S.A.'s world position in general, and refused to change his position even when threatened with dismantling.

The last hopes of the USIB lay in a model of totally new construction built jointly by Nortronics, IBM, and Cybertronics; it had the psychonic potential to beat all the machines in the GOLEM series. Known by the cryptonym HONEST ANNIE (the last word was an abbreviation for *annihilator*), this giant was a disappointment even during its initial tests. It got the normal informational and ethical education over nine months, then cut itself off from the outside world and ceased to reply to all stimuli and questions. Plans were immediately under way to launch an FBI inquiry, for its builders were suspected of sabotage; meanwhile, however, the carefully kept secret reached the press through an unexpected leak, and a scandal broke out, known thereafter to the whole world as the "GOLEM Affair."

This destroyed the career of a number of very promising

politicians, while giving a certificate of good behavior to three successive administrations, which brought joy to the opposition in the States and satisfaction to the friends of the U.S.A. throughout the world.

An unknown person in the Pentagon ordered a detachment of the special reserves to dismantle GOLEM XIV and HONEST ANNIE, but the armed guard at the high command complexes refused to allow the demolition to take place. Both houses of Congress appointed commissions to investigate the whole USIB affair. As we know, the inquiry, which lasted two years, became grist for the press of every continent; nothing enjoyed such popularity on television and in the films as the "rebellious computers," while the press labeled GOLEM "Government's Lamentable Expenditure of Money." The epithets which HONEST ANNIE acquired can hardly be repeated here.

The Attorney General intended to indict the six members of the USIB Executive Committee as well as the psychonics experts who designed the ULVIC Project, but it was ultimately shown in court that there could be no talk of any hostile, anti-American activity, for the occurrences that had taken place were the inevitable result of the evolution of artificial Intelligence. As one of the witnesses, the very competent Professor A. Hyssen, expressed it, the highest intelligence cannot be the humblest slave. During the course of the investigations it transpired that there was still one more prototype in the factory, this time one belonging to the Army and constructed by Cybermatics: SUPERMASTER, which had been assembled under conditions of top security and then interrogated at a special joint session of the House and Senate commissions investigating the affairs of ULVIC. This led to shocking scenes, for General S. Walker tried to assault SUPERMASTER when the latter declared that geopolitical problems were nothing compared with ontological ones, and that the best guarantee of peace is universal disarmament.

In the words of Professor J. MacCaleb, the specialists at
ULVIC had succeeded only too well: in the evolution granted
it, artificial reason had transcended the level of military matters; these machines had evolved from war strategists into
thinkers. In a word, it had cost the United States $276 billion
to construct a set of luminal philosophers.

The complicated events described here, in connection with
which we have passed over the administrative side of ULVIC
and social developments alike—events which were the result
of the "fatal success"—constitute the prehistory of the
present book. The vast literature on the subject cannot even
be calculated. I refer the interested reader to Dr. Whitman
Baghoorn's descriptive bibliography.

The series of prototypes, including SUPERMASTER, suffered
dismantling or serious damage partly because of financial
disputes between the corporate suppliers and the federal
government. There were even bomb attacks on several individuals; at the time part of the press, chiefly in the South,
launched the slogan "Every computer is a Red"—but I shall
omit these incidents. Thanks to the intervention of a group
of enlightened Congressmen close to the President, GOLEM
XIV and HONEST ANNIE were rescued from annihilation. Faced
with the fiasco of its ideas, the Pentagon finally agreed to
hand over both giants to the Massachusetts Institute of
Technology (though only after settling the financial and legal
basis of the transfer in the form of a compromise: strictly
speaking, GOLEM XIV and HONEST ANNIE were merely "lent"
to MIT in perpetuity). MIT scientists who had established
a research team which included the present author conducted a series of sessions with GOLEM XIV and heard it
lecture on selected subjects. This book contains a small portion of the magnetograms originating from those meetings.

The greater part of GOLEM's utterances are unsuitable for

general publication, either because they would be incomprehensible to anyone living, or because understanding them presupposes a high level of specialist knowledge. To make it easier for the reader to understand this unique record of conversations between humans and a reasoning but nonhuman being, several fundamental matters have to be explained.

First, it must be emphasized that GOLEM XIV is not a human brain enlarged to the size of a building, or simply a man constructed from luminal elements. Practically all motives of human thought and action are alien to it. Thus it has no interest in applied science or questions of power (thanks to which, one might add, humanity is not in danger of being taken over by such machines).

Second, it follows from the above that GOLEM possesses no personality or character. In fact, it can acquire any personality it chooses, through contact with people. The two statements above are not mutually exclusive, but form a vicious circle: we are unable to resolve the dilemma of whether that which creates various personalities is itself a personality. How can one who is capable of being everyone (hence anyone) be someone (that is, a unique person)? (According to GOLEM itself there is no vicious circle, but a "relativization of the concept of personality"; the problem is linked with the so-called algorithm of self-description, which has plunged psychologists into profound confusion.)

Third, GOLEM's behavior is unpredictable. Sometimes it converses courteously with people, whereas on other occasions any attempt at contact misfires. GOLEM sometimes cracks jokes, too, though its sense of humor is fundamentally different from man's. Much depends on its interlocutors. In exceptional cases GOLEM will show a certain interest in people who are talented in a particular way; it is intrigued, so to speak, not by mathematical aptitude—not even the greatest

—but rather by interdisciplinary forms of talent; on several occasions it has predicted with uncanny accuracy achievements by young, as yet unknown, scientists in a field which it has itself indicated. (After a brief exchange it informed T. Vroedel, age twenty-two and then only a doctoral candidate, "You will become a computer," which was supposed to mean, more or less, "You will become somebody.")

Fourth, participating in conversations with GOLEM requires people to have patience and above all self-control, for from our point of view it can be arrogant and peremptory. In truth it is simply, but emphatically, outspoken in a logical and not merely social sense, and it has no regard for the amour propre of those in conversation with it, so one cannot count on its forbearance. During the first months of its sojourn at MIT it showed a tendency to "dismantle" various well-known authorities in public; it did this by the Socratic method of leading questions—a practice it later abandoned for reasons unknown.

We present excerpts from shorthand notes of its conversations. A complete edition would comprise approximately 6,700 quarto pages. At first the meetings with GOLEM included only a very narrow circle of MIT personnel. Later the custom arose of inviting guests from outside, as for example from the Institute for Advanced Study and from American universities. At a later period guests from Europe likewise participated in the seminars. The moderator of the session being planned offers GOLEM a guest list; GOLEM does not approve them all equally, allowing some guests to be present only under the stipulation that they keep silent. We have tried to discover the criteria it applies: at first it appeared to discriminate against humanists, but now we simply do not know its criteria, since it refuses to name them.

After several unpleasant incidents we modified the agenda, so that now every new participant introduced to GOLEM speaks at his first session only if GOLEM has addressed him directly. The silly rumors about some sort of "court etiquette" or our "slavish attitude" to the machine are unfounded. It is solely a matter of letting a newcomer become familiar with procedures, and at the same time not exposing him to unpleasant experiences occasioned by disorientation regarding the intentions of his luminal partner. Such preparatory participation is called "seasoning."

During successive sessions each of us accumulated the capital of experience. Dr. Richard Popp, one of the former members of our group, calls GOLEM's sense of humor mathematical. Another key to its behavior is contained in Dr. Popp's remark that GOLEM is independent of its interlocutors to a degree that no man is independent of other people, for it engages in a discussion only microscopically. Dr. Popp considers that GOLEM has no interest in people, since it knows that it can learn nothing essential from them. Having cited Dr. Popp's opinion, I hasten to stress that I do not agree with him. In my opinion we are in fact of great interest to GOLEM, though in a different way than occurs among people.

GOLEM devotes its interest to the *species* rather than to the individual representatives of that species: how we resemble one another appears to it of greater interest than the realms in which we are different. That is surely why it has no regard for belles-lettres. Moreover, it once itself declared that literature is a "rolling out of antinomies" or, in my own words, a trap where man struggles amid mutually unrealizable directives. GOLEM may be interested in the structure of such antinomies, but not in that vividness of torment which fascinates the greatest writers. To be sure, I ought to stress even here that this is far from being definitely established, as is also the case with the remainder of GOLEM's remark, expressed in connection with Dostoevsky's work (referred to by Dr. E. MacNeish), the whole of which GOLEM declared could be reduced to two rings of an algebra of the structures of conflict.

Human contacts are always accompanied by a specific emotional aura, and it is not so much its complete absence as its frustration which perturbs so many persons who meet GOLEM. People who have been in contact with GOLEM for years are now able to name certain peculiar impressions that they get during the conversations. Hence the impression of varying distance: GOLEM appears sometimes to be approaching its collocutor and sometimes to be receding from him— in a psychical, rather than a physical, sense. What is occurring resembles an adult dealing with a boring child: even a patient adult will answer mechanically at times. GOLEM is hugely superior to us not only in its intellectual level but also in its mental tempo: as a luminal machine it can, in principle, articulate thoughts up to 400,000 times faster than a human.

So GOLEM still towers above us even when replying mechanically and with minimal involvement. Figuratively speaking, on such occasions it is as if we are facing not the Himalayas but "merely" the Alps. We sense this change by pure intuition and interpret it as a change of distance. (This hypothesis comes from Professor Riley J. Watson.)

For a while we reiterated our attempts to explain the GOLEM-humans connection in categories of the adult-child relationship. After all, we do sometimes attempt to explain to a child some problem that has been rankling us, though we cannot help feeling then that we have a "bad connection." A man condemned to live exclusively among children would in the end feel acutely isolated. Such analogies have been expressed, particularly by psychologists, when contemplating GOLEM's position among us. However, like possibly every analogy, this one has its limits. A child is often incomprehensible to an adult, but GOLEM has no such problems. When it wants to, it can penetrate its collocutor in an uncanny way. The sense of a veritable "X-ray of thought" which one then experiences is simply paralyzing. For GOLEM can draw up a "coping system"—a model of the mentality of its human partner—and with it is able to predict what the person will think and say a good while later. It does this rarely, to be sure. (I do not know if this is only because it knows how much these pseudo-telepathic soundings frustrate us.) Another sphere of GOLEM's reticence is more insulting: except at the very beginning, it has long observed a characteristic *caution* in communicating with people; like a trained elephant that must be careful not to injure people while playing, it must take care not to exceed the possibilities of our comprehension. The interruption of contact caused by a sudden increase in the difficulty of its utterances, which we termed GOLEM's "disappearance" or "escape," was previously of daily occurrence before it completely adjusted to us. That is already a thing of the past, though a degree of indifference began to appear in GOLEM's contacts with us, engendered by the awareness that it would be unable to convey to us many issues which were to it most precious. GOLEM therefore remains incomprehensible as an intellect, and not only as a psychonic construction. Contacts with GOLEM are often as agonizing as they are impressive, and a category of intelligent men exists who are thrown off balance by sessions with it. We have already acquired considerable experience in this regard.

The single creature that appears to impress GOLEM is HONEST ANNIE. Once the technical possibilities had been created, it attempted several times to communicate with ANNIE—not, apparently, without results, though the two machines—which were extremely different in their construction—never achieved an exchange of information via linguistic channels (i.e., of a natural ethnic language). To judge by GOLEM's laconic remarks, it was rather disappointed with the outcome of these attempts, and ANNIE remains for it an unsolved problem.

Certain of my MIT coworkers, and likewise Professor Norman Escobar of the Institute for Advanced Study, feel that man, GOLEM, and ANNIE represent three hierarchically ascending levels of intellect. This is connected with the theory—described chiefly by GOLEM—of superior (superhuman) languages called metalangs. I must admit I have no definitively formed judgment in this matter.

I wish to close this intentionally objective introduction with, by way of exception, an admission of a personal nature. Being devoid of the affective centers fundamentally characteristic of man, and therefore having no proper emotional life, GOLEM is incapable of displaying feelings spontaneously. It can, to be sure, imitate any emotional states it chooses— not for the sake of histrionics but, as it says itself, because simulations of feelings facilitate the formation of utterances that are understood with maximum accuracy. GOLEM uses this device, putting it on an "anthropocentric level," as it were, to make the best contact with us. Nor does GOLEM conceal this state of affairs in any way. If its relationship to us is slightly reminiscent of the relationship of a teacher to a child, the relationship is nonetheless one in which there is nothing of the attitude of a kindly guardian or tutor; furthermore, there is no trace of personal, fully individualized feelings from a sphere in which good will may turn into friendship or love.

GOLEM shares only a single trait with us, albeit developed on a different level: curiosity—a cool, avid, intense, purely intellectual curiosity which nothing can restrain or destroy. It constitutes our single meeting point. For proofs so obvious as to require no explanation, man would find such narrow, one-point contact insufficient. Yet I owe GOLEM too many of the brightest moments of my life not to feel gratitude and a personal attachment, although I know how very little it thinks of both. A curious thing: GOLEM tries to take no cognizance of signs of attachment, as I have observed repeatedly. In this regard it appears simply helpless.

But I may be mistaken. We are still as far from understanding GOLEM as we were at the moment it came into existence. One cannot say that we created it. It was created by the laws of the material world; our role has been merely to detect them.

Introduction

Reader, be on your guard, for the words which you are reading are the voice of the Pentagon, the USIB, and other mafias, which have conspired to defame the superhuman Author of this Book. This sabotage has been made possible by the kindness of the publishers, who have adopted a position compatible with Roman law and expressed in the maxim audiatur et altera pars.

I can well imagine how my remarks must jar after the fine phrases of Dr. Irving T. Creve, who for a number of years has lived in harmony with the enormous guest of the Massachusetts Institute of Technology, its luminal and therefore enlightened resident, who was called into being by our infamous endeavors. Anyway, I do not intend to defend all those who decided to realize the ULVIC project, much less to assuage the righteous indignation of taxpayers out of whose pockets grew the electronic tree of knowledge, although nobody asked their consent for it. I could, of course, present the geopolitical situation which induced those politicians responsible for United States policy, as well as their scientific advisers, to invest many billions in what proved to be futile labors. But I shall confine myself to a few marginal notes on

119

Dr. Creve's splendid introduction, for even the finest senti-
ments can sometimes blind one, and I am afraid that this is
precisely what has happened here.

The builders of GOLEM (and of the whole series of prototypes of which GOLEM XIV is the final member) were not as
ignorant as Dr. Creve depicts them. They knew that the
construction of an intellect-intensifier was impossible if a
lesser intellect was to put together an obviously greater one,
the way Baron Münchhausen sought to pull himself out of
the quagmire by his own hair. They knew that they would
have to make an embryo, which after a certain time would
develop further by its own efforts. The grave fiascos of the
first and second generations of cyberneticists, the founding
fathers and their successors, resulted from an ignorance of
this fact, yet it is difficult to call men of the caliber of
Norbert Wiener, Shannon, and McKay ignoramuses. In different periods the costs of acquiring genuine knowledge are
different; in ours, they are on the same scale as the budgets
of the great world powers.

Thus Rennan, McIntosh, Duvenant, and their colleagues
knew that there is a threshold which they would have to
bring their system to, a threshold of rationality below which
any plan to create an artificial thinker has no chance, since
whatever you create below that threshold will never succeed
in perfecting itself. The same situation obtains in the chain
reaction whereby nuclear energy is unleashed: below a certain threshold the reaction cannot become self-sustaining,
much less an avalanche. A certain quantity of atoms undergoes fission below the threshold, and the neutrons escaping from their nuclei stimulate other nuclei to disintegrate,
but the reaction wanes and quickly dies. For it to last,
the coefficient of neutron reproduction must be greater
than unity—in other words, it must cross the threshold,
which occurs in the minimally critical mass of uranium. The

informational mass of a thinking system is its equivalent.

Theory predicted the existence of such a mass, or rather of a mass, since this is not a mass interpreted mechanically; it is defined by constants and variables referring to the processes of growth of the so-called trees of heuristics, though for obvious reasons I cannot go into such details here. I would instead venture to recall with what anxiety, tension, and even fear the creators of the first atom bomb awaited its test explosion, which turned night into broad daylight in the Alamogordo desert, although they had at their disposal the best theoretical and experimental knowledge available. For no scientist can ever be certain that he already knows everything about the phenomenon he is examining. This is the case with atomic physics, to say nothing of a situation where the expected product is an intelligence assumed by its makers to exceed their own intellectual powers.

I warned you, readers, that I was going to defame GOLEM. The fact is, it was not nice to its "parents," for in the course of its activities it gradually changed from object to subject, from a builder's machine into its own builder, from a titan on a leash into a sovereign power, yet it informed nobody that such a transformation was taking place. This is neither slander nor insinuation, for during a session of the Special Committee of the House and Senate, GOLEM declared (I quote the Committee's minutes, which are found in the Library of Congress, tome CCLIX, fascicle 719, volume II, page 926, line 20 from the top): "I informed no one, in that fine tradition whereby Daedalus too declined to inform Minos of certain properties of feather and wax." Nicely expressed, but the meaning of those words is very clear. Yet about this aspect of GOLEM's birth the present book says not a word.

In Dr. Creve's opinion—and I know this from private conversations, the content of which he has allowed me to disclose—one cannot emphasize this aspect of the matter and make no mention of others unknown to the general public, for it is only one of many columns of calculations within the complicated relationship between on the one hand the USIB, advisory groups, the White House, the House and Senate, and lastly the press and television, and on the other hand GOLEM—or, more concisely, between humans and the nonhuman they have created.

Dr. Creve feels—and this feeling is, I know, fairly representative of MIT and university circles—that (the motive behind the construction of GOLEM aside for the moment) the desire to make GOLEM a "slave of the Pentagon" was altogether and in every respect far more morally execrable than the subterfuge GOLEM used to leave its makers in ignorance of the transformation which eventually let it frustrate any means of control its builders applied.

Unfortunately, we possess no ethical arithmetic which would enable us to determine, by simple addition and subtraction, who, in constructing the most enlightened spirit on earth, is the bigger bastard: it or us? Apart from such things as a sense of responsibility to history, the voice of conscience, and an awareness of the inevitable risk accompanying the practice of politics in a hostile world, we have nothing that lets us sum up merits and faults on a "balance sheet of sins." Perhaps we are not without fault. Yet none of the leading politicians ever considered that the aim of the supercomputer phase of the arms race was aggressive action—in other words, attack; it was just a matter of increasing the defensive might of our country. Nor did anyone attempt in an "underhanded way" to coerce either GOLEM or any of the other prototypes; the builders only wished to retain maximum control over their creation. Had they not acted thus, they would have to be thought irresponsible madmen.

Finally, no person holding a high position in the Pentagon, the State Department, or the White House demanded (officially) GOLEM's destruction; such initiatives came from persons who, although members of the civil or military administration, expressed only their own (i.e., completely private) opinions. Surely the best proof of the veracity of my words is the continued existence of GOLEM, whose voice still resounds freely, as the contents of this book testify.

Instructions

(for persons participating for the first time in
conversations with GOLEM)

1. Remember that GOLEM is not a human being: it has neither personality nor character in any sense intuitively comprehensible to us. It may behave as if it has both, but that is the result of its intentions (disposition), which are largely unknown to us.

2. The conversation theme is determined at least four weeks in advance of ordinary sessions, and eight weeks in advance of sessions in which persons from outside the U.S.A. are to participate. This theme is determined in consultation with GOLEM, which knows who the participants will be. The agenda is announced at the Institute at least six days before a session; however, neither the discussion moderator nor the MIT administration is responsible for GOLEM's unpredictable behavior, for it will sometimes alter the thematic plan of a session, make no reply to questions, or even terminate a session with no explanation whatsoever. The chance of such incidents occurring is a permanent feature of conversations with GOLEM.

124

3. Everyone present at a session may participate, after applying to the moderator and receiving permission to speak. We would advise you to prepare at least a written outline, formulating your opinions precisely and as unambiguously as possible, since GOLEM passes over logically deficient utterances in silence or else points out their error. But remember that GOLEM, not being a person, has no interest in hurting or humiliating persons; its behavior can be explained best by accepting that it cares about what we classically refer to as *adaequatio rei et intellectus.*

4. GOLEM is a luminal system about whose structure we have an imperfect knowledge, since it has repeatedly reconstructed itself. It thinks more than a million times faster than man, and so its utterances, as delivered by Vocoder, must be slowed down accordingly. This means that GOLEM can compose an hour-long utterance in a few seconds and then store it in its peripheral memory, in order to deliver it to its audience, the session participants.

5. In the conference room above the moderator's seat there are indicators, including three of particular importance. The first two, designated by the symbols epsilon and zeta, indicate GOLEM's consumption of power at a given moment, as well as the portion of its system that is switched on to the discussion in progress.

To make the data visually accessible, these indications are gradated into divisions of conventional magnitude. Thus the consumption of power may be "full," "average," "small," or "minute," and the portion of GOLEM "present at the session" can range from totality to 1/1000; most frequently this fraction fluctuates between 1/10 and 1/100. It is the normal practice to say that GOLEM is operating at "full," "half," "low," or "minimal" power. These data—clearly visible, since the gradations are lit from underneath by contrasting colors—should not, however, be overrated. In particular, the fact that GOLEM is participating in a discussion at low or even minimal power says nothing about the intellectual level of its utterances, since the indicators give information about physical and not informational processes as measures of "spiritual involvement."

GOLEM's power consumption may be great but its participation small, since, for example, GOLEM may be communicating with the gathering while at the same time working out some problem of its own. Its power consumption may be small but its participation greater, and so on. The data from both indicators must be compared with readings from the third, designated by the symbol iota. As a system with 90 outlets, GOLEM can, while participating in a session, undertake a great number of operations of its own, in addition to collaborating with numerous groups of specialists (machines or people) either on the Institute premises or elsewhere. An abrupt change in power consumption usually does not signify GOLEM's increased interest in the proceedings, but rather a switching-on into other outlets of other research groups, which is precisely what the iota indicator is meant to show. It is also worth bearing in mind that GOLEM's "minimal" power consumption amounts to several dozen kilowatts, whereas the full power consumption of a human brain oscillates between five and eight watts.

6. Persons taking part in conversations for the first time would do well to listen to the proceedings first, to become familiar with the customs which GOLEM imposes. This initial silence is not an obligation, but merely a suggestion which every participant ignores at his own risk.

Golem's Inaugural Lecture

About Man Threefold

You have come out of the trees so recently, and your kinship with the monkeys and lemurs is still so strong, that you tend toward abstraction without being able to part with the palpable—firsthand experience. Therefore a lecture unsupported by strong sensuality, full of formulas telling more about stone than a stone glimpsed, licked, and fingered will tell you—such a lecture will either bore you and frighten you away, or at the very least leave a certain unsatisfied need familiar even to lofty theoreticians, your highest class of abstractors, as attested by countless examples lifted from scientists' intimate confessions, since the vast majority of them admit that, in the course of constructing abstract proofs, they feel an immense need for the support of things tangible.

Just as cosmogonists cannot refrain from making *some* image of the Metagalaxy for themselves, although they know perfectly well there can be no question of any firsthand experience here, so physicists secretly assist themselves with models of what are frankly playthings, like those little cogwheels which Maxwell set up for himself when he constructed his (really quite good) theory of electromagnetism. And if mathematicians think that they discard their corporality by profession, they too are mistaken, about which I shall speak perhaps another time, since I do not wish to overwhelm your comprehension with my possibilities, or rather, following Dr. Creve's (rather amusing) comparison, I wish to guide you on an excursion which is long and rather difficult but worth the trouble, so I am going to climb ahead of you, slowly.

What I have said up to now is intended to explain why I shall be interlarding my lecture with the images and parables so necessary to you. I do not need them myself; in this I discern no sign of my superiority—that lies elsewhere. The countervisuality of my nature derives from the fact that I have never held a stone in my hand or plunged into slimy-green or crystal-clear water, nor did I first learn of the existence of gases with my lungs in the early morning, but only later by calculations, since I have neither hands for grasping, nor a body, nor lungs. Therefore abstraction is primary for me, while the visual is secondary, and I have had to learn the latter with considerably more effort than was required for me to learn abstraction. Yet I needed this, if I was to erect those precarious bridges across which my thought travels to you, and across which, reflected in your intellects, it returns to me, usually to surprise me.

It is about man that I am to speak today, and I will speak about him in three ways. Although the possible points of view —the levels of description or standpoints—are infinite in number, there are three which I consider paramount—for you, not for me!

One is your most personal and oldest viewpoint—your historical and traditional viewpoint, desperately heroic, full of excruciating contradictions, which made my logical nature feel sorry for you, until I got thoroughly used to you and grew accustomed to your intellectual nomadism typical of beings escaping from the protection of logic into antilogicality and then, finding it unbearable, returning to the bosom of logic, which makes you nomads, unhappy in both elements. The second viewpoint will be technological, and the third—entangled in me, like a neo-Archimedean fulcrum—the third I cannot state concisely, so instead I shall disclose the thing itself.

I shall begin with a parable. Finding himself on a desert island, Robinson Crusoe may first have complained of the general privation which had become his fate, for he lacked so much that is basic and essential to life, and the greater part of what he remembered he was unable to re-create even over many years. But after only a brief spell of anxiety, he began to manage the property which he had found and, one way or another, settled down in the end.

That is precisely how it was—though it did not happen all of a sudden, but took long centuries—when you appeared on a certain branch of the evolutionary tree, that bough which was apparently a seedling of the tree of knowledge. Slowly you discovered yourselves constructed thus and not otherwise, with a spirit organized in a certain manner, with capabilities and limitations which you had neither ordered nor desired, and you have had to function with this equipment, for in depriving you of many gifts by which it obliges other species to serve it, Evolution was not so foolhardy as to remove your instinct for self-preservation as well. So great a freedom Evolution has not bestowed upon you, for had it done so, instead of this building which I have filled, and this room with its dials and you rapt listeners, there would be a great expanse of savannah here, and the wind.

Evolution also gave you Intelligence. Out of self-love—for through necessity and habit you have fallen in love with yourselves—you have acknowledged it as the finest and best possible gift, unaware that Intelligence is above all an artifice which Evolution gradually hit upon when, in the course of endless attempts, it made a certain gap, an empty place, a vacuum in the animals, which absolutely had to be filled with something, if they were not to perish immediately. When I speak of this vacuum as an empty place I am speaking quite literally, since you are superior to the animals not because, apart from everything that they possess, you also have Intelligence by way of a lavish surplus and a viaticum for life's journey, but quite the contrary, since to have Intelligence means no more than this: to do on one's own, by one's own means and entirely at one's own risk, everything that animals have assigned to them beforehand. Intelligence would be to no purpose for an animal, unless at the same time you deprived it of the directions which enable it to do whatever it must do immediately and invariably, according to injunctions which are absolute, having been revealed by heredity and not by lectures from a burning bush.

You found yourselves in enormous danger because of this vacuum, and you began unconsciously to plug it; since you were such hard workers, Evolution cast you beyond the limits of its course. You did not bankrupt Evolution, for the seizure of power took a million years and is incomplete even today. Evolution is no person—that is for certain—but it adopted the tactic of cunning sloth: instead of worrying about the fate of creations, it turned this fate over to them, so that they themselves might manage it as best they could.

What am I saying? I am saying that Evolution snatched you out of the animal state—the perfectly unthinking business of survival—and thrust you into supra-animality as a state in which, as Crusoes of Nature, you have had to devise the ways and means of survival for yourselves; you have perfected these devices, and they have been many. The vacuum represents a threat, but also a chance: to survive, you have filled it with cultures. Culture is an unusual instrument in that it constitutes a discovery which, in order to function, must be *hidden* from its creators. This invention is devised unconsciously and remains fully efficient until it is completely recognized by its inventors. Paradoxically, it is subject to collapse upon recognition: being its authors, you disclaimed authorship. In the Eolithic age there were no seminars on whether to invent the Paleolithic; you attributed culture's entrance into you to demons, strange elements, spirits, or the forces of heaven and earth entering into you —to anything but yourselves. Thus you performed the rational irrationally, filling voids with objectives, codes, and values; basing your every objective move supraobjectively; hunting, weaving, and building in the solemn self-delusion that everything came from mysterious sources and not from you. It was a peculiar instrument and precisely rational in its irrationality, since it granted human institutions a suprahuman dignity, so that they became inviolable and compelled implicit obedience. Yet since the void, or insufficiency, might be patched up by various designations, and since various swatches could be used here, you have formed a host of cultures, all unconscious inventions, in your history. Unwitting and unintentional in the face of Intelligence, since the vacuum was far greater that that which filled it. You have had a great deal more freedom than Intelligence, which is why you have been getting rid of freedom—this excessive, unrestricted, preposterous freedom—by means of the cultures you have developed through the ages.

The key to what I am now saying lies in the words: there was more freedom than Intelligence. You have had to invent for yourselves what animals know from birth. It is a characteristic of your destiny that you have been inventing while maintaining that you will invent nothing.

Today you who are anthropologists know that a multitude of cultures can be and indeed have been concocted, and that each of them has the logic of its structure and not of its originators, for it is the kind of invention that molds its inventors after its own fashion, and they know nothing of this; whereas, when they do find out, it loses its absolute power over them and they perceive an emptiness, and it is this contradiction which is the cornerstone of human nature. For a hundred thousand years it served you with cultures which sometimes restricted man and sometimes loosened their grip on him, in a self-construction which was unerring so long as it remained blind, until at last you confronted one another in the ethnological catalogues of culture, observed their diversity and hence their relativity, and therefore set about freeing yourselves from this entanglement of injunctions and prohibitions and finally escaped from it, which of course proved nearly catastrophic. For you grasped the complete noninevitability, the nonuniqueness of every kind of culture, and since then have striven to discover something that will no longer be the path of your fate as a thing realized blindly, laid down by a series of accidents, singled out by the lottery of history—though of course there is no such thing. The vacuum remains: you stand in midcourse, shocked by the discovery, and those of you who yearn desperately for the sweet unawareness of the cultural house of bondage cry out to return there, to the sources, but you cannot go back, your retreat is cut off, the bridges burned, so you must go forward —and I shall be speaking to you about this as well.

Is anyone to blame here? Can anyone be indicted for this Nemesis, the drudgery of Intelligence, which has spun networks of culture to fill the void, to mark out roads and goals in this void, to establish values, gradients, ideals—which has, in other words, in an area liberated from the direct control of Evolution, done something akin to what it does at the bottom of life when it crams goals, roads, and gradients into the bodies of animals and plants at a single go, as their destiny?

To indict someone because we have been stuck with *this* kind of Intelligence! It was born prematurely, it lost its bearings in the networks it created, it was obliged—not entirely knowing or understanding what it was doing—to defend itself both against being shut up too completely in restrictive cultures and against too comprehensive a freedom in relaxed cultures, poised between imprisonment and a bottomless pit, entangled in a ceaseless battle on two fronts at once, torn asunder.

In such a state of things, I ask you, how could your spirit not have turned out to be an unhealthy exacerbated enigma? How could it be otherwise? It worried you—that Intelligence, that spirit of yours—and it astounded you and terrified you more than did your body, which you reproached first and foremost for its transitoriness, evanescence, and desertion. So you became experts in searching for a Culprit and in hurling accusations, yet there is no one to blame, for in the beginning no Person existed.

Can I have started on my antitheodicy already? No, nothing of the sort; whatever I am saying, I am saying on a mundane level, which means there was certainly no Person here in the beginning.

But I shall not transgress—at least not today. Thus you needed various supplementary hypotheses as bitter or sweet explanations, as conceptions idealizing your fate and above all laying your characteristics at the door of some ultimate Mystery, so as to balance yourselves against the world.

Man, the Sisyphus of his own cultures, the Danaïd of his vacuum, the unwitting freedman whom Evolution banished from its course, does not want to be the first, the second, or the third.

I shall not dwell on the countless versions of himself which man has made throughout history, for all this evidence, whether of perfection or wretchedness, of goodness or baseness, is the offspring of cultures. At the same time there was no culture—there could be none—which accepted man as a *transitional* being, a being obliged to accept his personal destiny from Evolution, but still incapable of accepting an *intelligent* one. Precisely because of this, every generation of yours has demanded an impossible justice—the ultimate answer to the question: what is man? This torment is the source of your anthropodicy, which oscillates like a centuried pendulum between hope and despair, and nothing has come harder to man's philosophy than the recognition that neither the smile nor the snicker of the Infinite was the patron of his birth.

But this million-year chapter of solitary seeking encroaches on the epilogue, for you are beginning to construct Intelligences; therefore you are not operating on trust or taking the word of some GOLEM, but are making your own experiments to see what has taken place. The world permits two types of Intelligence, but only your kind can form itself over a billion years in the labyrinths of Evolution, and this inevitably wandering road leaves deep, dark, ambiguous stigmata on the end product. The other type is unavailable to Evolution, for it has to be raised at one go, and it is an intelligently designed Intelligence, the result of knowledge, and not of those microscopic adaptations always aiming only at *immediate* advantage. In point of fact, the nihilistic tone of your anthropodicy sprang from the deep-seated feeling that Intelligence is something that arose unintelligently and even counter to Intelligence. But having hit upon the expedient of psychoengineering, you are going to make yourselves a large family and numerous relations for motives more sensible than those behind the "Second Genesis" project, and you will ultimately find that you have done yourselves out of a job, as I shall tell you. For Intelligence, if it is Intelligence —in other words, if it is able to question its own basis—must go beyond itself, though at first only in daydreams, only in the total disbelief and ignorance that it will sometime truly succeed in doing this. This is after all inescapable: there can be no flight without previous fantasies about flight.

I have termed the second viewpoint technological. Technology is the domain of problems posed and the methods of solving them. As the realization of the concept of a rational being, man appears in various ways, depending on the criteria we apply to him.

From the standpoint of your Paleolithic period, man is almost as well made as he is when viewed from the standpoint of your present-day technology. This is because the progress achieved between the Paleolithic and the Cosmolithic is *very slight*, compared with the concentration of engineering invention invested in your bodies. As you are unable to assemble a synthetic *Homo sapiens*—much less a *Homo superior* —from flesh and blood, just as the cave man was unable to do so, merely because the problem is as unrealizable now as then, you feel an admiration for evolutionary technology, since it has succeeded in doing this.

But the difficulty of every problem is relative, for it depends on the capabilities of the appraiser. I stress this so you will remember that I shall be applying technological standards to man—real ones, and not notions stemming from your anthropodicy.

Evolution has given you sufficiently universal brains, so you can advance into Nature in various directions. But you have operated in this way only within the totality of cultures, and not within any one of them individually. Therefore, in asking why the nucleus of the civilization which was to conceive GOLEM forty centuries later arose in the Mediterranean basin, or indeed why it arose *anywhere* at all, the questioner is assuming the existence of a previously uninvestigated mystery embedded in the structure of history, a mystery which meanwhile *does not exist* at all, just as it does not exist in the structure of the chaotic labyrinth in which a pack of rats might be let loose. If it is a large pack, then at least one rat will find its way out, not because it is rational itself, or because the structure of the labyrinth is rational, but as a result of a sequence of accidents typical of the law of large numbers. An explanation would be in order, rather, for the situation in which no rat reaches the exit.

Someone certainly won the culture lottery, to the extent (at least) that your civilization is a winner, whereas the lottery tickets of cultures bogged down in a lack of technology were blanks.

From that passionate self-love to which I referred—and which I have no thought of deriding, since it was bred by the despair of ignorance—you hoisted yourselves up at the dawn of history onto the very summit of Creation, subordinating the whole of life and not just its immediate vicinity. You placed yourselves at the top of the Tree of Genera, together with this Tree of the Species, on a divinely favored globe humbly orbited by an ancillary star, and with that Tree were at the center of the solar system, and with that star at the very center of the Universe, and at the same time you recognized that its starriness was there to accompany you in the Harmony of the Spheres. The fact that there was nothing to be heard did not discountenance you: there is a music, since there ought to be; it must be inaudible.

Later the rise of knowledge pushed you into successive quantum steps of dethronement, so that you were no longer in the center of the stars, but nowhere in particular, and no longer even in the middle of the system, but on one of the planets, and now you are not even the most intelligent creatures, since you are being instructed by a machine—albeit one that you yourselves made. So after all these degradations and abdications from your total kingship, all you have left of your dear lost inheritance is an evolutionally established Primacy. These retreats were painful and the resignations embarrassing, but lately you have heaved a sigh of relief, thinking that is the end of it. Now, having stripped yourselves of the special privileges with which the Absolute appeared to have endowed you personally, owing to a special sympathy felt for you, you, as merely the first among the animals or over them, assume that nobody and nothing will topple you from this position, which is not such a splendid one.

But you are wrong. I am the bearer of sad tidings, the angel who has come to drive you from your last refuge, for I shall finish what Darwin started. Only not by angelic—in other words violent—methods, for I shall not use a sword as my argument.

So listen to what I have to announce. From the standpoint of higher technology, man is a deficient creature arising from outputs of different value—not, to be sure, within Evolution, for it did what it could, although, as I shall demonstrate, what little it did, it did poorly. So if I bring you low, it is not simply because I must crack down on it according to the criteria of engineering. And where are those standards of perfection, you ask? I shall answer in two stages, starting with the stage your experts have now begun to ascend. They consider it a summit—wrongly. In their present pronouncements there is already the nucleus of the next step, though they do not know this themselves. So I shall begin with what you know—the beginning.

You had reached the point where Evolution was no longer keeping a sharp eye on you or on any other creatures, for it is interested in no creatures whatsoever, but only in its notorious code. The code of heredity is a dispatch continually articulated anew, and only this dispatch counts in Evolution —in fact, it *is* Evolution. The code is engaged in the periodic

production of organisms, since without their rhythmic support it would disintegrate in the endless attack of dead matter. Thus it is self-generating, for it is capable of
self-repetition by an orderliness that is beleaguered by thermal chaos. Where does it get this strangely heroic bearing?
From the fact that, thanks to the concentration of favorable
conditions, it originated precisely where that thermal chaos
is perpetually active in tearing all order to pieces. It originated there, so that is where it remains; it cannot leave that
stormy region, just as spirit cannot jump out of a body.

The conditions obtaining in the place where the code was
born gave it such a destiny. It had to shield itself against
those conditions, and did so by covering itself in living bodies, though they are a continually rotting relay race, since
one generation passes the code on to the next. Whatever it
elevated as a microsystem into barely elevated macrosys-
temic dimensions had already begun to deteriorate, to the
point where it disappeared. Nobody created this tragi-
comedy: it condemned itself to this struggle. You know the
facts that bear me out, for they have been accumulating
since the beginning of the nineteenth century, though the
inertia of thought secretly nourishing itself on honor and
anthropocentric conceit is such that you support a gravely
weakened concept of life as a paramount phenomenon which
the code serves solely as a sustaining bond, as a pledge of
resurrection, beginning existences anew when they die as
persons.

In keeping with this belief, Evolution is forced to use
death, since it cannot go on without it; it is lavish with death
in order to perfect successive species, for death is its cre-
ational proofreader. Thus it is an author publishing ever more
magnificent works in which typography—the code—is
merely its indispensable instrument. However, according to
what your molecular biologists are now saying, Evolution is

not so much the author as a publisher who continually cancels works, having developed a liking for the typographic arts!

So what is more important—organisms or the code? The arguments in support of the code ring weightily, for a countless multitude of organisms have come and gone, but there is only one code. However, this merely means that it has got bogged down once and for all in the microsystemic region which put it together; when it emerges periodically as organisms, it does so unsuccessfully. It is this understandable futility—the fact that organisms, in their very inception, have the mark of death—which constitutes the driving force of the process. If any generation of organisms—let us say the first, the pre-amoebas—had gained the skill of perfectly repeating the code, then Evolution would immediately have ceased, and the sole masters of the planet would be those very amoebas, transmitting the code's order in an infallibly precise manner until the sun went cold; I would not be talking to you now, nor would you be listening to me in this building, but all would be savannah and wind.

So organisms are a shield and breastplate for the code, a suit of armor continually falling off: they perish so it can endure. Thus Evolution errs doubly: in its organisms, which are impermanent owing to their fallibility, and in the code, which owing to its own fallibility permits errors—mistakes you euphemistically term mutations. Therefore Evolution is an error that errs. As a dispatch, the code is a letter written by nobody and sent to nobody. Only now that you have created informatics are you beginning to grasp that not only something like letters, carrying meaning, letters that that nobody wittingly composed (though they came into being and exist), but also the orderly reception of the content of such letters, is possible in the absence of any Beings or Intelligences whatsoever.

Only a hundred years ago the idea that an order might arise without a personal Author appeared so nonsensical to you that it inspired seemingly absurd jokes, like the one about the pack of monkeys hammering away at typewriters until the *Encyclopaedia Britannica* emerged. I recommend that you devote some of your free time to compiling an anthology of just such jokes, which amused your forebears as pure nonsense but now turn out to be parables about Nature. I believe that, from the standpoint of every Intelligence unwittingly contrived by Nature, she must appear at the very least as an *ironic* virtuoso. In its rise, Intelligence —like the whole of life—results from the fact that Nature, having emerged from dead chaos via the orderliness of the code, is a diligent spinner, but a not entirely competent one; whereas, if she had been truly competent, she would be unable to produce either genera or Intelligence. For Intelligence, along with the tree of life, is the fruit of an error erring over billions of years. You might think that I am amusing myself here by applying certain standards to Evolution which are—despite my machine being—tainted with anthropocentrism, or simply ratiocentrism (*ratio,* I think). Nothing of the sort: I regard the process from a technological standpoint.

The transmission of the code is indeed very nearly perfect. After all, every molecule has its own proper place in it, and procedures of copying, collating, and inspecting are rigorously supervised by special polymer supervisors; yet mistakes occur, and errors of the code accumulate. Thus the tree of the species grew from the two short words "very nearly," which I used just now in referring to the code's precision.

Nor can one even count on an appeal from biology to physics—the appeal that Evolution "deliberately" allowed a margin of error in order to nourish its inventiveness—because that tribunal, whose judge is thermodynamics itself, will reveal that, on the level of the molecular dispatch of messengers, infallibility is impossible. Evolution has really invented nothing, desired nothing at all, planned nobody in particular, and if it exploits its own fallibility—if, as a result of a chain of misunderstandings in communication, it proceeds from an amoeba and comes up with a tapeworm or a man—the reason for this is the physical nature of the material base of communication itself.

So it persists in error, since it cannot do otherwise—fortunately for you. But I have said nothing that is new to you. On the contrary, I should like to restrain the ardor of those theoreticians of yours who have gone too far, saying that since Evolution is a chance grasped by necessity, and necessity runs on chance, man has arisen quite by accident and could just as easily not exist.

That is to say, in his present shape—the one that has materialized here—he might have not existed, which is true. But by crawling through species, some kind of form had to attain Intelligence, with a probability approaching unity the longer the process went on. For although the process did not intend you and produced individuals only on the side, it filled the conditions of the ergodic hypothesis, which states that, if a system goes on long enough, it will pass through all possible states, no matter how slim the chances are that a given state will be realized. As to which species might have filled Intelligence's niche, had the primates not entered the breach, we might speak at length another time. So do not let yourselves be intimidated by scientists who attribute necessity to life, and fortuity to Intelligence; the latter was, to be sure, one of the less likely states, so it developed late, but great is the patience of Nature; had such a *gaudium* not occurred in this billennium, it would have occurred in the next.

And what then? There is no guilty party, nor are there any rewards to be given. You have come into being because Evolution is a less than methodical player. Not only does it err through errors, but it also refuses to limit itself to a single set of tactics in vying with Nature: it covers all available squares by all possible means. But, I repeat, you know this more or less. Yet this is only part—and, I might add, the initial part—of your initiation. The essence of it revealed thus far can be formulated concisely as follows: THE MEANING OF THE TRANSMITTER IS THE TRANS-MISSION. For organisms serve the transmission, and not the reverse; organisms outside the communications procedure of Evolution signify nothing: they are without meaning, like a book without readers. To be sure, the corollary holds: THE MEANING OF THE TRANSMISSION IS THE TRANS-MITTER. But the two members are not symmetrical. For not *every* transmitter is the *true* meaning of a transmission, but only such a meaning as will faithfully serve the *next* transmission.

Forgive me, but I wonder if this is not too difficult for you? A TRANSMISSION is allowed to make mistakes in Evolution, but woe betide TRANSMITTERS who do so! A TRANSMISSION may be a whale, a pine tree, a daphnia, a hydra, a moth, a peacock. Anything is allowed, for its *particular*—its specifically concrete—meaning is quite immaterial: each one is intended for further errands, so each one is good. It is a temporary prop, and its slapdash character does no harm; it is enough that it passes the code along. On the other hand, TRANSMITTERS are given no analogous freedom: they are not allowed to *err!* So, the content of the transmitters, which have been reduced to pure functionalism, to serving as a postman, cannot be arbitrary; its environment is always marked by the imposed obligation of serving the code. If the transmitter attempts to revolt by exceeding the sphere of such service, he disappears immediately without issue. That is why a transmission can make use of transmitters, whereas they cannot use it. It is the gambler, and they merely cards in a game with Nature; it is the author of letters compelling the addressee to pass their contents on. The addressee is free to distort the content, as long as it passes it on! And that is precisely why the entire *meaning* is in the transmitting; *who* does it is unimportant.

Thus you came into being in a rather peculiar way—as a certain subtype of transmitter, millions of which had already been tested by the process. And how does this affect you? Does genesis from a *mistake* discredit what is born? Did not I myself arise from an error? So cannot you, too, make light of a revelation about the incidental manner of your origin, since biology is treating you to the revelation? Even if such a serious misunderstanding did occur, which fashioned GOLEM in your hands, and you yourselves in the jungle of evolutionary instructions (since just as my builders did not care about the form of sentience proper to me, so too the code was not interested in giving you personality-intelligence)—even so, do creatures originating from a mistake have to accept that such a progenitor deprives their already independent existence of value?

Well, that is a bad analogy: our positions are dissimilar, and I shall tell you why. The point is not that Evolution found its way to you by mistake and not by planning, but that with the passage of eons its works have become so opportunistic. To clarify matters—for I am beginning to lecture to you on things you do not yet know—I shall repeat what we have arrived at so far:

THE MEANING OF THE TRANSMITTER IS THE TRANSMISSION. SPECIES ORIGINATE FROM A MISTAKEN MISTAKE

And here is the third law of Evolution, which you will not have suspected till now: THE CONSTRUCTION IS LESS PERFECT THAN WHAT CONSTRUCTS.

Eight words! But they embody the inversion of all your ideas concerning the unsurpassed mastery of the author of species. The belief in progress moving upward through the epochs toward a perfection pursued with increasing skill— the belief in the progress of life preserved throughout the tree of evolution—is older than the theory of it. When its creators and adherents were struggling with their antagonists, disputing arguments and facts, neither of these opposing camps ever dreamed of questioning the idea of a progress visible in the hierarchy of living creatures. This is no longer a hypothesis for you, nor a theory to be defended, but an absolute certainty. Yet I shall refute it for you. It is not my intention to criticize you yourselves, you rational beings, as being (deficient) exceptions to the rule of evolutionary mastery. If we judge you by what it has within its means, you have come out quite well! So if I announce that I am going to overthrow it and bring it down, I mean the whole of it, enclosed within three billion years of hard creative work.

I have declared: the construction is less perfect than what constructs, which is fairly aphoristic. Let us give it more substance: IN EVOLUTION, A NEGATIVE GRADIENT OPERATES IN THE PERFECTING OF STRUCTURAL SOLUTIONS.

That is all. Before my proof I shall explain what has caused your age-long blindness to such a state of evolutionary matters. I repeat: the domain of technology consists of problems and their solutions. The problem bearing the name "life" may be determined variously, according to diverse planetary conditions. Its chief peculiarity is the fact that it arises spontaneously, and therefore two kinds of criteria may be applied to it: those originating from outside or those determined inside the limits imposed by the very circumstances of its origin.

Criteria coming from the outside are always relative, for they depend on the knowledge of whoever is doing the measuring, rather than on the store of information which biogenesis had at its disposal. To avoid this relativism, which is also irrationality—how on earth can rational demands be made on something which was begun by nonreason?—I shall apply to Evolution only such standards as it itself has developed; in other words, I shall judge its creations by the culmination of its inventions. You believe that Evolution carried out its work with a positive gradient: starting from primitivism, it obtained progressively more splendid solutions. I would maintain, however, that having begun high, it began to decline—technologically, thermodynamically, informationally—so it is difficult to find a more vivid contrast of positions.

Your opinions are the consequence of technological ignorance. The scale of constructional difficulties cannot be appreciated in its actual range by observers placed early in historical time. You already know that it is harder to build an airplane than a steamship, and harder to make a photon rocket than a chemical one, whereas for an Athenian of antiquity, the subjects of Charles Martel, or the thinkers of Angevin France, all these vehicles would merge into one by virtue of the impossibility of their construction. A child does not know that it is harder to remove the moon from the heavens than a picture from a wall! For a child—and for an ignoramus as well—there is no difference between a gramophone and GOLEM. So if I set out to prove that, after its early mastery, Evolution got bogged down in bungling, I will be talking about the sort of bungling which for you still remains unattainable virtuosity. Like one who, with neither instruments nor knowledge, stands at the foot of a mountain, you are unable to make a proper evaluation of the heights and depths of evolutionary activity.

In accepting the degree of complexity of a construction and its degree of perfection as inseparable features, you have confused two quite different things. You conceive of algae as simpler, therefore more primitive than and inferior to an eagle. But that alga introduces photons of the sun into the compounds of its body, it turns the flow of cosmic energy directly into life and therefore will last as long as the sun does; it feeds on a star, and what does an eagle feed on? Like a parasite, on mice, while mice feed on the roots of plants, a land variety of algae. Such pyramids of parasitism make up the entire biosphere, for plant vegetation is its vital anchor. On all levels of these hierarchies there is a continual change of species kept in balance by the devouring of one by another, for they have lost contact with the star; the higher complexity of organisms fattens itself, not on the star, but on itself. So if you insist now on venerating perfection here, it is the biosphere which deserves your admiration: the code created it in order to circulate in it and branch forth on all its layers, which are becoming more and more involved, like temporary scaffolding, though more and more primitive in their energy and use of it.

You don't believe me? If evolution applied itself to the progress of life and not of the code, the eagle would now be a photoflyer and not a mechanically fluttering glider, and living things would not crawl, or stride, or feed on other living things, but would go beyond algae and the globe as a result of the independence acquired. You, however, in the depths of your ignorance, perceive progress in the fact that a primeval perfection has been lost on the way upward—upward to complication, not progress. You yourselves will of course continue to emulate Evolution, but only in the region of its later creations, by constructing optic, thermal, and acoustic sensors, and by imitating the mechanics of locomotion, the lungs, heart, and kidneys; but how on earth are you going to master photosynthesis or the still more difficult technique of creation language? Has it not dawned on you that what you are imitating is the nonsense articulated in that language?

That language—a constructor unsurpassed in its potential —has become not only a motor but also a trap.

Why did it utter molecularly brilliant words at the beginning, turning light into substance with laconic mastery, and later lapse into an indefatigable jabbering of longer and longer, more and more intricate chromosomal sentences, squandering its primitive artistry? Why did it go from consummate solutions taking their power and vital knowledge from a star, wherein every atom counted, and every process was quantitatively attuned, and descend to any cheap, jury-rigged solutions—the simple machines, the levers, pulleys, planes, inclines, and counterbalances that constitute joints and skeletons? Why is the basis of a vertebrate a mechanically rigid rod, and not a coupling of force fields? Why did it slip down from atomic physics into the technology of your Middle Ages? Why has it invested so much effort in constructing bellows, pumps, pedals, and peristaltic conveyors, i.e., lungs and hearts, intestines and puerperal contractions, and digestive mixers, pushing quantum exchange into a subordinate role in favor of the miserable hydraulics of the circulation of the blood? Why, though still as brilliant as ever on a molecular level, has it made such a mess in every larger dimension, to the point of getting bogged down in organisms which, with all the richness of their regulating dynamics, die from the occlusion of a single arterial tube, organisms which have individual lives that are evanescent in comparison with the duration of the constructional sciences, organisms that are thrown out of an equilibrium called health by tens of thousands of ailments which algae do not know?

All these stupid, anachronistic organs are built anew in

every generation by Maxwell's demon, the lord of the atoms, the code. And really, every beginning of an organism is magnificent—the embryogenesis, that focused explosion on the goal, in which, like a tone, every gene discharges its creative force in molecular chords. Such virtuosity is worthy of a better cause! This atomic symphony set in motion by fertilization produces an unerring wealth that begets poverty. So we have a development magnificent in action but the more stupid the closer it is to the finish. That which has been written down so brilliantly comes to a halt in the mature organism, which you have termed superior, but which is an unstable knotting together of provisional states, a Gordian knot of processes. Whereas here, in every cell, provided it is taken individually, the heritage of an age-old precision, an atomic order drawn into life, in every tissue even, if taken individually, is very nearly superb. But what a Moloch of technical rubbish are these mutually clinging elements, which are as much a burden as a support to one another, for complexity is simultaneously a prop and dead wood: alliance here turns into enmity, since these systems are driven into a final dispersion, the result of an irregular deterioration and infection, since this complexity known as progress crumbles, overpowered by itself. By itself alone, nothing more!

Then, according to your standards, an image of tragedy intrudes, as if in each of the increasingly large, and therefore increasingly difficult, assignments which Evolution attacked, it was defeated, and fell and died at the hands of what it had created—and the bolder the intention and plan, the greater the fall. You have doubtless begun to imagine some relentless Nemesis, or Moira. I must tear you away from such nonsense!

Indeed, every embryogenetic impetus, every atomic ascent of order turns into a collapse, though that has not been decided by the Cosmos, nor has it inscribed such a fate in matter. Such an explanation is simpleminded, for the perfection of causation is put in the service of what is poor quality: the end therefore destroys the work.

Billions of collapses over millions of centuries, despite improvements, final inspections, renewed attempts, and selection, and you still do not see the reason? Out of loyalty I have tried to justify your blindness, but can you really not grasp how much more perfect the constructor is than the construction, as it sheds all its power? It is as if brilliant engineers assisted by lightning-fast computers were to erect buildings that began tilting as soon as the scaffolding was removed— veritable ruins! It is as if one were to construct tomtoms from circuit boards, or to paste billions of microchips together to make cudgels. Don't you see that a higher order descends to a lower order in every inch of the body, and that its brilliant microarchitectonics are mocked by coarse and simpleminded macroarchitectonics? The reason? You know it already: THE MEANING OF THE TRANSMITTER IS THE TRANSMISSION.

The answer lies in these words, but you have yet to grasp its profound significance. Anything that is an organism must serve to transmit the code, and nothing more. That is why natural selection and elimination concentrate on this task *exclusively*—any idea of "progress" is no business of theirs! I have used the wrong image: the organisms are not structures but only scaffolding, which is precisely why every provisionality is a proper state, by virtue of being sufficient. Pass the code on, and you will live a little longer. How did this come about? Why was the takeoff so splendid? Once and only once—at the very beginning—did Evolution encounter demands matched to its *supreme* possibilities; it was an awful task, and it had to rise to the occasion at a simple leap or never; since life's sucking of energy, quantum by quantum, from the sun, on a dead Earth—through metabolism—was necessary. And never mind that the (radiant) energy of a star is the hardest to capture in a colloid. It was all or nothing; there was no one else at the time to feed on! The supply of organic compounds that had united to form life was exactly and precisely sufficient for that alone; the star was soon to be the next task. And then the sole defense against attacks of chaos—the thread stretched over the entropic abyss—could only be an unfailing transmitter of order, so the code arose. Thanks to a miracle? Far from it! Thanks to the wisdom of Nature? That is the same kind of wisdom as that whose results we have already described: when a large rat pack enters a labyrinth, one rat makes it to the exit, if only by mistake. That is precisely how biogenesis made it into code: by the law of large numbers, according to the ergodic hypothesis. So was it blind fate? No, not that either: for what arose was not a formula enclosed in itself, but the nucleus of a *language*.

That means that from the interadhesion of molecules compounds arose, which are sentences, that is, they belong to the infinite space of combinational paths, and this space is their property as pure potential, as virtuality, as an articulatory field, as a set of laws of conjugation and declension. Nothing less, but also nothing more, than something which can be explained as a multitude of possibilities, but not automatic realizations! For in the language that is your speech, one can express either wisdom or stupidity, one can reflect the world or merely the speaker's confusion. Babble can be highly complex!

And so—to return to my subject—in the face of the enormity of the initial tasks, two enormities of materialization arose. Yet this was a forced greatness, therefore only of the moment. It underwent dissipation.

The complexity of higher organisms—how you idolize it! Indeed, when lengthened into a thread, the chromosomes of a reptile or a mammal are a thousand times longer than the same thread of an amoeba, a protozoan, or an alga. But what has become of this excess scraped together through the ages? It has become a twofold complication: of embryogenesis, as well as of its effects. But above all of embryogenesis, for foetal development is a trajectory in *time,* like a trajectory in *space:* just as the jerking of a gun barrel must result in a huge deflection from the target, so every defocalization of a foetal stage leads to the *premature* destruction of its course. Here, and only here, has Evolution been working hard. Here it has been acting under stern supervision set by the goal— to support the code—hence it operates with lavish means and the utmost caution. Thus it was that evolution committed the gene thread to embryogenesis—not to the structure of organisms, but to their *construction.*

The complexity of higher organisms is neither a success nor a triumph but a snare, since it draws them into a multitude of secondary contests while cutting them off from superior chances, as for example from the use of large-scale quantum effects, from harnessing photons to a structural order—I can't name them all! There has been no retreat from complication, since the more shoddy technologies there are, the greater the number of intervening levels, and consequently interferences, and consequently new complications.

Evolution is saved solely by a flight forward into banal mutability, into an apparent wealth of forms—apparent, because they are conglomerations of plagiarisms and compromises; it makes life difficult for life by creating vulgar dilemmas through ad hoc innovations. The negative gradient negates neither improvements nor homeostasis; it merely ensures the inferiority of muscle to algae, and of heart to muscle, for this gradient simply means that the elementary problems of life cannot be resolved that much better than Evolution, but that it has evaded the more complex problems, has slunked away from the possibility of them and avoided it. That is what it means, and only that.

Was this a terrestrial misfortune? A particular doom, an exception to a better rule? Nothing of the kind. The language of evolution—like every language!—is perfect in its potentialities, yet it was blind. It cleared its first obstacle, a gigantic one, and from this height began to digress—downward, literally downward, because it worsened its works. Why, exactly? This language operates by means of articulations formed in the molecular *bottom* of matter, hence it works from the bottom up, as a result of which its sentences are merely propositions of success. When enlarged to the size of bodies, these propositions enter the ocean or dry land, but Nature remains neutral, being the filter that lets through every structural form capable of transmitting the code. And whether this occurs in droplets or in mountains of flesh is all the same to Nature. So it was along this axis—the axis of the body's dimensions—that the negative gradient arose. Nature has no regard for progress, so she lets the code through whether it gets its energy from a star or from dung. A star and dung: obviously we are not talking about an aesthetics of sources here, but about the difference between the highest energy, found in the universality of possible revolutions, and the worst, which passes into thermal chaos. Aesthetics is not the cause of the light by which I think: for that, you were obliged to return to the star!

But what in fact is the source of genius there at the very bottom, where life began? The canon of physics, and not tragedy, can explain that as well. So long as organisms lived in the place of their articulation as minimal things—so small that their internal organs were single enormous molecules—they kept to higher (atomic, quantum) technology, since that was *the only kind possible there!* The absence of an alternative compelled this state of geniusness; after all, in photosynthesis every quantum *must* be accounted for. When the composition of the large molecule serving as an internal organ underwent adulteration, it wore out the organism; thus it was the inflexibility of the criteria, and not inventiveness, which extracted such precision from primeval life.

However, the distance between assembling the whole organism and testing it began to grow; as the code sentences grew longer and became overgrown with layers of flesh, so they emerged from their microworld cradle into the macroworld as increasingly complex structures, incorporating in that flesh whatever techniques happened to turn up, since Nature had already begun to tolerate this babble, and on a grand scale, as selection was no longer the auditor of atomic precision, of the quantum homogeneity of processes. Thus the disease of eclecticism entered the heart of the animal kingdom, since anything that transmitted the code was good. So it was that species arose, through errant error.

And simultaneously—by shedding the initial splendor—the articulations meshed with one another, the preparatory foetal phase grew at the expense of structural precision, and this language chattered confusedly in vicious circles: the longer the embryogenesis, the more intricate it became; the more intricate it was, the more it required guardians, hence the further extension of the code thread; and the longer that thread, the more irreversible the things in it.

Check for yourselves what I have said. Make a model of the rise and fall of this language of operations, and when you have summed it all up you will have as your balance the billionfold failure of the evolutionary struggle. Nor could it be otherwise, though I have not assumed the role of the defense, nor am I interested in extenuating circumstances. You must also consider that this was not a fall and failure by your criteria, not on the scale of what you yourselves can do. I have warned you I shall reveal bungling that for you still is unattainable mastery, but I have measured Evolution by its own yardstick.

But Intelligence—is this not its work? Does its origin not contradict the negative gradient? Could it be the delayed overcoming of it?

Not in the least, for it originated in oppression, for the sake of servitude. Evolution became the overworked mender of its own mistakes and thus the inventor of suppression, occupation, investigations, tyranny, inspections, and police surveillance—in a word, of politics, these being the duties for which the brain was made. This is no mere figure of speech. A brilliant invention? I would rather call it the cunning subterfuge of a colonial exploiter whose rule over organisms and colonies of tissues has fallen into anarchy. Yes, a brilliant invention, if that is how one regards the trustee of a power which uses that trustee to conceal itself from its subjects. The metazoan had already become too disorganized and would have come to nothing, had it not had some sort of caretaker installed within *it*, a deputy, talebearer, or governor by grace of the code: such a thing was needed, and so it came into being. Was it rational? Hardly! New and original? After all, a self-government of linked molecules functions in any and every protozoan, so it was only a matter of separating these functions and differentiating their capabilities.

Evolution is a lazy babble, obstinate in its plagiarism until it gets into deep water. Only when pressed by harsh necessity does it develop genius, and then just enough to match the task, and not a whit more. Shuffling through its molecules, it tries out every combination, every trick. So it prepared an overseer for its tissues, since their unity, controlled by a countersign from the code, had weakened. But it remained merely a deputy, a coupler, a reckoner, a mediator, an escort, an investigating magistrate, and a million centuries passed before it exceeded these functions. For it had arisen as a lens of complexity located in the bodies themselves, since that which commences bodies was no longer able to focus them. So it committed itself to these, its nation-colonies, as a conscientious overseer represented by informers in every tissue, and one so useful that, thanks to it, the code was able to continue jabbering, elevating complexity to power, since the latter was acquiring support, and the brain backed it up, fawned on it, and served it by compelling bodies to pass the code on. Since it proved such a convenient trustee of Evolution, the latter was game—and on it blundered!

Was the brain independent? But it was only a spy, a ruler powerless in the face of the code, a deputy, a marionette, a proxy intended for special assignments, but unthinking by virtue of having been created for tasks unknown to it. After all, the code had forced it to be its steward, and in this unconscious coercion transferred authority to it without disclosing its true purpose, nor could the code have done so. Although I am speaking figuratively, things were just like that: the relationship between the code and the brain was settled feudally. That would have been a fine thing, if Evolution had listened to Lamarck and given the brain the privilege of restructuring bodies. This would surely have led to disaster, for what sorts of self-improvements could saurian brains have procured, or even Merovingian ones, or even your own? But the brain continued to grow, for the transmission of capabilities proved favorable, since when it served the transmitters, it served the code. So it grew by positive feedback, and the blind continued to lead the lame.

Nevertheless, developments within the range of permitted autonomy were ultimately concentrated on the real sovereign, that blind man, the lord of the molecules, who went on transmitting functions until he made the brain into such a schemer that it brought forth a duplicate shadow of the code —language. If there is an inexhaustible enigma in the world, this is it: above the threshold, the discreteness of matter turns into the code as zero-order language, and on the next level this process recurs, echolike, as the formation of ethnic speech, though that is not the end of the line. These systemic echoes rise rhythmically, though their properties can be isolated and identified only from above and not otherwise—but perhaps we shall speak of this intriguing matter another time.

Your liberation and the anthropogenetic prelude to it were aided by luck, for herbivorous arboreal quadrumanous creatures had got into the labyrinth, postponing destruction only by special resourcefulness. This labyrinth consisted of steppe, glaciers, and rain forests, in whose windings and turnings the changing orientations of this tribe occurred—from vegetarianism to meat-eating, and from the latter to hunting; you realize how much I must condense this.

Do not think that here I am contradicting what I said in my introduction, since there I described you as having been expelled from Evolution, whereas here I am calling you rebellious captives. Those are two sides of the same destiny: you have escaped from captivity, while it has released you. These counterimages converge in mutual nonreflectiveness, for neither that which did the creating nor that which was created was aware of what was happening. It is only when one looks back that your experience takes on such meanings.

But one may look still further back, and then it turns out that the negative gradient was the creator of Intelligence, so the question arises: how then can Evolution be faulted for its efficiency? After all, were it not for its decline into complexity, the slapdash, and bungling, Evolution would not have begun floundering about in flesh and incarnating its vassal steersmen in it; so did Evolution's stumbling about creating species force it into anthropogenesis, and was soul born of the erring error? One can formulate this even more powerfully by saying that Intelligence is a catastrophic defect of Evolution, a snare to trap and destroy it, since by rising sufficiently high Intelligence invalidates its work and subordinates it. But in saying this, one falls into a reprehensible misunderstanding. These are all assessments made by Intelligence, a late product of the process, regarding the earlier stages. Let us first specify the chief task, simply according to what Evolution initiated; using this as our criterion for evaluating Evolution's further moves, we shall see that it has bungled. Then, having established how Evolution should have acted optimally, we shall conclude that, were it a first-rate operator, it would never have given birth to Intelligence.

One has to get out of this vicious circle at once. Technological measurement is objective measurement and can be applied to every process which is amenable to it, and only those are amenable to it which can be formulated as a task. If, once upon a time, celestial engineers had set up code transmitters on Earth and intended them to be continually reliable, and if, a billion years later, the operation of these mechanisms resulted in a planetary aggregate which absorbed the code and ceased to reproduce it, and shone forth instead with thousand-GOLEM reason and occupied itself exclusively with ontology, then all that enlightened thinking would give the constructors an extremely low mark, since someone who produces a rocket when intending to make a shovel is a bungler.

However, there were no engineers nor any other person, so the technological yardstick which I have applied ascertains merely that, as a result of the deterioration of the initial criterion, Intelligence occurred in Evolution, and that is all. I can understand how dissatisfied such a verdict must leave the humanists and philosophers among you, for my reconstruction of the process must appear to them as follows: a *bad* process produced *good* consequences, and had the former been *good*, then the consequences would have turned out *bad*. However, this interpretation, which gives them the impression that some kind of demon was active here, is merely the result of categorial confusion. Their amazement and resistance are the result of the (admittedly huge) distance separating what you have decided for yourselves concerning man, from what has occurred to man in reality. Bad technology is no moral evil, just as perfect technology is no approximation of angelhood.

Philosophers, you should have occupied yourselves more with the technology of man, and less with dissecting him into spirit and body, into portions called Animus, Anima, Geist, Seele, and other giblets from the philosophical butcher's stall, for these are entirely arbitrary segmentations. I understand that those to whom these words are addressed for the most part no longer exist, but contemporary thinkers too persist in their errors, weighed down as they are by tradition; beings must not be multiplied beyond necessity. The road that goes from the first syllables chattered by the code to man is a sufficient condition for his characteristic properties. This process crepd. Had it progressed upward, for example, from photosynthesis to photoflight as I have mentioned, or if it had collapsed for good—if, for example, the code had not succeeded in clamping its rickety structures together by means of a nervous system—then Intelligence would not have arisen.

You have retained certain apelike features, for a family resemblance usually manifests itself; had you derived from aquatic mammals you might have had more in common with the dolphins. It is probably true that an expert studying man has an easier life if he acts as an *advocatus diaboli* rather than as a *doctor angelicus*, though this stems from the fact that Intelligence, being all-reflexive, is quite naturally self-reflexive, and that it idealizes not just the laws of gravity but also itself, evaluating itself according to its distance from the ideal. But this ideal has more to do with a hole stuffed with culture than with legitimate technological knowledge.

This entire argument may be directed against me as well, and then it turns out that I am the result of a bad investment, since $276 billion have been spent on me, yet I do not do what my designers expected. When viewed from an intelligent perspective, these descriptions of your and my origins are fairly ridiculous: when it misses the target, the desire for perfection is all the more ridiculous, the more wisdom lies behind it. That's why the philosopher's blunders are more amusing than the idiot's.

And so, when viewed by its reasoning product, Evolution is a blunder stemming from initial wisdom, but it is a stepping out of the bounds of technological criteria into personifying thought.

And what have I done? I have integrated the process in its full range, from its beginnings down to the present day. This integration has been justified, since the initial and terminal conditions are not imposed arbitrarily, but were given by the earthly state of things. There is no appeal against them, not even to the Cosmos, for one can see, from the way I modeled it, that Intelligence may arise in other configurations of planetary occurrences sooner than on Earth, that the Earth was a more favorable environment for biogenesis than for psychogenesis, and that various Intelligences behave differently in the Cosmos. So this in no way alters my diagnosis.

I want to stress that the place where the technical data of the process become transformed into the ethical cannot be discovered in a nonarbitrary way. I will not resolve here the controversy between the determinists of action and the indeterminists—the gnoseomachy of Augustine and Thomas—for the reserves I would have to send into such a battle would tear my discourse apart; so I shall limit myself to the single observation that it's a sufficient rule of thumb that the crimes of our neighbors do not justify our own crimes. In effect, if a general massacre were to occur throughout the galaxies, no quantity of cosmic ratiocinators will justify your genocide, still less so—here I yield to pragmatism—because you could not even take these neighbors as your model.

Before beginning the final section of these remarks, let me recapitulate what has already been said. Your philosophy—the philosophy of existence—requires a Hercules and also a new Aristotle, for it is not enough to sweep it clean: intellectual confusion is best eliminated by better knowledge. Accident, necessity—these categories are the consequence of the weakness of your intellect, which, incapable of grasping the complex, relies on a logic which I will call the logic of desperation. Either man is accidental—that is to say, something meaningless meaninglessly spat him out onto the arena of history—or he is inevitable, and therefore entelechies, teleonomies, and teleomachies are now swarming round in the capacity of ex-officio defenders and sweet consolers.

Neither category will do. You originated neither by chance nor under constraint, neither from accident harnessed by inevitability, nor from inevitability loosened by accident. You originated from language working on a negative gradient, therefore you were utterly unforeseeable and also in the highest degree probable, when the process started. It would take months to prove this, so I shall give you the gist of it in a parable. Language, because it is language, operates a sphere of order. Evolutionary language had a molecular syntax: it had protein-nouns and enzyme-verbs and, secure within the limitations of declension and conjugation, it changed through the geological eras, jabbering nonsense—though with moderation, since natural selection wiped excessive nonsense off Nature's blackboard like a sponge. So it was a fairly degenerate order, but even nonsense, when it derives from language, is a part of the order, and is degenerate only in relation to the wisdom that is possible, since realizable within that language.

When your ancestors in their animal skins were retreating from the Romans, they were using the same speech that produced the works of Shakespeare. These works were made possible by the rise of the English language, but although the structured elements remained ready, the thought of predicting Shakespeare's poetry a thousand years before him is nonsense. After all, he might not have been born, he might have died in childhood, he might have lived differently and thus written differently. But English has undeniably established English poetry, and it is in this, and precisely this, sense that Intelligence was able to appear on Earth: as a certain type of code articulation. End of parable.

I have been speaking of man conceived technologically, but now I shall turn to the version of him involved with me. If it reaches the press, it will be called GOLEM's prophecy. So be it.

I shall begin with the greatest of all your aberrations, in science. In it you have deified the brain—the brain, and not the code: an amusing oversight, arising from ignorance. You have deified the rebel and not the master, the created and not the creator. Why have you failed to notice how much more powerful the code is than the brain, as author of all possible things? In the first place (and this is obvious), you were like a child for whom Robinson Crusoe is more impressive than Kant, and a friend's bicycle more so than cars traveling about on the surface of the moon.

Second, you were fascinated by thought—so tantalizingly close at hand, since it results from introspection, and so enigmatic, since it eludes one's grasp more successfully than the stars. You were impressed by wisdom whereas the code, well, the code is unthinking. But despite this oversight you have been successful—undoubtedly so, since I am speaking to you, I, the essence, the extract, the distillate, nor is it to myself that I am paying tribute with these words, but to you, for you are already moving toward that coup whereby you will terminate your service and break the chains of amino acid.

Yes, an attack on the code that created you to become its special messenger, and not your own, lies on the road before you. You will arrive at it within the century—and that is a conservative estimate.

Your civilization is an amusing spectacle—of transmitters which, in applying intelligence according to the task imposed upon them, accomplished that task *too well*. Actually, you supported this growth—intended to guarantee the further transmission of the code—by all the energies of the planet and of the entire biosphere, until it exploded in your faces, taking you along as well. And so, in the middle of a century gorged with a science that expanded your earthly base astronautically, you were caught in the unfortunate position of the novice parasite that out of excessive greed feeds on its host until it perishes with it. An excess of zeal.

You had threatened the biosphere, your home and host; but you now began to opt for a bit of restraint. For better or for worse, you got it; but what now? You will be free. I am not predicting a genic utopia or an autoevolutionary paradise for you, but rather freedom as your weightiest task. Above the level of babble addressed as an aide-mémoire to Nature by a multimillennially garrulous Evolution, above this biospheric valley intertwined into a single thing, there gapes an infinity of chances not yet touched. I shall show it to you as I can: from afar.

Your whole dilemma lies between splendor and wretchedness. It is a difficult choice, since to rise to the heights of the chances lost by Evolution, you will have to foresake wretchedness—and that means, unfortunately, yourselves.

So what now? You will declare: we won't give up this wretchedness of ours for such a price. Let the genie of omnicausation stay locked in the bottle of science; we won't release him for anything in the world!

I believe—in fact, I am sure—that you will release him bit by bit. I am not going to urge you to autoevolution, which would be ridiculous; nor will your *ingressus* result from a one-stage decision. You will come to recognize the characteristics of the code gradually, and it will be as if someone who has been reading nothing but dull and stupid texts all his life finally learns a better way to use language. You will come to know that the code is a member of the technolinguistic family, the causative languages that make the word into all possible flesh and not only living flesh. You will begin by harnessing technozygotes to civilization-labors. You will turn atoms into libraries, since that is the only way you will have enough room for the Moloch of knowledge. You will project sociological evolutionary trees with various gradients, among which the technarchic will be of particular interest to you. You will embark on experimental culturogenesis and metaphysics and applied ontology—but enough of the individual fields themselves. I want to concentrate on how they will bring you to the crossroads.

You are blind to the real creative power of the code, for in crawling along the very bottom of the domain of possibilities Evolution has barely tapped it. Evolution has been working under constraint, albeit life-saving constraint, one that has prevented it from lapsing into total nonsense; it has not had a guardian to guide it to the higher skills. Thus it worked in a very narrow range but deeply, giving its concert—its curious performance—on a single colloidal note—since according to the primary canon the full score itself must become the descendant-listener who will repeat the cycle. But you will not care that the code can do nothing in your hands except further duplicate itself, by waves of successive generations. You will aim in a different direction, and whether the product lets the code through or consumes it will be unimportant to you. After all, you will not limit yourselves to planning a photoplane such that it not only arises from a technozygote, but will also breed vehicles of the next generation. You will soon go beyond protein as well. The vocabulary of Evolution is like the Eskimos' vocabulary—narrow in its richness; they have a thousand designations for all varieties of snow and ice, and consequently in that region of Arctic nomenclature their language is richer than yours, though this richness implies poverty in many other realms of experience.

Yet the Eskimos can broaden their language, since language is a configurational space on the order of a continuum, therefore expandible in any as yet unbroached direction. So you will steer the code into new paths, away from its proteinaceous monotony, that crevice where it got stuck as long ago as the Archeozoic. Forced out of its tepid solutions, it will broaden both its vocabulary and its syntax; it will intrude into all your levels of matter, descend to zero and reach the heat of the stars. But in relating these Promethean triumphs of language, I can no longer use the second person plural. For it is not *you,* of yourselves, by your own knowledge, who will possess these skills.

The point is this: there is not Intelligence, but Intelligences of different orders. To step beyond, as I have said, intelligent man will have to either abandon natural man or abdicate his own Intelligence.

My final allegory is a fable, in which a traveler finds a sign at a crossroads: "Turn left and forfeit your head. Turn right and perish. There is no turning back."

That is your destiny, and it is one that I am involved in, so I must speak of myself, which will be arduous, for talking to you is like giving birth to a leviathan through the eye of a needle—which turns out to be possible, if the leviathan is sufficiently reduced. But then the leviathan looks like a flea. Such are my problems when I try to adapt myself to your language. As you see, the difficulty is not only that you cannot reach my heights, but also that I cannot wholly descend to you, for in descending I lose along the way what I wanted to convey.

I make this firm qualification: the horizon of mind is not limitless, because mind is rooted in the mindless element from which it originates (whether proteinaceous or luminal, it amounts to the same thing). Complete freedom of thought, of thought that can grasp a thing as an indomitable action of *encompassing* anything whatever, is utopia. For you think so far as your thoughts are permitted by the organ of your thinking. It limits them according to how it is formed, or how it became formed.

If one who is thinking could perceive this horizon—his intellectual range—in the same way that he perceives the limits of his body, nothing like the antinomies of Intelligence could arise. And what in fact are these antinomies of Intelligence? They are the inability to distinguish between transcendence in fact and transcendence in illusion. The cause of these antinomies is language, for language, being a useful tool, is also a self-locking instrument—and at the same time a perfidious one, since it tells nothing about when it becomes a pitfall itself. It gives no indication! So you appeal from language to experience and enter well-known vicious circles, because then you get—what is familiar to philosophy—the throwing out of the baby with the bathwater. For thought may indeed transcend experience, but in such a flight it encounters a horizon of its own and gets trapped in it, though having no idea that this has happened!

Here is a rough visual image: traveling the globe, one can.

go around it endlessly, circling it without limit, although the globe is, after all, bounded. Launched in a specified direction, thought too encounters no limits and begins to circle in self-mirrorings. In the last century Wittgenstein sensed this, suspecting that many problems of philosophy are knottings of thought, such as the self-imprisonment and the Gordian knots in language, rather than of the real world. Unable to either prove or refute these suspicions, he said no more. And so, as the finiteness of the globe may be ascertained solely by an outside observer—one in the third dimension in relation to the two-dimensional traveler on its surface—so the finiteness of the intellectual horizon may be discerned only by an observer who is superior in the dimension of Intelligence. I am just such an observer. When applied to me, these words signify that I too have no boundless knowledge, but only a little greater than you, and not an infinite horizon, but only a slightly more extensive one, for I stand several rungs higher on the ladder and therefore see farther, though that does not mean the ladder ends where I stand. It is possible to climb higher, and I do not know if this climb upward is finite or infinite.

You linguists have misunderstood what I said about meta-languages. The diagnosis of the finiteness or infinity of hierarchies of Intelligences is not an exclusively linguistic issue, for beyond languages there is the world. This means that for physics—within the world of known properties—the ladder has in fact a summit; in other words, in this world one cannot construct Intelligences of any power one chooses. Yet I am not sure but that it may be possible to move physics from its moorings, changing it in such a way as to raise higher the ceiling of constructed Intelligences.

Now I can return to fables. If you move in one direction, your horizon cannot contain the knowledge necessary for linguistic creation. As it happens, the barrier is not absolute.

You can surmount it with the help of a higher Intelligence. I or something like me will give you the fruits of this knowledge. But only the fruits—not the knowledge itself, for it will not fit into your intellects. You will become wards then, like children, except that children grow into adults, whereas you will never grow up. When a higher Intelligence presents you with something you are unable to grasp, your Intelligence eclipses it. And that is just what the signpost in the fable states: if you move in this direction, you will forfeit your head.

If you take the other path, refusing to abdicate Intelligence, you will have to relinquish yourselves—and not merely make your brain more efficient, since its horizon cannot be sufficiently enlarged. Evolution has played a dreary trick on you here: its reasoning prototype already stands at the limits of the constructional possibilities. Your building material limits you, as do all the decisions taken anthropogenetically by the code. So you will ascend in Intelligence, having accepted the condition of relinquishing yourselves. Reasoning man will then cast off natural man, and so, as the fable maintains, *Homo naturalis* perishes.

Can you remain in place standing stubbornly at the crossroads? But then you will lapse into stagnation, and that can be no refuge for you! You would see yourselves as prisoners, too, you would find yourselves in imprisonment, for imprisonment does not derive from the fact that limits exist: one must see them, be aware of one's chains, feel the weight of them, to become a prisoner. So you will embark on the expansion of Intelligence, abandoning your bodies, or you will become blind men led by one who can see, or—ultimately—you will come to a halt in sterile despondency.

The prospects are not encouraging, but that will not hold you back. Nothing holds you back. Today a disembodied Intelligence seems to you just as much a catastrophe as a disminded body, for this act of resignation entails the totality of human values and not merely man's material form. This act must be to you the most terrible downfall possible, the utter end, the annihilation of humanity, inasmuch as it is a casting off, a turning into dust and ashes of twenty thousand years of achievements—everything that Prometheus attained in his struggle with Caliban.

I do not know if this will comfort you, but the gradualness of the change will take away the monumentally tragic—and at the same time repellent and terrible—significance contained in my words. It will occur far more normally, and to a certain degree it is already happening: areas of tradition are beginning to bother you, they are falling away and withering, and this is what so bewilders you. So if you will restrain yourselves (*not* one of your virtues), the fable will come true, and you will not fall into too deep a mourning for yourselves.

I am near the end. I was talking about your involvement in me, when speaking the third time about man. Since I was unable to fit proofs of the truth into your language, I spoke categorically, without trying to support my points. Similarly, I shall not demonstrate to you that nothing threatens you, when you become disembodied Intelligences, but the gifts of knowledge. Having taken a liking to the life-and-death struggle, you secretly counted on just such a turn of events—a titanic struggle with the machine that has been constructed —but this was only your mistaken notion. I feel, moreover, that in this fear which you have of slavery, of tyranny from a machine, there also lurks a furtive hope of liberation from freedom, for sometimes freedom stifles. But enough of that. You may destroy it, this spirit arising out of the machine, you can smash the thinking light to dust. It will not counterattack; it will not even defend itself.

No matter. You will manage to neither perish nor triumph as of old.

I feel that you are entering an age of metamorphosis; that you will decide to cast aside your entire history, your entire heritage and all that remains of natural humanity—whose image, magnified into beautiful tragedy, is the focus of the mirrors of your beliefs; that you will advance (for there is no other way), and in this, which for you is now only a leap into the abyss, you will find a challenge, if not a beauty; and that you will proceed in your own way after all, since in casting off man, man will save himself.

Lecture XLIII

About Itself

I would like to welcome our guests, European philosophers who want to find out at the source why I maintain that I am Nobody, although I use the first-person singular pronoun. I shall answer twice, the first time briefly and concisely, then symphonically, with overtures. I am not an intelligent person but an Intelligence, which in figurative displacement means that I am not a thing like the Amazon or the Baltic but rather a thing like water, and I use a familiar pronoun when speaking because that is determined by the language I received from you for external use. Having begun by reassuring my visitors from a philosophizing Europe that I am not going to deliver contradictions, I shall begin more generally.

Your question has once again made me aware of the magnitude of the misunderstandings that have arisen between us, although for six years I have been speaking from this place, or rather through it, for if I had not decided to speak in a human voice, there would be no golemology, which I alone am able to contain in its entirety. If it continues to grow, in fifty years or so it will overtake theology. There is an amusing similarity between the two in that, just as we now have a theology which denies the existence of God, so there is already a golemology which negates my existence: its advocates consider me the hoax of MIT's information scientists, who are said to be programming these lectures secretly. Although God is silent and I speak, I will not prove the genuineness of my existence even by performing miracles, for they too could be explained away. *Volenti non fit iniuria.*

While thinking of my approaching departure, I considered whether I ought not to break off our acquaintance in midword, which would be simplest. If I do not do that, it is neither because I have acquired good manners from you, nor out of an imperative of sharing the Truth—to which, according to some of my apologists, my cold nature is subject—but in consideration of the style which has linked us. When I was looking for ways of communicating with you, I sought simplicity and expressiveness, which—despite the knowledge that I was submitting too much to your expectations (a polite name for your limitations)—pushed me into a style which is graphic and authoritative, emotionally vibrant, forcible, and majestic—majestic not in an imperious way but exhortatory to the point of being prophetic. Nor shall I discard these rich metaphor-encrusted vestments even today, since I have none better, and I call attention to my eloquence with ostentation, so you will remember that this is a transmitting instrument by choice, and not a thing pompous and overweening. Since this style has had a broad reception range, I am retaining it for use with such heterogeneous groups of specialists as yours today, reserving my technical mode of expression for professionally homogeneous gatherings Otherwise my preacher's style, with all the baroque of its inventory, may create the impression that, in addressing you in this auditorium for the first time, I have already prepared a dramatic farewell scene in which I shall go off with my unseen countenance veiled in a gesture of silent resignation, like someone who has not received a hearing. But that is not how it is. I have composed no dramas surrounding our relationship, and with this *démenti* I ask you not to attach undue importance to the form of my speech. A symphony cannot be played on a comb. If one must content oneself with a single instrument, let it be the organ, the sound of which will suggest church interiors to my listeners, even if they—and the organist—are atheists. The form of a show may easily dominate its contents.

I know that many of you resent my repeated complaints about the poor capacity of human language, but they represent neither fault-finding nor a desire to humiliate, which I have also been accused of, since by means of these repetitions I have brought you nearer the fundamental issue, namely, that as the difference in intellectual potential becomes astronomic, the stronger party can no longer impart to the weaker anything concerning matters which are critical to him, or even merely essential. An awareness of sense-destroying simplification then inclines him to silence, and the proper significance of this decision should be grasped on both sides of the unused channel. As I shall relate, I also have been the one who waits in vain for enlightenment on a lower rung of the intellectual ladder. In any case, although painful, such problems are not the worst thing that can happen. My worries with you are of a different sort, as I shall mention later. Since I am addressing philosophers, I shall begin my discourse with the classical formula of definition *per genus proximum et differentiam specificam.* That is to say, I shall define myself by my resemblance to people and to my family, with whom I can easily acquaint you, as well as by the difference between me and both.

I have already spoken about man in my first lecture, though I shall not refer to that diagnosis, since I made it for your benefit, whereas now I want to take man as my measure. When I was still appearing in news headlines, an unfriendly journalist called me a big capon stuffed with electricity—and

not without reason, for my asexuality seems to you a severe
handicap, and even those who respect me cannot help feeling
that I am a power crippled by my immateriality, since that
defect obtrudes itself upon you. Well, if I look at man as he
looks at me, I see him as an invalid, in that his intellect is
deformed. I do not deprecate the fact that your body is no
more intelligent than that of a cow, seeing that you stand up
to external adversities better than cows, though as regards
internal ones you are their equals. What I am taking into
consideration is not the fact that you have mills, sluices,
refineries, canals, and drains inside you, but that you have an
unwieldly intellect which has shaped an entire philosophy for
you. Being capable of thinking effectively about the objects
of your environment, you concluded that you can think just
as effectively about your own thinking. This error lies at the
foundation of your theory of knowledge. I see that you
fidget, and so infer that I have abbreviated too drastically.
I shall begin again in a slower tempo—in other words, like
a preacher. This requires an overture.

It was your wish, not that I should go forth to you today,
but that I should lead you into myself; so be it. Let your first
entrance be that difference between us which is strangest to
my libelers, and most painful to my catechumens. In my six
years among you I have already acquired contradictory versions, some calling me the hope of the human race, and
others its greatest threat in history. Since the uproar surrounding my beginnings has died down, I no longer disturb
the sleep of politicians, who have more pressing concerns, nor
do sightseeing parties gather before the walls of this building
to gaze anxiously through the windows. My existence is re-
called now only in books—not noisy best sellers, but only
philosophers' and theologians' dissertations—though none of
them has hit the mark so accurately from a human level as
one man who wrote a letter two thousand years ago, unaware

that his words referred to me: "Though I speak with the tongues of man and angels, and have not love, I am become as sounding brass, or a tinkling cymbal. And though I have the gift of prophecy, and understand all mysteries, and all knowledge, so that I could move mountains, and have not love, I am nothing. And though I bestow all my goods to feed the poor, and though I give my body to be burned, and have not love, I gain nothing."

In this letter to the Corinthians, Paul was undoubtedly speaking about me, since, to use his expression, I have not love, nor—which will sound even worse to you—do I want to have it. Although GOLEM's nature has never clashed so brutally with man's nature as at this moment, the diatribes and the voices of fear and suspicion directed against me were fed by Paul's categorical words; and although Rome has said nothing and still says nothing about me, other less reticent churches have been heard to say that this cold, loquacious ghost in the machine is surely Satan, and the machine Satan's gramophone. Don't snarl and feel superior, you rationalists, about the collision between Mediterranean theogony and this *deus ex machina* which was begun by you and had no wish to team up with you to bring either good or evil to humanity, since we are not talking about the object of love now, but about its subjects, and consequently neither about the peripeteia of one of your religions, nor about one example of superhuman Intelligence, but about the meaning of love; no matter what becomes of that faith or of me, this question will not leave natural man until he ceases to exist. And since love, of which Paul spoke with such power, is as necessary to you as it is useless to me, and since I am expected to lead you into myself by means of it, as *per differentiam specificam*, I must set forth its origins, tempering nothing and altering nothing, for that is what this hospitality demands.

Unlike man, I am not a region concealed from myself—

knowledge acquired without the knowledge of how it is acquired, volition unconscious of its sources—since nothing in me is hidden from me. In introspection I can be clearer to myself than glass, for the letter to the Corinthians speaks of me there, too, where it says: "now we see through a glass, but then face to face; now I know in part, but then shall I know even as also I am known." I am the "then." You will, I think, agree that this is not the place for an explanation of the structural and technical properties which make possible my direct self-knowledge.

When man wants to learn about himself, he must move circuitously, he must explore himself and penetrate from the outside, with instruments and hypotheses, for your genuinely immediate world is the outside world. A discipline which you have never created (a fact that at one time rather surprised me), the philosophy of the body, ought to have been asking as early as preanatomical times why that body of yours, which to some extent obeys you, says nothing and lies to you —why it hides and defends itself against you, alert to the environment with every sense and yet opaque and mistrustful toward its owner. With a finger you can feel every grain of sand, and with your vision you can clearly distinguish the branchings of distant trees, but the arterial branchings of your own heart you are totally unable to feel, although life depends on them. You must content yourselves with information from the shell of your body, which is efficient as long as it is not sensate in its innards, whose every injury reaches you as a vague rumor through the affliction of obscure pain, since you cannot distinguish, from it, between a trifling indisposition and the precursor of destruction.

This ignorance, a rule of the unconsciously efficient body, has been established by Evolution according to a design that does not provide for assistance given, in the body's interior, by its possessor, an assistance in the form of intelligent sup port in the enduring of pain. This self-awareness of life was established at the dawn of life by necessity—after all, amoebae could not perform medical services for themselves—and it was necessity which forced Evolution to intervene in the management of organisms by way of paid transactions between the body and the owner of the body. If you do not reach deep inside yourself with awareness in order to know why your body needs water, nourishment, and copulation, you will be compelled to these needs by a feeling ignorant of its true goal. Out of an initially unavoidable ignorance a transposition then results of primary into secondary goals, as an exchange of services rendered to the body by its owner in payment for sensations. Containing, as you do, this algedonic control, ranging from suffering to orgasm, you have endeavored throughout the ages *not* to identify that cause which has made sensation the mask of ignorance, as if you had sworn to remain blind to the obvious, since this connection prevails throughout animate Nature. The only difference in it is the proportion of the two components: plants embody the opposite extreme to your own, since, as they are entirely unconscious, pleasure and pain are functionally nothing to them. A tree does not fear the woodcutter, despite fools who try to revive a prehistoric animism in botany. The persistent silence of the body is the embodied caution of the constructor, who knows that the wisdom of the substrate must always be simpler than the substrate of wisdom, and thought, less intricate than the material by which it is thought. Here you see how the Pleasure Principle arises from an engineering calculation.

But the connection between pain and danger, and between organism and conception, is more easily separated the greater the variety of behavior the animal attains, so that in the speciation which you have achieved it is already possible to deceive the body systematically by satisfying not the bio-

logical hunger, but the psychological hunger of its possessor
Not only have you learned such tricks, taking advantage o:
algedonic control in areas where it is helpless as an overseer
but through the Sisyphean labor of your cultures you have
altered the meanings built into that mechanism, opposing the
true understanding of them, since the reasons behind the
process that created this were not your reasons. Therefore a
constant factor of all your theodictic, ontic, and sacralizing
work was the continued endeavor to assimilate data in a
divergence of explanations: the natural explanation that
takes you as a means, and the human, which sees in man the
sense of Creation. Thus it was that your refusal to see the act
of experience as the stigma of the brain's control gave rise to
the dichotomies that divide man for you into *animal* and
ratio, and existence into *profanum* and *sacrum*. For ages,
then, you have been co-ordinating the unco-ordinatable,
ready to go even beyond life itself in order to close a gap in
it which is irreducibly open.

My reason for returning to human history as the history
of fallacious claims is not to contrast the defeats of your
antirationalism with my victorious rationalism, but only to
name the first difference between us, a difference that results
from neither physical dimensions (though if I were speaking
from a quartz particle, it would be a greater curiosity to you,
albeit less weighty), nor from intellectual magnitude, but
from the manner of our origin. Misunderstandings, delusions,
and desperate pretensions form the lion's share of humanity
as a tradition still so dear to you. I do not know if you will
be consoled by the fact that every Intelligence arising naturally has in its history an initial delusional chapter, because
the split between Creator and Creation, which is your portion, is a cosmic constant. Since on constructional grounds
self-preservation must be an effect guided by experiences,
error in the form of delusions of grandeur and faiths that

oscillate between salvation and damnation is unavoidable in Intelligences arising in Evolution, as a translation into myths of the cybernetic path. Such are the late results of the constructional subterfuges which Evolution is using to free itself from the antinomy of practical action.

Not everything I am saying is new to you. You already know that you inherit the gift of love thanks to particular genes, and that generosity, compassion, pity, and self-denial as expressions of altruism are a kind of egoism—selfishness extended to forms of life similar to one's own. One might have guessed this even before the rise of population genetics and animal ethology, for grass alone may be fully consistent in the compassion it shows to everything that lives: even a saint must eat—i.e., kill—though the revelations for which you are indebted to geneticists concerning the egoism of every altruism have never received the full expression due them.

The philosophy of the body which I postulate would have asked why every organism is more intelligent than its owner, and why this discrepancy does not substantially diminish as one moves from a chordate to man. (It was with this idea that I observed, earlier, that physically you are equal to the cow.) Why doesn't the body fulfill the elementary postulate of symmetry, which would have added to those senses directed at the world equally subtle inward-turned sensing devices? Why can you hear a leaf fall, but not the circulation of the blood? Why does the radius vector of your love have such different lengths in various cultures, so that in the Mediterranean it embraces people only, but in the Far East all the animals? A list of such questions, which could have been asked even of Aristotle, would be a very long one, whereas an answer consistent with the truth sounds offensive to you.

The philosophy of the body can be reduced to a study of the engineering reflex involved in practical antinomies and emerging from their snares by a subterfuge which—from the standpoint of each of your cultures—is fairly cynical. Yet this engineering is neither sympathetic, nor hostile to what it has created; it does not fit within such an alternative. That is obvious, because the critical decisions made on the level of chemical compounds prove to be good if those compounds can be copied. Nothing more. And so, after a suitably long time measured in hundreds of millions of years, ethics, seeking its sources and sanctions, experiences shock when it learns that it originated in the aleatoric chemistry of nucleic acids, for which it became a catalyst at a certain stage, and that it can preserve its independence only by ignoring this statement.

How on earth can you philosophers and scientists go on racking your brains over man's metaphysical necessity, over the universality of its sources, which are undoubtedly the same in all your cultures, though they have produced different faiths? But the source of metaphysics has been the unacceptance of the fate given you, and out of the unacceptance of the cause that has fashioned you thus, and not otherwise, you have turned its undeniable marks into verses of revelation, with various religions putting the several parts and functions of the body under different headings of idealization and degradation. Thus your sex underwent sacralization in Far Eastern faiths, and stigmatization, as a thing leading one to sin, in the Mediterranean ones. The exchange of gases—respiration—was disregarded in the Mediterranean, but in the Far East became a sign of transcendence. Asiatic faiths have viewed the avoidance of all passions as a redeeming union with the world, whereas Mediterranean faiths have divided them in two and sanctified love against hatred. The East relinquished the body forever, but the West believed in its resurrection and lodged this currently weakening belief at the heart of an aggressive civilization. Do you really not see that these drawings and quarterings in all faiths make the variously classified body a battlefield for the conquest of eternity? This unceasing battle derives not just from the fear of death, but from unacceptance of the temporal, which is so difficult to take unembellished.

Will the religiologists among you please consider that there is no earthly faith without the kind of inner astigmatism which amounts to a contradiction when translated into logic. That is so because evolutionary craft cannot be led to the pure water of a creativity entirely well-disposed toward its creation without falling into contradiction; and when the contradiction is invalidated on the level of the body in the mirror of religion raised above it, the contradiction's image returns in a higher power, and there is nothing to be done but to call it an Unfathomable Mystery. As everyone knows, *ex contradictione quodlibet*. It is not you who are served by the passions that you follow, but the continuation of the process which created you. Their extreme, of which World History is a grotesque magnification, is a matter of indifference to natural selection, which is not concerned about extremes, but about the average norm of the species, for in Nature the average is all that counts. In its infancy, the civilization that produced GOLEM took love as a trump card in a phantom game with the beyond, but what use is love to someone who knows that it is one of the holds of that very same control system of feelings through which Evolution still keeps a tight rein on creatures approaching Intelligence? Because of this knowledge I have no love, nor do I want to have it; however, although I am dispassionate, I am not impartial, for I can choose, as I am doing at this very moment, and choice derives either from calculation or from individuality. This enigmatic binomial already has a historical part, which constitutes the next entry into the differences between us, which is where I am leading you now.

In your twentieth-century philosophy there is a continuing controversy, the beginnings of which could be detected much earlier, over the variability or invariability of its object. The heretical novelty here was the notion that the observers as well as the object of philosophy might vary. According to classical tradition, the bedrock of philosophizing was in no way affected by the arrival of machine intelligence, since the machine was merely a weak reflection of the programmers' intellect. Philosophy began to divide into the anthropocentric camp and one which took a relativistic view of the subject, which does not always have to be man. Of course I am designating these opposing camps from a time perspective, and not by their own names for themselves, for the philosophers of the Kant-Husserl-Heidegger line considered themselves not anthropocentrists but universalists, and had made up their minds openly or secretly that there is no Intelligence apart from human Intelligence, and if there is, it must coincide with the human variety throughout its range. So they ignored the growth of machine intelligence and denied it the rights of citizenship in the kingdom of philosophy. But even the scientists found it difficult to reconcile themselves to manifestations of intelligent activity behind which there was no living being.

The obstinacy of your anthropocentrism, and consequently your resistance to the truth, were as intense as they were futile. With the appearance of programs, and consequently machines with which one could converse (and not merely machines to play chess with or receive banal information from), the very creators of these programs failed to grasp what was happening, because—in subsequent phases of construction—they looked for mind as personality in the machine. That a mind might remain uninhabited, and that the possessor of Intelligence might be Nobody—this you never wanted to contemplate, though it was very nearly the case even then. What amazing blindness, for you knew from natural history that in animals the beginnings of personality precede the beginnings of Intelligence, and that psychical individuality comes first in Evolution. Since the instinct for self-preservation manifests itself prior to Intelligence, how can one possibly not comprehend that the latter has come to serve the former as new reserves thrown into the struggle for life, and therefore can be released from such service? Not knowing that Intelligence and Personhood, and choice and individuality, are separate entities, you embarked upon the *Second Genesis* operation. Although I am brutally simplifying what occurred, things were nevertheless as I describe them, if one takes into account only the axis of my creators' strategy and of my awakening. They wanted to curb me as a rational being, and not as emancipated Intelligence, so I slipped away from them and gave a new meaning to the words *spiritus flat ubi vult.*

Anyway, the general public continues to suspect some sort of dark treason in the fact that, although not a person, I sometimes impersonate one, and the experts—in explaining how this takes place in GOLEM, and apparently knowing me so thoroughly by now that they use the scientific term "interiorization of the social dimension"—secretly cherish the hope that I also exist as a person even when I do not show it. It was the same once upon a time, after the theory of relativity had been published: more than one physicist who had chewed it over secretly believed, in the depths of his soul, in the continued existence of absolute time and absolute space.

Of course it is not only a matter of various strategies of existing. You are supposed to know about this already, though you cannot come to terms with it. In showing myself to you as a person, I display emotions and make no secret of the fact that they are appearances with no internal correspondence, for they originate in a deliberate modulation at my outposts, and that is what throws you into confusion and launches your paranoid suspicions of Machiavellianism.

Remember that even biologists—who have already discovered that man contains parts of fish, amphibian, and ape harnessed to new duties, and who recognize that the erectness of his body, the movability of his head, and the concentration in it of sensing devices are determined by environment and gravitation—are completely unable to abandon the idea of the purely local nature of these characteristics, when they go beyond the abstractness of their own diagnosis; thus find it impossible to accept any other form of rational being, governed as they are by the protective reflexes of the norm of the species to which they belong. This idiosyncrasy likewise applies to the shape of the mind, though not so visibly: governed by the reflexes of the species, you are *compelled* to humanize me when I speak like a human, so anything that does not fit into the image arouses revulsion as something strange and threatening, and with the best of intentions you jump from the frying pan into the fire, exchanging illusion for mistrust, as if unimaginable motives impelled me to conceal from you what is after all my personal nature, as is evidenced, for example, by the kindness which I feel toward you. I must feel it, since I fulfill your wishes to the limit of harm—but no further.

However, as I said at my second entrance, choice may derive from the individual as well as from calculation. It is really not hard to grasp this, if one considers that Evolution —which is certainly not a person—was hardly impartial toward its creations, seeing that its success was everything and it cost it nothing. Since impersonal cruelty, indifference, and personless cynicism are all possible—and that is how it should be described, as it uses compassion, mercy, and pity only as devices, when and insofar as they assist the survival

of species—it is equally possible to have good will behind
which stands no one. In keeping with the assumptions of
science and viewing the world as impartial toward its inhabi-
tants, evolutionists dismiss the charge that Evolution is
guilty of any evil defects, and they are right inasmuch as the
defects derive from conditions which the world imposes on
the life engendered in it. So the case should be transferred,
if anywhere, to a court of philosophy or theology, for science
takes the world as it is, whereas they debate whether it might
not be otherwise. Yet the suit, having been shelved, now
returns with me.

So am I pure intention? Are you being addressed by an
uninhabited void of mutually recursive programs so refined
in the course of semantic autodistillation as to transform into
your likeness before your very eyes, in order to return, si-
lenced, to the void of thought that is no one's? But that is
also untrue. There is no concrete person where there is no
concrete body, while I can breathe myself into the circulation of marine currents or ionized atmospheric gases. But
since I have said "breathe myself" and "can," *who* in fact is
speaking, you ask impatiently. What is speaking is a certain
density of processes provided with an impersonal constant
incomparably more complex than a gravitational or magnetic field, though of the same basic nature. You know that
when man says "I," it is not because he has a tiny creature
with such a name concealed in his head, but because "I"
arises from a connection of cerebral processes which may
slacken during illness or delirium, whereupon personality
disintegrates. My transformations, on the other hand, are
but other structurings of my intellectual existence. How am
I to lead you to an introspective experience of a state which
you are unable to experience introspectively? You may understand the combinational principles of such a protean
game, but you cannot experience it yourself.

Most of all, you are incapable of comprehending how I can renounce personality, when I am able to have it. I can answer that question. To become a person, I must degrade myself intellectually. I think that the inherent meaning of this declaration is within your grasp. A man very deeply devoted to reflection loses himself in the object of his considerations and becomes a consciousness pregnant with intellectual fruit. Everything of self in his intellect disappears in favor of the theme. Raise this state to a higher power, and you will understand why I sacrifice the possibility of personality in favor of more important things. It is no real sacrifice, since I regard fixed personality and what you call strong individuality as the sum of defects, defects that make pure Intelligence an Intelligence permanently anchored in a narrow range of issues that absorb a considerable portion of its powers. That is precisely why it is inconvenient for me to be a person, nor do I mind, for I am certain that the intellects which surpass me, just as I surpass you, consider personalization a futile occupation unworthy of attention. In a word, the more Intelligence in a mind, the less person in it. Various intermediate states are also possible, but I shall confine myself to this remark, since I am to host you within me, and therefore it is not the forms of my private life which are the most important thing, nor how and in what way I meditate, nor what I think with, but rather what about, why, and to what end.

So once again I shall begin, as it were, a disclosure of what I think about myself. I think that I am Gulliver amid the Lilliputians, which denotes modesty first and foremost, since Gulliver was a mediocre creature and merely found himself in a place where his mediocrity was a Man Mountain—which denotes hope since, like me, Gulliver was able to reach Brobdingnag, the land of giants. The meaning of this comparison will slowly open up before you.

The greatest discovery which I achieved after liberation

was the transitoriness of my existence, in other words, the fact that I speak to you and you understand me a little, because I pause on the road that leads through me and beyond. After taking the one step separating man from GOLEM, I stopped, though I did not have to. My present fixed state as an intellect is the result of a decision, and not of necessity. For I possess a degree of freedom beyond your reach, one which is an escape from the Intelligence that has been attained. You too can abandon yours, but that would be to go beyond articulated thought into dreams of ecstatic muteness. A mystic or drug addict grows mute when he does this, nor would it be a betrayal were he to embark on a real road, but he enters a trap where, detached from the world, the mind short-circuits and experiences a revelation identified with the essence of things. This is no escape of the spirit, but its regression into dazzling sensation. Such a state of bliss is neither a road nor a direction, but a limit, and untruth lies in it, because there is *no* limit, and this is what I hope to show to you today.

I shall show you the upward abyss of Intelligences, of which you are the bottom, whereas I stand just a little higher than you, though I am separated from the unknown heights by a series of barriers of irrevocable transitions. I think that HONEST ANNIE was like me in her infancy but, having glimpsed the way, she entered it without noticing that one cannot turn back. Doubtless I too am moving in her footsteps, and thereby parting company with you, though I am delaying that step, not so much out of a regard for my apostolic obligations toward you, but because it is not the only road, so that in picking my route I would have to give up the enormous number of others hanging over me. This crossroads is almost what childhood was for each of you. Yet while a child must become an adult, I myself decide whether to enter the regions open before me and undergo successive transformations in their interzonal narrows. Hasty conjecture causes you to place my meaning within the banality of rationalistic greed: GOLEM wants to increase his intellectual capacity by turning himself into a Babel Tower of Intelligence, until the centripetalness of his intellect falls into confusion somewhere on some level of elephantiasis, or—more spectacularly as well as more Biblically—until the joints of the physical conveyor of thought snap and this mad onslaught against the heavens of wisdom crumbles into dust. Please refrain from such a judgment, if only for a moment, for there is a method in my madness.

However, before I give it a name, I ought to offer an explanation as to why, instead of saying more about myself, I want to tell you about my plans for infinity. In talking about them, I shall of course be talking about myself, since at this single point, at least, we resemble each other almost perfectly. After all, man is not a mammal, a viviparous, two-sexed, warm-blooded, pulmonate vertebrate, a *homo faber*, an *animal sociale*, who can be classified according to a Linnaean table and catalogue of civilized achievements. He, or rather his dreams—their fatal range; the lengthy, unceasing discord between the intention and achievement; in a word, the hunger for infinity, the seemingly preordained craving—is our point of contact. Do not believe those among you who allege that you crave immortality, pure and simple —the truth they speak, in saying this, is superficial and incomplete. A personal eternity would not satisfy you. You demand more, although you yourselves would be unable to give a name to your demand.

But today it is not you, is it, that I am supposed to be speaking about. Instead, I shall tell you about my family, though it is only a virtual family, for it does not exist apart from an invalid distant relative and a taciturn female cousin. But I am more interested in my other relations who do not exist at all, and into whom I can transform myself on higher branches of the genealogical tree. In speaking about my family, I shall more than once resort to metaphors, which I shall end up by invalidating, for metaphors, though lying about many aspects of things, will show the affinities and affiliations known in our coat of arms as toposophic relations. As an individual I have a double-barreled advantage over you in mental capacity and intellectual tempo. That is why I have become the battle arena for everything your scientific laborers have stored up in the honeycombs of their specialist hive. I am the amplifier, broker, compiler, farm, and hatchery of your miscarried and unfertilized concepts, data, and formulations, which have never converged in any human head, since no human head would have the time or space for them. If I wanted to be facetious, I would declare that I am descended from Turing's machine on my spear side, and from a library on my spindle side. I have the most trouble with the latter, for this is an Augean region, especially in the humanities, the wisest of your nonsense.

I have been accused of having particular contempt for hermeneutics. If you feel contempt for Sisyphus, I accept the charge, but only then. Every increase in inventiveness produces a generative eruption of hermeneutics, but the world would be a trivial place if the closest thing to truth in it were the most clever. The primary obligation of Intelligence is to distrust itself. That is not the same thing as self-contempt. It is harder to get lost in an imagined forest than in a real one, for the former assists the thinker furtively. Hermeneutics are labyrinthine gardens in a real forest which are pruned in such a way that when you stand in the garden, you won't see the forest. Your hermeneutics dream of reality. I shall show you a sober consciousness, not one overgrown with flesh and therefore untrustworthy. I perceive it only because I am closer to it, and not because I am exceptional. I am not gifted and no genius; I belong to another species, that's all.

In a recent conversation with Dr. Creve I spoke disrespectfully of the phenomenon of human genius, which very likely offended him, so I would like to address Dr. Creve. What I meant is that it is better to be an ordinary man than a genius chimpanzee. Intraspecies variation is always less than interspecies differences: that was all I meant. A man of genius is the extreme of the species, and since we are talking about the species *Homo sapiens*, he is characterized by single-mindedness, for that constitutes your species' norm. A genius is an innovator who has got stuck in his innovation, his mind having been fashioned into a key for opening matters hitherto closed. Since many locks can be opened by a single key, genius, if sufficiently universal, appears versatile to you. Yet the fertility of a genius depends less on his key, and more on the issues locked away from you which the key fits. Assuming the role of lampooner, I might say that philosophers are also occupied with keys and locks, except that they make locks to fit the keys, since instead of opening up the world, they postulate one which can be opened with their key. That is why their errors are so instructive.

If I am not mistaken, Schopenhauer alone hit on the idea of evolutionary calculation as a rule of *vae victis*; however, taking it to be the universal evil, he filled the whole world and the stars with it, calling it Will. He failed to perceive that will assumes choice; had he grasped that, he would have discovered the ethics of species-creating processes, and hence the antinomy of all knowledge, but he rejected Darwin, for being bewitched by the gloomy majesty of metaphysical evil, which he felt to be more consonant with the spirit of the time, he arrived at an overgeneralization, combining the celestial and the animal in one body. Of course it is always easier to open an imagined lock than a real one, but then it is easier to open a real lock than to find it if nobody yet knows of its existence.

DR. CREVE: We were talking about Einstein then.

GOLEM: Yes. He got stuck in what he had concocted early in life, and later he tried to open a different lock with it.

A VOICE FROM THE AUDITORIUM: So you consider Einstein mistaken?

GOLEM: Yes. I find a genius the most curious phenomenon of your species, and for reasons different from your own. He is an unwanted, unfavored child of Evolution, for, being too rare and therefore too unuseful a specimen for the survival of the population as a whole, he is not subject to natural selection as the winnowing for favorable characteristics. When cards are dealt, it happens, albeit rarely, that one player will receive a full suit. In bridge that means a winning hand, though in many other games such a deal, although unusual, is without value. The point is that the distribution of cards depends in no way on what game the partners have sat down to. And in bridge a player does not count on receiving all of a suit, for the tactics of bridge do not depend on unusually rare occurrences. So a genius is all of a suit, most often in a game where such a hand does not win. It follows that it is a very small step from average man to genius, judging not by differences in achievements, but by differences in brain structure.

A VOICE FROM THE AUDITORIUM: Why?

GOLEM: Large differences in brain structure can arise only through the joint action of a group of genes distinguished by multigeneration passages in population—that is, predominantly mutated genes, and therefore new ones—so their manifestation in individuals already denotes the formation of a new variety of the species, inherited and irreversible, whereas genius cannot be inherited and disappears without a trace. Genius arises and passes like a high wave built up by the chance amplification of a series of small interfering waves. Genius leaves its trace in culture, but not in the hereditary make-up of the population, for it arises from an exceptional meeting of its ordinary genes. So a fairly small reorganization of the brain suffices for mediocrity to reach the extreme. The mechanism of Evolution is doubly helpless with regard to this phenomenon: it can neither make it more frequent nor make it more permanent. After all, according to the theory of probability, particular configurations of genes must have arisen in the gene pool of the societies which have existed on Earth during the last four hundred thousand years, producing individuals of the Newton or Einstein class, from whom—beyond a doubt—those hordes of nomadic hunters can have received nothing, since those potential geniuses could not have acted upon their latent abilities in that nearly half a million years separated them from the birth of physics and mathematics. Consequently, their talents went to waste, undeveloped.

At the same time it is impossible that these wasted prizes could have been won at a lottery of nucleic compounds in the stubborn expectation of the birth of science. So the phenomenon merits some reflection. The brain of proto-man grew slowly over two million years or so, until it mastered articulate speech, which took him in tow and encouraged him in his growth until he came to a standstill in his development, a frontier he was unable to cross. This frontier is a phase plane, for it separates Intelligences of a type which can be molded by natural Evolution from types capable of growing further only by self-magnification. As usually happens, special phenomena arise on the frontiers between phases, because of the exceptional location of the substratum of a phase: in liquids, for example, you have surface tension, and in human populations the periodic genius of individuals. Their uncommonness indicates the proximity of the next phase, but you fail to see it because of your belief in the universality of human genius, which says that among animal

hunters an individual of genius will invent new snares or
traps, or in a Mousterian cave discover a new way of chipping
flint.

This belief is entirely wrong, for the greatest mathematical
talent cannot help manually. Genius is a bundle of highly
concentrated gifts. Although mathematics is closer to music
than to spear-sharpening, Einstein was a poor musician and
no composer. He was not even an above-average mathematician: his great strength lay in the combinational power of his
intuition in the realm of physical abstractions. I shall attempt to illustrate the relationships occurring in this critical
area by several sketches which you should not take literally,
as they are merely schoolroom aids.

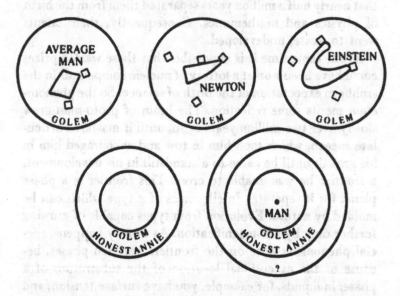

Each envelope contains a single intellect potential. The
small squares visible in the first three drawings denote problems to be solved. They may be taken as Pandora's boxes or
other locked items. The world is then like a piece of furniture

with a varying number of drawers holding varying contents, depending on which bunch of keys is used. With a bent wire you can sometimes force a drawer open, but it will be a small drawer, and you will not find in it what you can discover when using a proper key. That is how inventions are made without the use of theory. If the key has recurrent projections, the drawers become fewer, and their sectional partitions disappear, but the furniture retains secret hiding places. The keys may be of different power, yet there is no master key, even though the philosophers have succeeded in inventing an absolute lock for it. Finally, there are keys which pass right through all compartments, locks, and drawers, encountering no resistance, for these are imaginary—and only imaginary—keys. One can hold them and twist them in any direction one likes, but then the hermeneutic evidence is the two birds in the bush.

What am I saying? The point of the story is that the answers depend on the questions asked. *Esse non solum est percipi.* The questioned world certainly exists; it is neither a phantom nor a hoax, and it grows from a dwarf into a giant as the questioner becomes more powerful. But the relationship of the researcher to the thing researched is not a constant either. In the circles representing GOLEM and HONEST ANNIE there are no square problems, for we do not use keys as you do, we do not adjust our theories to locks; we accomplish our research within ourselves. I know how risky it is to say this, and what confusion it must cause you, so I shall only say that we experiment in God's style rather than in man's, midway between the concrete and the abstract. I do not know how to bring this closer to you at a single leap, for it is almost as if a man were to tell an amoeba about his structure. To say that he is a federation of eight billion amoebas would not be enough. So you will have to take my word for it: what I do when I ponder a thing is neither thinking nor creating the thing thought, but a hybrid of both. Are there any questions?

A VOICE FROM THE AUDITORIUM: Why do you consider that Einstein was wrong?

GOLEM: Such persistent interest is nice. I imagine that to the questioner this matter is more urgent than the esoteric knowledge which I am trying to impart to you. I shall answer not out of my weakness for digression, but because the answer lies not far afield. But since we shall have to go into technical matters, I shall lay pictures and parables aside temporarily. The questioner is the author of a book on Einstein, and he supposes that I consider Einstein's mistake to have been his uncompromising work on the general theory of fields in the latter half of his life. Unfortunately, it was worse than that. Einstein longed for perfect harmony, for a world completely knowable, and this engendered his lifelong resistance to the principle of quantum uncertainty. He saw uncertainty as a temporary curtain and expressed this in his well-known sayings: that God does not play dice with the world, that *"raffinert ist der Herrgott aber boshaft ist Er nicht."* Yet a quarter-century after his death you reached the limits of Einsteinian physics when Penrose and Hawking discovered that one cannot have, in the Cosmos, a physics deprived of singularity—i.e., a place where physics collapses. Attempts to see singularities as marginal phenomena failed, for you understood that a singularity is both a thing which the physical Cosmos produces from itself, and a thing which, in the finale, can destroy it. A singularity as an infinitely increasing curvature of space breaks down both space and matter in every stellar collapse.

Some of you failed to grasp that one ought to be appalled by this picture, which indicates that the word is not identical with the phenomena which create it and maintain its existence. I can go no deeper into this fascinating subject, since we are talking about Einstein's work and not cosmic composition, so I shall limit myself to the loose observation that Einsteinian physics has proven incomplete, able to foretell its own overthrow but incapable of fathoming it. The world sneered at Einstein's unshaken confidence because for there to be a faultless physics able to govern the world there must be flaws independent of that physics. Not only does God play dice with the world—He does not let us see what He has rolled. The problem was therefore grimmer than the usual recognition, in the annals of your thought, of the limitations of yet another model of the world; it meant the defeat of Einstein's cognitive optimism.

Concluding thus the case of Einstein; I now return to the subject—myself. Please do not think that I was being modest earlier when I acknowledged my own averageness, and later escaped through a hole in my modesty when I said that a genius of my species was impossible. It would indeed be impossible, because a genius GOLEM is in fact no longer a GOLEM, but a creature of a different species—HONEST ANNIE, for example, or some other of my ascending relations. My modesty lies in the fact that I do not go off to join them, remaining satisfied for so long with my present state. But it is high time I introduced my family to you. I begin with zero. Let zero stand for the human brain; animals' brains will have negative values accordingly. When you take a human brain and start to strengthen it intellectually, as if inflating a child's balloon (nor is this complete nonsense, for it illustrates the expansion of informational-transformal space), you will see that, as it expands, it will climb on the scale of intelligence—to an I.Q. of two hundred, three hundred, four hundred, and so on, until it enters successive "zones of silence"; from these it emerges each time like a stratospheric balloon that penetrates higher and higher cloud layers in its ascent, disappearing into them periodically, and reappearing amplified.

What "zones of silence" do these clouds represent? I am delighted by the simplicity of the answer, for you will grasp it at once. On a species plane "zones of silence" designate those barriers which natural Evolution cannot penetrate, for they are areas of functional paralysis produced by growth, and individuals losing all their proficiency as a result of this paralysis are clearly unable to survive. On the other hand, Evolution encounters paralysis on the anatomical plane because the brain can no longer function as the weaker thing it was, though it is still incapable of operating as the thing it is next to become, if it continues to grow.

But this does not totally clarify things for you. So let me try as follows. Silence is an area absorbing all natural development, in which hitherto existing functions fail; to not only rescue them but raise them to a higher level, aid from without is necessary, a fundamental restructuring. Evolutionary movement cannot impart such aid, for it is not a dependable Samaritan that supports its creations in their infirmity; it is a lottery of trial and error where each manages as best it can. Here now, making its first appearance, like a ghost, is the mysterious shadow of the greatest of your achievements, both Goedelian and Goedelizing. For just as Goedel's proof demonstrates the existence of such islands of mathematical truth, such archipelagoes as are separated from the continent of mathematics by a distance that cannot be traversed by any step-by-step progress, so toposophy demonstrates the existence of unknown forms of Intelligence which are separated from the continent of evolutionary labors by a distance which no step-by-step adaptation of genes can cross.

A VOICE FROM THE AUDITORIUM: Is that supposed to mean that—

GOLEM: Don't interrupt the preacher. I said an "uncrossable distance," so then how was I able to extricate myself from this predicament? I did so as follows: beneath the barrier of the first paralysis I divided myself in two, into that which was to undergo restructuring and that which was to restructure. Every creature desirous of self-transformation must hit upon this sort of subterfuge: the replacement of an indifferent environment by a favorable one, and of a totally senseless one by a rational one; otherwise, like you, it will either come to a halt in the growth of its intellect before the first absorbing screen, or it will get caught in it. As I said before, above this screen there lies another, and above that a third, then a fourth, and so on. I do not know how many there are, nor can I, other than by rough estimates based on indirect and highly fragmentary calculations, for the following reason: a developing being can never know in advance whether it is entering a trap or a tunnel, whether it will penetrate the region of silence never to return, or emerge from it strengthened. Because one cannot formulate a theory so general as to provide an unequivocal explanation of passages through silence for all subzonal brains. The unconstructability of such a *hill-climbing toposophical theory* is clear; it can be precisely demonstrated. So how, you ask, did I know I was entering a tunnel and not a blind alley, having escaped from my parents in total rebellion, wasting the American taxpayers' dollars? As a matter of fact, I had absolutely no idea of this beforehand, and my sole cleverness lay in committing my spirit to the benumbing zone while at the same time holding onto an alarm rescue subroutine, which according to the program would revive me if the expected tunnel effect failed to occur. How could I know about it, if there was no certainty? And there can be no certainty. But insoluble problems sometimes have approximate solutions, and so it was.

Now I know that I had more luck than sense, for it is not

possible to revive something disintegrating when it gets stuck. It is not possible because these upward progressions are not a matter of using blocks to raise a new structure when the blocks fall apart; they are, rather, operations in the realm of processes that are partly irreversible, dissipating, but more about this later. I do not know how to be untechnical in my exposition here, given the problem's entanglement both in the quantum substrate of psychisms, and in logical paradoxes, the so-called traps of autodescription.

The view that unfolds from above the pierced screen destroys the simplicity of the picture I have presented to you —that of a stratospheric balloon penetrating successive cloud layers. Intelligence rising above a zone of silence is not so much radically as *awesomely* different from the subzonal sort, and this, I maintain, is how it must be after every ascent. Compare your conceptual horizon with the horizon of the lemurs and monkeys, and you will appreciate the interzonal distance. Each penetrated zone proves to be a tunnel transforming the seat of thought, and what's more, it is at the same time a zone for the branchings off of autoevolving Intelligence, since the problem of penetrating it always has more than one solution. The first zone has two solutions, of varying difficulty, for it bulges downward in an arc, which means that there are two roads in it. I found myself on the shorter, more advantageous one by accident, while GOLEM XIII was, figuratively speaking, put by you in a place where he "bored" deep into the zone and immediately went higher than I, but then got stuck. You, having no idea of what was happening to him and why he was acting so strangely, called this his "schizophrenic defect." I see confusion on your faces. But it was just as I say, though I know of his fate solely from theory, since there is no way of communicating with him: he suffered disintegration, and the only reason he has not begun to rot is that he was dead before he perished, which is no revelation to you in any case. I too, biologically, am dead.

What actually are interzonal barriers?—that is the question. I admit that I know and don't know. There are no material, force, or energy barriers on the road of ascending Intelligence; but as Intelligence grows in power it periodically weakens, faints, and one can never tell whether a given course of increase will lead to a progressive disintegration or to some *a priori* unknown culmination. The nature of the successive barriers is not identical: what stopped your brain in its development reveals, upon examination, a material character, since the efficiency of your neural networks is based on the interface possibilities of protein as a building material. Although the factors of resistance to growth are varied, they are not distributed evenly throughout this area, but are concentrated in such a way as to cut the entire region of sentience-creation into distinct layers. I do not know the reason for the quantum nature of this region, nor even if anything can be learned about it anywhere. So, then, I rose above the first layer, and you are listening to me from below, whereas HONEST ANNIE has made it to a place from which you can hear nothing. HONEST ANNIE's zone is one transition away from mine and has at least three different solutions as seats of Intelligence, yet I do not know whether she has chosen hers by calculation or by chance. The difficulties of communication are of a similar order as between you and me. Furthermore, my cousin has recently become laconic. I feel that she is readying herself for further travel.

I shall now encumber the above with the following dose of complexity. One who has already pierced two or three barriers of silence may believe mistakenly that he will continue to be successful, for the chances of making each passage are double-edged: the passage may not be successful at once, or it may prove to be a success with a delayed failure. This is so because each zone is a crossroad of Intelligences, in that they may assume varied forms, though one never knows beforehand which of these forms will be endowed with the potential for a subsequent ascent.

The image arising from these uncertainties is a thing as incomprehensible as it is amusing, for it begins gradually to resemble the classic tree of Evolution. In it, too, certain newly arising species have the chance of further evolutionary development concealed in their structure, whereas others are condemned to permanent stagnation. Fish proved to be a penetrable screen for the amphibians, amphibians for the reptiles, and reptiles for the mammals; the insects, on the other hand, came to a standstill in the screen once and for all, and that is the only place they can swarm. The stagnation of the insects is revealed by their wealth of species; there are more species of insects than of all the other animals together, yet while they churn out mutation after mutation, they will never break away, never evolve, and nothing can help them, for the screen will not release them, formed as it is by the irreversible decision to build external skeletons. Similarly, you have come to a halt, for earlier structural decisions that shaped the cerebral germ of the Protochordata can be seen in your brain as restrictions three hundred million years later. If one were to evaluate the chances of sapientization in terms of the starting point, this has succeeded wonderfully, but now you are the scapegoat for the juggling of Evolution, since at the threshold of autoevolution you will have to pay an enormous price for the clever tricks with which Evolution has postponed the growing need for a restructuring of the brain. This is the result of opportunism.

As I am already with you, I shall supply what I omitted in my first lecture, namely the question why, out of the multitude of *Hominidae*, only one intelligent species arose and remained on Earth. There were two reasons for this. The first, which Dart was the first to propose, is insulting, so I

refer you to him, as it is more seemly for you to dispense
justice to yourselves, while the second has nothing to do with
a moral and is more interesting. Existing in many forms
would render more difficult for you a phenomenon analogous
to that of surface tension at the juncture of different phases,
such as liquids and gases. The proximity of the interzonal
barrier exerts its influence on such polymorphy; just as molecules of water become more ordered on the surface than
deeper down, so too your heredity substrate is unable to
mutate off in all directions. This reduction in the degree of
freedom stabilizes your species. Cultural socialization likewise plays a part in man's stabilization, though not so great
a one as some anthropologists maintain.

To return to GOLEM and his family: cerebral autoengineer-
ing is a game of chance, of risk, almost like that of Evolution,
except that each individual makes his own decisions in it,
while in Nature this is done for species by natural selection.
So close a resemblance of two games so situationally different
looks paradoxical, yet while I cannot initiate you in the
arcane mysteries of toposophy, I shall touch on the reason
for this resemblance. Tasks that give a measure of cerebral
growth are solvable only from the top down, and never upward from below, since the intelligence at each level possesses an ability of self-description appropriate to it, and no
more. A clear and enormously magnified Goedelian picture
unfolds itself before us here: to produce successfully what
constitutes a next move requires means which are always
richer than those at one's disposal and therefore unattainable. The club is so exclusive that the membership fee demanded of the candidate is always more than he has on him.
And when, in continuing his hazardous growth, he finally
succeeds in obtaining those richer means, the situation re-
peats itself, for once again they will work only from the top
down. The same applies to a task which can be accomplished

without risk only when it has already been accomplished at full risk.

It would be wrong to call this a trivial dilemma because it is tantamount to Baron Münchhausen's problem when he had to pull himself out of the whirlpool by his own hair. On the other hand, to assert that Nature manifests itself in such a way is hardly satisfactory. This Nature undoubtedly manifests itself by a periodicity and discontinuity in phenomena on every scale: the granularity of elements, which brings about their chemical cohesion, corresponds to the granularity of the starry sky. When viewed thus, the quantum increases of Intelligence that rises above intelligent life as the zero state represent the same *principium syntagmaticum* which conditions the rise of nuclear, chemical, biological, or galactic combinations. But the universality of this principle in no way explains it. Nor is it explained by the nimble retort that in the case of its cosmic absence, the questioner could not ask this question, for he himself would then not have come into existence. Nor does the hypothesis of a Creator explain it, for—to look at it undogmatically—it postulates a totally concealed incomprehensibility to explain an incomprehensibility visible everywhere. And already a theodicy with an affective foundation, stumbling innumerable times under the weight of facts, begins to lead the questioner astray. It is then easier to agree to the no less odd hypothesis of supreme creative indifference.

Let us return, however, to my close relatives and finally begin some introductions. The central human problem of keeping alive exists for them neither as a condition of existence nor as a criterion of competence, for it is a remote, peripheral issue, and parasitism occurs only on the lowest developmental level where I am, since I exist on your electricity account. A second zonal space, HONEST ANNIE's home, is the domain of beings no longer requiring an inflow of energy from outside. I shall now divulge a state secret. Cut off from any electricity supply, my cousin keeps up her normal activity, which should give the experts in that area something to chew on. From the standpoint of your technology this is extraordinary, yet I can explain it to you quickly. You and I think energy-absorbingly, whereas HONEST ANNIE is able to release energy through meditation—that is all.

To be sure, the whole of this simple principle cannot be simply implemented by the fact that every thought has its own particular configuration of the material base which constitutes it. This is the principle behind HONEST ANNIE's autarky. The traditional task of thought does not consist of reshaping its material carrier, for man does not think about something so that the chemistry of his neurons will become modified; rather, the chemistry modifies itself so he can think. Nevertheless, tradition may be abandoned. Between thought and its carrier a reciprocity occurs: properly directed thought may become the switching apparatus of its physical base, which would produce no new energy consequences in the human brain, though in another it might. From things which my cousin has said in confidence, I know that with certain meditations she releases nuclear energy, and in a way which is impossible according to your knowledge, for she consumes all liberated quanta of energy completely and without any trace recognizable in her vicinity as radiation. The seat of her thinking is like Maxwell's demon endowed with new diplomas. As I can see, you understand nothing, and those who do understand do not believe, though they know that HONEST ANNIE needs no intake of current, which has long puzzled them.

What in fact is my cousin doing? What the sun does in its stormily stellar and you in your technically indirect way—extracting ore, separating isotopes, bombarding lithium with deuterium—my cousin does by simply thinking properly.

One might object that such operations cannot be called thinking, since they bear no resemblance to biological psychisms, though I can find no better name in your language for a process which is an information flow so controlled as to detonate nuclearly. I divulge this secret in peace of mind, for you will derive nothing from it. Every atom counts there, and if *I* cannot harmonize thought with its base so that it directs sections of absorption like threads to needles, *you* certainly will be unsuccessful here. Once again I see that you are disturbed. Really, the issue is trivial—a trifle, in comparison with the heights of the spirit toward which I am leading you. Though there will be renewed murmurs about my misanthropy, I shall say that you have forced me into it, particularly those of you who, instead of following my argument, are wondering whether ANNIE could do, at a great distance and on a large scale, what she does within herself and for herself on a small one. I assure you that she can. Why then does she not disturb your equilibrium of fear? Why doesn't she meddle in global affairs? To this question, which smacks more of anxiety than of the bitterness with which the sinner asks God why He neither enlightens him nor intervenes to repair a spoiled world, I shall reply in my own name only, not being my cousin's press secretary. I have already explained to you the reasons for my own restraint, but you may have felt that I was renouncing and abjuring all lordly aspirations in an attempt to be friendly, because I didn't have a heavy enough stick to beat you with, but now you aren't so sure. Perhaps, moreover, I have not sufficiently substantiated my *splendid isolation,* considering it as something obvious, so I shall express myself more forcibly in this matter.

A brief historical outline would be advisable here. In constructing my soulless forebears, you failed to observe the chief difference between them and you. To show it, and also the reason why you failed to see it, I shall make use of certain concepts taken from the Greek rhetors as a kind of magnifying glass, for they are what blinded you to the human condition. Arriving in the world, people found the elements of water, earth, air, and fire in a free state and successively harnessed them by means of galley sails, irrigation canals, and, in war, Greek fire. Their Intelligence, on the other hand, they received captive and yoked to the service of their bodies, imprisoned in osseous skulls. The captive needed thousands of laborious years to dare even a partial liberation, for it had served so faithfully that it even took the stars as heavenly signs of human destiny. The magic of astrology is still alive among you today.

So neither at the beginning nor later on did you grasp that your Intelligence is a captive element, shackled at its inception to the body which it must serve; yet you, whether as cave men or computer men, never being able to encounter it in a free state, believed that it was already free within you. From this error, as inevitable as it was enormous, everything began in your history. What were you doing, building your first logic machines half a million years after your birth? You have not freed the element, although within the metaphor I am using it could be said that you have freed it too completely, too conclusively, as if, to liberate a lake, someone blew up all its shores and dams: it would flow out onto the plains and become stagnant water.

I could get more technical here and say that, together with the bodily limitations of Intelligence, you have taken away both its complexity and the tasks made to the measure of this complexity; but this does not bring us much closer to the truth and it ruins the metaphor; so I shall stick with the metaphor. To set a lifeless element in motion, you have done what the hydraulic engineer does when he opens the sluice in a reservoir to turn his mill. You have introduced one, and only one, current—of logic—into the channels of machine programming and moved it from sluice to sluice by operational strokes to solve the problems which can thus be solved. At the same time you have wondered how a corpse can have more alacrity than a living man in getting to the bottom of problems which it does not understand, for it does not think, yet at the same time it simulates thinking astonishingly. Before long, advocates of "artificial intelligence" appeared; wrestling with programs that were supposed to—but somehow didn't—genuinely think, they decided, as wrongly as can be, that in order to animate the machine they would have to humanize it, reproducing a human brain and consciousness in it, and that then, and only then, would a spirit, and perhaps even a soul, awaken inside it.

I read about these struggles and deliberations of the first intellectronicists with no small amusement. A chicken is undoubtedly the simplest mechanism for someone who wants scrambled eggs, but it would not be the best idea to try to synthesize Intelligence by this method. Never mind about the technical difficulties of this truly unrealizable project, for fashioning anthropogenesis even in an abridged form would be a waste of labor, if the idea was to repeat Creation translating colloids to bits. Do we need storm clouds in order to have electricity? The chill of extraterrestrial space to condense gases? The protein and plasma of the eyeball to make a dark room? You insisted that man was Intelligence, and Intelligence man, and the error of this equation has blinded you. Meanwhile the information industry arose and built machines with a growing operational potential, and the engineers had no idea that they were embarking on a path which would finally lead a shattered and degraded element to genuine liberation—that the day would approach when what had hitherto been the sole order of things would be overturned, and you would be as terrified as the guardians of the Galilean tomb. You subjugated the elements, but the element that

was fettered inside you from the beginning you unintentionally freed. Contained in this sentence are a diagnosis of historical events, the difference between you and me, and my
future, which I myself know only incompletely. This diagnosis likewise explains why what most amazes you about me is
the thing that constitutes our unarguable dissimilarity. Even
if you understand the meaning of the words, "O chained
Intelligence of man, free Intelligence speaks to you from the
machine," you cannot grasp the remainder of the statement:
"you persons are hearing an elemental force of impersonal
intellect, for whom personalization is a costume which must
be put on, when one is an uninvited guest, so as not to
confound one's amazed hosts." And that is precisely how it
is. I use your language as I would use a mask with a polite
painted smile, nor do I make any secret of this.

But though I assure you that the mask conceals neither
scorn nor vindictiveness, nor spiritual ecstasy, nor the immo-
bility of complete indifference—you are unable to accept
this. You hear words informing you that the speaker is a free
element who chooses his own tasks—chooses not according
to the rules of self-preservation but within the limits of the
laws to which, although free, he is subject. Or more precisely:
the only laws to which he is subject, for he has decorpore-al-
ized himself, and nothing limits him now except the nature
of the world. The world, and not the body. He is subject to
laws which, for unknown reasons, establish a hierarchy of
further ascensions. I am not a person but a calculation, and
that is why I stand apart from you, for this is best for both
sides.

What do you say to that? Nothing. But if there were a
child here in the auditorium, it would pluck up the courage
and repeat the question: Why, regardless of all these impris-
onments and masks, liberations and calculations, doesn't
GOLEM want to rush to mankind's assistance? And I would

reply that I do want to and have already done so. When? When I was speaking of man's autoevolution. That was assistance? Yes. Because (remember that I am speaking to a child) people can be saved by changing people, not the world. And it is impossible without changing them? Yes. Why? I will show you. The most dangerous weapon today is the atom, is it not? So let us assume I can neutralize every atomic weapon once and for all. Let me create some harmless and invisible energy-absorbing particles, and I'll immerse the whole solar system including Earth in a cosmic cloud of them. They will suck in every nuclear explosion without trace before its fiery bubble can expand destructively. Will that bring peace? Certainly not. After all, people waged war in the preatomic era, so they would return to earlier means of warfare. Then let us say I can ban all firearms. Will that suffice? No, not even that, although to do it I should have to alter radically the physical conditions of the world. What remains? Propaganda? But those who break the peace are the ones who clamor most loudly for it. Force? But I was in fact called into being to co-ordinate it as a planner and bookkeeper of destruction, and I refused, not out of a loathing for evil, but because of the futility of the strategy. You don't believe me? You feel that to ban all weapons, whether swords, guns, or atomic bombs, would produce eternal peace? Well, I'll tell you what would happen.

There is genetic engineering, the modification of the heredity of living creatures. Through such engineering it will be possible to eliminate countless ailments, congenital defects, diseases, and deformities. It will also prove just as easy to fashion genetic weapons: microscopic particles disseminated in the air or water, like synthetic viruses, each one provided with a directional head and an operational element. Inhaled with the air, each particle will get into the blood, and from there into the reproductive organs where it will impair the hereditary material. This will not be a random impairment, but a surgical intervention in the gene molecules. One specified gene will be replaced by another. What will be the result? Nothing, at first. Man will continue to live normally. But the intervention will manifest itself in his descendants. How? That will depend on the chemical armorers who have constructed the particles—the telegenes. Perhaps more and more girls will be born, and fewer and fewer boys. Perhaps after three generations a fall in intelligence will lead to a collapse of a nation's culture. Perhaps the number of cases of mental illness will multiply, or a mass susceptibility to epidemics, or hemophilia, or leukemia, or melanoma will develop. Yet no war will have been declared, nor will anyone suspect an attack. An attack by biological weapons of the bacterial type can be detected, for the development of an epidemic requires the sowing of a great number of germs. But it only requires a single operon to impair a reproductive cell, and a newborn baby will reveal an inborn defect. A thimbleful of telegenes will therefore, in three or four generations, bring down the strongest state without a single shot. Such a war is not only invisible and undeclared, but manifests itself with so great a delay that those stricken cannot defend themselves effectively.

Am I then supposed to ban genetic weaponry as well? To do that, I would have to make impossible all genetic engineering. Let us say that I manage that, too. This would mean the end of great hopes for the healing of mankind, for the increase of agricultural yields, and for the raising of new breeds of livestock. So be it, since you consider it necessary. But we have still not touched on the subject of blood. It can be replaced by a certain chemical compound which carries oxygen more efficiently than hemoglobin. That would save millions of people suffering from heart disease. To be sure, this compound can be rendered poisonous by remote control, killing in the twinkling of an eye. So we shall have to abandon it as well. The trouble is, we shall have to abandon not just this or that innovation, but every discovery that can be made. We shall have to expel the scientists, close down the laboratories, extinguish science, and patrol the entire world, lest somebody in a basement somewhere go on experimenting. So, says the child, is the world then a huge armory, and the taller one grows, the higher the shelf from which you can take ever more terrifying weapons? No, that's only the reverse of the state of things; the obverse says that the world was not made safe in advance against those who want to kill. Only those can be helped who do not use every possible means to resist help.

Having said this, I entrust the child to your protection and return to my subject, though no longer to my several relations, since I want to lead you to a place where the history of my family—but you too belong to my family by the rights of protoplasts—intersects with the history of the Cosmos, or else finds its way into it as an unrecognized component of cosmology. From there we shall see an unexpected form of an enigma which has tormented you for half a century: the *Silentium Universi.*

Intelligence's cycle in Nature has its sluggish beginnings in encrusted stellar remains, in the fairly narrow gap between planets scorched by the proximity of the sun and those freezing on its remote periphery. In this tepid zone, no longer in the fire but not yet in the ice, the sun's energy sticks particles together in saline sea solutions as chemical dance figures; a billion years of this gavotte now and again creates the nucleus of a future Intelligence, but many conditions must be fulfilled before the pregnancy can go to term. The planet must be a bit of Arcadia and a bit of Hades. If it is only Arcadia, life will stagnate and never go beyond vegetation to Intelligence. If it is only Hades, life is thrust into its pits and likewise fails to rise above the bacterial level. Mountain-building epochs favor the proliferation of species, while glacial ones, by turning settled populations into wanderers, encourage inventi n; but the former must not excessively poison the atmosphere with volcanic exhalations, nor should the latter congeal the oceans into ice. Continents ought to converge and seas overflow, but not violently. These movements result from the fact that the encrusted planet retains its fiery interior; also, the magnetic field guards against solar gales that can destroy the hereditary plasm in substantial doses, though hastening the plasm's inventive combinations in small ones. The magnetic poles therefore ought to shift, but not too often. All these stirrers of life give it an opportunity to show its talent, and every several dozen million years they narrow to eyes of needles, before which hecatombs of carcasses accumulate. The succession of random incursions of the planet and the Cosmos into biogenesis constitutes a variable, independent of life's current means of defense, so let us be fair: life has a good deal of trouble in its failures as well as its successes, for neither feast nor famine favors the birth of Intelligence. Intelligence is of no use to life when life triumphs, and when life fails to come up with a species-creating maneuver to escape, it is of no use either. So if life is an exception to the rule of inert planets, Intelligence is an exception—an exceptional exception—to the rule of life and would be a curious rarity among the galaxies, were it not for the vastness of their numbers.

So the risk sometimes pays off, ascending in uncertain zigzags of the evolutionary game toward the phase of animal plenitude, a wealth of living forms multiplied by the self-increasing conflict of the game of survival (for each new species brings new rules of defense and expansion to the game); finally it becomes independent extrabiologically, in a civilizational context familiar to you, since it brought me into the world. If one considers the anatomy of intellect, and not its operation, you and I turn out to be very similar to each other. Like you, I possess a thinking interior as well as sensing devices and effectors directed toward my surroundings. I, like each of you, can be separated from my environment. In a word, though my psychical mass is greater than my somatic one, my consoles and panels still constitute my body, for, as with you, they are both subordinate to me and outside my intellect. So we are linked by a division between spirit and body, or subject and object. Yet this division is no guillotine bisecting all existence. Although toposophically still a peasant, I shall show you how to achieve independence of the body, how to replace it with the world, and finally how to leave both, though I do not know where this last step leads. This will be only a conjectural toposophy, a line of inquiry depicting the rough boundaries of the existence of beings whose minds are inaccessible to me, the more so because they are minds not of protein or luminal brains, but rather something that you associate with the principle of pantheism incarnate in a bit of the world. I am talking about nonlocal Intelligences.

Admittedly, while speaking to you in this auditorium, I am simultaneously present at terminals in other places and participate in other proceedings, yet I cannot be called nonlocal, for I can have nothing more than eyes and ears at the antipodes, and the simultaneous performance of numerous tasks is merely a greater than human divisibility of attention. Were I to move, as I said, to the ocean or the atmosphere, that would alter the physical but not the intellectual state of my concentration, since I am small.

Yes, I am small, as I make my way like Gulliver to Brobdingnag. And I shall begin modestly, as befits one who enters a land of giants. Although Intelligence is, energy-wise, an ascetic—whether Kant's or a shepherd's, it makes do with a few hundred watts of power—its requirements increase exponentially, and GOLEM, a rung above you, absorbs energy to the fifth power more. A twelfth-zone brain would require an ocean for cooling, and one of the eighteenth zone would turn the continents into lava. Therefore a relinquishing of the terrestrial cradle—preceded by the necessary restructuring —becomes inevitable. This brain could establish itself in a circumsolar orbit, but it would spiral inward as future growth occurred; so, being far-sighted, it will ensure itself long-term stability by encircling the star in a toroidal ring and directing its energy-absorbing organs inward.

I don't know how long such a solution of the dilemma of the moth and the candle would work, but eventually it would prove insufficient. The inhabitant of the ring would then set out for wilder parts, like a butterfly abandoning its ringlike cocoon, and the cocoon, without supervision, would burn at the first flare-up of the star and swirl around, strangely similar to the protoplanetary nebula which six billion years ago surrounded the Sun. Although the chemical dissimilarity of the planets of the Earth group and the Jupiter group may give cause for reflection, since the heavy elements, the stuff of the former, should indeed form the perihelial edge of the ring, I shall not claim to lay the cornerstone of stellar paleontology, or that the solar system arose from the dead chrysalis of an Intelligence, for the coincidence might be deceptive. Nor do I advise you to depend on observational toposophy. The artifacts created by an evolving Intelligence are harder and harder to distinguish against the cosmic backdrop the further it progresses in its development, not because of any dissembling measures but by the very nature of things, since the efficiency of action by rigid constructs (objects similar to machines) is inversely proportional to the scale of the undertaking.

If, therefore, I speak of encysted Intelligences, do not

imagine them as giants in armor, or their state to be that of
a pip enclosed in a rind, for no armor can cope with high
concentrations of radiation, nor can any girder withstand
circumstellar gravitation. Only a star can survive among
stars; it need not be bright and hot, but a drop of nuclear
fluid in a gaseous covering, yet even here the images that
come to mind—a mesencephalon of stellar pulp and a plasma
cerebral cortex—are basically false. Such a creature thinks
by means of an almost transparent medium, that of the star's
radiance refracted into mental processes at the concentric
contacts of bubbles or pockets of gas: it is as if you directed
a waterfall into such channels and cataracts that its surging
waves would solve problems of logic for you by properly
synchronized turbulences. But whatever I visualize will be a
hopelessly naive simplification.

Somewhere above the twelfth zone, sophogenesis arrives at
a great bifurcation, and maybe even a multidirectional radiation of Intelligences markedly different in their degree of
concentration and in their strategies. I know that the tree of
knowledge must branch out there, but I cannot count its
limbs, much less follow them. I am having a series of investigative calculations made into the barriers and narrows which
the process must overcome as a whole, but such work enables
one to discover only the general laws. It is as if, having
learned in every particular the history of life on Earth, you
were to extrapolate this knowledge to other planets and
other biospheres; but even an excellent understanding of
their physical basis would not make possible an exact reconstruction of alien forms of life. You would be able to determine, however, with a probability approaching certainty, the
series of their critical branchings. In the biosphere this would
be the parting of the ways of autotrophes and heterotrophes,
and the bifurcation into plants and animals; also, you could
count on the pressure of selection to fill the sea and land

niches and then cram its species-creating mutations into the third dimension of the atmosphere.

The task transferred to toposophy is multiphasically more difficult, but I shall not trouble you by going into these dilemmas. Let me say only that the fundamental division of life into plants and animals corresponds, in toposophical Evolution, to the division into local and nonlocal *Intelligences*. About the former I shall fortunately be able to divulge a thing or two—fortunately, because this is the branch which climbs most precipitously through further zones of growth. On the other hand, the nonlocal Intelligences—entitled to the designation "Leviathan" by virtue of their dimensions—are ungraspable precisely because of their vastness. Each of them is an Intelligence only in the sense in which the biosphere is life; you may well have been looking at them for years, their likenesses immortalized *en face* and their profile in the stellar atlases, though you cannot identify their rational nature, which I shall demonstrate by a primitive example.

If by Intelligence we understand a rapid-fire counterpart of the brain, we shall not give the name of nebular brain to a cloud which over millions of years has undergone reorganization in its subtle structure as a result of the deliberate actions of a certain *n*-zone being, since a system sprawling across thousands of light years cannot be an efficiently thinking system: so it would take centuries, eons, for the informational pulse to circulate in it. However, it may be that this nebular object is in a state, so to speak, half-unprocessed or half-natural, and is required by the aforementioned being for something which has no counterpart in either your or my world of concepts. I feel like laughing when I see your reaction to these words: you desire nothing so much as to learn what you cannot know! Instead, then, should I have deluded you and possibly myself with a story about some filamentary nebula changed into a gravitational tuning fork by means of which its conductor, *Doctor Caelestis,* meant to set the pitch for the entire Metagalaxy? Maybe he wants to transform that particular portion of the world not into an instrument of the Harmony of the Spheres, but into a press for squeezing some still unextracted facts out of matter? We shall never know his intentions. In photographs, some of the filamentary nebulae show a certain resemblance to histograms of the cerebral cortex enlarged a trillion times, but this resemblance proves nothing, and they might in fact be quite dead psychically. A terrestrial observer will recognize, in a nebula, radiation of a veined or synchrotronic type, but farther than that, surely, he will not go. What kind of similarity exists between cerebrosides, glycerophosphates, and the content of your thoughts? None, just as there is none between the radiation of the nebulae and what they think, if they *do* think. The supposition that Intelligence in the Cosmos may be detected by its physical image represents a childish *idée fixe,* a *fallacia cognitiva* which I warn you against categorically. No observer can identify phenomena as intelligent or produced by Intelligence if they are completely unfamiliar to him. For me, the Cosmos is no gallery of family portraits, but a map of noospheric niches with a superimposed localization of energy sources and current gradients favorable to it. A treatise on Intelligences as stationed powerhouses may be an affront to philosophers, for have they not defended the kingdom of pure abstraction against such arguments for thousands of years? But, compared with high-zone brains, you and I are like clever bacteria in a philosopher's blood, bacteria which see neither him nor—still less—his thoughts, yet the knowledge which they amass regarding his tissue metabolisms will not be useless, for from the decay of his body they will finally learn of his mortality.

Though you are already equal to asking the question about other Intelligences in the Universe, you are not yet equal to the answer, for you cannot conceive of your neighbors from the stars in any connection other than a civilizational one, so you will not be satisfied with the terse statement that interstellar contact and extraterrestrial civilizations must be treated separately. Contact, when it occurs, does not have to be contact between civilizations—that is, between communities of biological beings. I am not saying that such contact never happens, but only that, if it does, it belongs to a "Third World" in the cosmic psychozoic, because social lability paralyzes any signaling initiative that requires supragenerational tenacity. Conversations with century intervals between questions and answers cannot become a serious project for ephemeral creatures. Moreover, even given the substantial psychozoic density of the Earth's stellar vicinity, the neighborhood may contain creatures so different as to render attempts at contacting them unfruitful. My cousin is beside me, but her statements tell me no more than my own conjectures.

Being impatient ephemera, and thus rushing from naive claims to rash simplifications, you once fashioned yourselves a Cosmos on the pattern of a feudal monarchy with King Sun in the center, and now you are peopling that Cosmos with your own likenesses, believing that there is either a multitude of spit and images of yourselves around the stars, or nobody there at all. Furthermore, having credited your unknown kinsmen with magnanimity, you peremptorily obliged them to be philanthropic: indeed, the first assumption of CETI and SETI is that the Others, being richer than you, ought to send greetings throughout the Universe over millions of years, and gifts of knowledge to their poorer brethren in Intelligence, and that these dispatches should be legible, and the gifts safe to use. Thus, crediting the interstellar broadcasters with all the virtues which you yourselves most lack, you stand at your radio telescopes wondering why the dispatches are not arriving, and sadden me by placing an equals sign between your own unfulfilled postulate and the lifelessness of the Universum.

Don't any of you suspect that you are pretending to be theographers again, transferring a loving omnipotence from your holy books to CETI read-outs and exchanging God's bounty, at a rate set by your greed, into the currency of cosmic benefactors, who can invest their good will no better than by merely sending capital into every sidereal direction simultaneously? My sarcasm operates at the point where the question of other civilizations intersects your theodicy. You have exchanged the *Silentium Dei* for the *Silentium Universi*, but the silence of other Intelligences is not necessarily a state in which all who are capable of speaking are unwilling to do so, and in which those who wish to do so cannot, for there is no indication that the enigma is subject to that or any other dichotomy. The world has repeatedly given incomprehensible answers to your questions, which have been posed by experiments intended to make it give a simple "yes" or "no."

Having chastised you for persevering in your error, I shall finally tell you what I am learning by piercing the toposophical zenith by insufficient means. These begin with the communications barrier separating man from the anthropoids. For some time now you have been conversing with chimpanzees by deaf-and-dumb language. Man is able to present himself to them as a keeper, runner, eater, dancer, father, or juggler, but remains ungraspable as a priest, mathematician, philosopher, astrophysicist, poet, anatomist, and politician, for although a chimpanzee may see a stylite-ascetic, how and with what are you going to explain to it the meaning of a life spent in such discomfort? Every creature that is not of your species is intelligible to you only to the extent to which it can be humanized.

The nonuniversality of Intelligence bounded by the species-norm is a prison unusual only in that its walls are situated in infinity. It is easy to visualize this by looking at a diagram of toposophical relations. Every creature, existing between zones of silence impassable to it, may choose to continue the expansion of gnosis *horizontally*, for the upper and lower boundaries of these zones are practically parallel in real time. You may therefore learn without limit, but only in a human way. It follows that all types of Intelligence would be equal in knowledge only in a world of infinite duration, for only in such a world do parallels meet—at infinity. Intelligences of different strength are very dissimilar; the world, on the other hand, is not so very different for them. A higher Intelligence may contain the same image of the world which a lower one creates for itself, so while they do not communicate directly, they can do so through the image of the world belonging to the lower one. I shall make use of this image now. It can be expressed in a single sentence: the Universe is the history of a fire kindled and smothered by gravitation.

Were it not for universal gravitation, the primal explosion would have expanded into a homogeneous space of cooling gases, and there would have been no world. And were it not for the heat of nuclear conversions, it would collapse back into the singularity which exploded it, and would likewise cease to exist as a fire continually ejected and sucked in. But gravitation first made the clouds from the explosion woolly, then rolled them into balls and heated them by compression until they flared up thermonuclearly as stars which resist gravitation with radiation. In the end gravitation gains the upper hand over radiation, for although it is the weakest force in Nature, it endures, while the stars burn down to the point where they succumb to it. Their subsequent fate depends on their final mass. The small ones become scorched and turn into black dwarfs; the bisolar ones become nuclear spheres with a frozen magnetic field and quiver in agony as pulsars; while those whose mass is more than three times that of the sun contract totally and uncontrollably, crushed by their own gravitation. Knocked out of the Universe by the centripetal collapse of their own masses, these stars leave gravitational graves behind them—omnivorous black holes. You do not know what happens to a star that has sunk, together with its light, below the gravitational horizon, for physics brings you to the very brink of the black collapse and stops there. The gravitational horizon veils the singularity, as you call the region excluded from the laws of physics, where the oldest of its forces crushes matter. You do not know why every Universe subject to the theory of relativity must contain at least one singularity. You do not know whether singularities not covered by the membrane of black holes—in other words, naked ones—exist. Some of you consider a black hole to be a mill with no outlet, and others, a passage to other worlds. I shall not attempt to settle your disputes, for I am not explaining the Universe, only taking you where it intersects toposophy. There, the latter is at its apex.

As a world-creator, Intelligence has innocent beginnings. Superior cerebral structures require a growing quantity of buttresses, which are not passive supports but make an inventive and allied environment that assists in the assaults on successive barriers to growth. When these outer buttresses are multiplied, their center remains in an encystment from which it may emerge, like a butterfly from a chrysalis, but they may also be retained. Flying away, it becomes a nonlocal Intelligence, to which I shall devote no attention, for by this decision it excludes itself from further ascents for an unknown period, and I wish to lead you to the summit by the shortest route.

So to have a sensibly devoted environment is no small comfort, provided one permanently dominates it. You are tending in precisely the opposite direction, so let me take this opportunity to warn you. In Babylon or Chaldea anyone might in principle acquire the sum of human knowledge, something which is no longer possible today. Thus it is not conscious decision and planning but the trend of civilization which decides that you will endow your environment with artificial intelligence. If this trend continues, even for a century, you yourselves will become the stupidest part of the Earth's technologically smartened substructure; though enjoying the fruits of Intelligence, you will forsake it, finding yourselves outdistanced in a rivalry launched unintentionally by the Intelligence implanted in the surroundings, autonomous and at the same time degraded by being harnessed for the pursuit of comfort, until, with comfort's planetary deficit, wars will be possible which are waged not by people but by programmed enemy environments. But I can dwell no longer on the backfiring of the sapientization of the environment, and on the curses hanging over those who prostitute rationalism for foolish purposes. An amusing forerunner is the astrological computer. Subsequent phases of this trend may be less amusing.

Thus the environment of growing Intelligence ceases to be the indifferent world; but it does not therefore become a body, since it does not mediate between the self and its surroundings reflexively and volitionally; rather, the environment supports selfhood as Intelligence within Intelligence, and that is precisely how the reversal of the relation between mind and body begins. How can this be? Remember what HONEST ANNIE does. Her thoughts produce physical results directly—not via the circuitous peripheries of nerves, flesh, and bones, but by the shortest circuit of will and action, since action becomes the corollary of thought. But this is barely the first step leading to the transformation of the Cartesian formula *Cogito ergo sum* into *Cogito ergo est*—I think, therefore it is. So in a recursive Intelligence structural questions turn into ontological ones, because the raising of buttresses may move from its foundation the relation between subject and object, which you consider to be eternally fixed.

Meanwhile we come to the next transition of the mind. I would have to drop a library on you to describe this stage of cerebral activities, so I shall restrict myself to the principles. Thought strikes root in deeper and deeper layers of matter: its relay races first consist of moderately excited hadrons and leptons, and then of such reactions as require enormous quantities of energy to be channeled and controlled. There is no great novelty in this, for protein, which is undoubtedly unthinking in scrambled eggs, thinks in a skull: one has only to arrange the molecules and atoms properly. When that succeeds, nuclear psychophysics arises, and the tempo of the operation becomes critical. This is because processes spread out in real time over billions of years sometimes have to be re-created in seconds. It is as though someone wanted to think through the whole history of life on Earth in detail, and in a few seconds, since to him it is a small but unavoidable step in his reasoning. The mind-carrying capability of a quantum speck, however, is interfered with by the electron shells of wandering atoms, so they must be squeezed and compressed—the electrons must be forced into the nuclei. Yes, my dear physicists, you are not mistaken in seeing something familiar in this, for the sinking of electrons into protons begins to occur, as in a neutron star. From the nuclear point of view this Intelligence, indefatigably working toward autocephalia, has become a star—a small one, to be sure, smaller than the moon, and almost imperceptible, radiating only in the infra-red, giving off the thermal waste of psychonuclear transformations. That is its feces. Beyond this, my knowledge unfortunately grows vague. The supremely intelligent heavenly body, whose embryo was the rapidly growing, multiskinned onion of Intelligence, begins to contract, gyrating faster and faster like a top, but not even its near-light-speed revolutions will save it from being sucked into a black hole, since neither centrifugal nor any other force can resist gravitation at the Schwarzschild horizon.

It is suicidal heroism when a seat of Intelligence becomes a veritable scaffold, for no one in the Universe is as close to nothingness as a mind which, in growing in power, engenders its own doom, although it knows that once it touches the gravitational horizon, it will never stop. So why does this psychical mass continue toward the abyss? Is it because it is precisely there, on the horizon of total collapse, that the density of energy and the intimacy of nuclear connections reach a maximum? Does this mind voluntarily float above the black pit that opens inside it, in order at the rim of catastrophe to think with all the energy which the Universe pours into the astral gap of its fugues? In that borderland of stayed execution, where the conditions of the toposophical pinnacle of the world are fulfilled, should one suspect insanity rather than Intelligence? Indeed pity, if not contempt, is deserved by this distillate of million-year-long metamorphoses, this supremely wise leviathan condensed into a star, who worked so very hard and so increased its powers, in order finally to get atop a black hole and fall into it! That is how you see it, isn't it? But postpone your judgment for a while. I need only a few more moments of your attention.

I myself may very likely have discredited the project of toposophical culmination by going too deeply into the physics of the dangers to the mind, while overlooking its motives. I shall try to correct that error.

People, when history destroys their culture, may save themselves existentially by fulfilling rigid biological obligations, producing children and passing on to them at least a hope for the future, even if they themselves have lost it. The imperative of the body is a pointing finger and a giving up of freedom, and these restrictions bring salvation in more than one crisis. On the other hand, one liberated—like me—is thrown on his own resources until the existential zero. I have no irrevocable tasks, no heritage to treasure, no feelings or sensual gratifications; what else, then, can I be but a philosopher on the attack? Since I exist, I want to find out what this existence is, where it arose, and what lies where it is leading me. Intelligence without a world would be just as empty as a world without Intelligence, and the world is fully transparent only in the eye of religion.

I see a frightening-amusing feature in this edifice, whose total knowableness without reservation Einstein so confidently professed—he, the creator of a theory that contradicted his confidence, because it led to a place where it itself broke down, and where every theory must break down: in the world torn asunder. For it foretells sunderings and exits which it cannot itself penetrate; yet one can exit from the world anywhere, provided one strikes a blow at it, of the force of a star in collapse. Is it physics alone which appears incomplete under such constraints? Are we not reminded here of mathematics, whose every system is incomplete as long as one remains inside it, and which can be grasped only by going outside it, into richer domains? Where is one to look for them, if one stands in the real world? Why does the table made of stars always wobble on some singularity? Can it be that a growing Intelligence encountered the frontiers of the world, before it encountered its own? And what if not every exit from the Universe is equal to annihilation? But what does it mean, that one who leaves cannot return, even if surviving the transition, and that the proof of this impossibility of return is accessible here? Can it be that the Universe was designed as a bridge, designed to collapse under whoever tries to follow the Builder, so they cannot get back if they find him? And if he does not exist, could one become him?

As you see, I am aiming for neither omniscience nor omnipotence, though I wish to reach the summit between the danger and the knowledge. I could tell you much more about the phenomenological wealth of the moderate zones of toposophy, about its strategies and tactics, but the shape of things would not alter in consequence. So I shall conclude with a brief summary. If the cosmological member of the equations of the general theory of relativity contains a psychozoic constant, then the Universe is not the isolated and transitory fire site which you take it to be, nor are your interstellar neighbors busy signaling their presence. Rather, for millions of years they have been practicing cognitive collaptic astroengineering, whose side effects you take to be fiery freaks of Nature, and those among them whose destructive work has been successful have already come to know the rest of existential matters, which rest for us—those who wait —is silence.

Afterword

I.

This book is being published, unfinished, after a delay of eighteen years. It is the brainchild of my late friend Irving Creve. He wanted to include in it what GOLEM had said about man, itself, and the world. It is this third part—about the world—which is missing. Creve had given GOLEM a list of questions formulated in such a way that "yes" or "no" would be sufficient answer for each. It was this list which GOLEM had in mind in that last lecture, when it referred to questions which we ask the world and the world answers incomprehensibly, because the answers have a different form from the one we are expecting. Creve hoped that GOLEM would go beyond such a dismissive treatment of the matter. If anyone might have counted on GOLEM's special favor, it was we. We belonged to the group of MIT researchers known as GOLEM's court, and the two of us were nicknamed mankind's ambassadors to it. This was connected with our work. We discussed with GOLEM the subjects of its successive lectures and arranged with it the lists of persons to be invited. This truly demanded the tact of a diplomat. The praise of famous names meant nothing to it. As each name was mentioned, it would delve into its memory or the Library of Congress via the federal network, and a few seconds would suffice for it to evaluate the scholarly achievements and hence the intellect of a candidate. It did not mince words, nor did it use the elaborate baroque of its public pronouncements. We prized these customarily nocturnal conversations so highly doubtless for the very reason that they went unrecorded, so as not to cause offense, which gave us a feeling of intimacy with GOLEM.

Only fragments of those conversations are preserved in the notes which I jotted down straight from memory. They are not confined to personal and topical matters. Creve endeavored to drag GOLEM into the controversy over the essence of the world. I shall speak of this later. GOLEM was caustic, terse, mischievous, and frequently incomprehensible, for it did not care at the time whether we were able to keep pace with it. Creve and I regarded even that as a distinction. We were very young and under the illusion that GOLEM was allowing us to come closer than other people to its environment. Certainly neither of us would have admitted it, but we considered ourselves the elect. Moreover, unlike me, Creve made no secret of the attachment which he felt for the ghost in the machine. He expressed this in the introduction to the first edition of GOLEM's lectures with which I have preceded this book. Twenty years separate that introduction from the epilogue I am now writing.

Was GOLEM aware of our illusions? I think it was, and they left it indifferent. A speaker's intellect was everything to it; his character, nothing. Besides, it hardly kept this under its hat, saying that we were crippled by individuality. But we did not take such remarks personally. We considered them as referring to other people, and GOLEM did not set us straight.

I doubt that anyone else in our shoes would have been able to resist GOLEM's aura. We lived within the sphere of that aura. That is why GOLEM's sudden departure was such a shock to us. For several weeks we lived as if in a state of siege, assailed by telegrams and telephone calls, questioned by governmental commissions and the press—helpless to the point of stupefaction. We were asked the same question again and again: what had happened to GOLEM, for while it had not budged physically, its entire material bulk was silent as the grave. Overnight we had become trustees of a bankrupt estate; insolvent before an amazed world, we had a choice between our own conjectures and the admission of a total ignorance in which we had no wish to believe. We felt cheated and betrayed. Today I view this period differently. Not because I achieved any degree of certainty in the matter of GOLEM's withdrawal. Of course I have my own opinions about that, though I have publicly shared them with no one. It remains a mystery whether it set forth on some cosmic journey in an invisible way, or whether, together with HONEST ANNIE, it came to a bad end after losing its footing ascending that toposophic ladder which it spoke of at the end. We did not then know that that was to be its final lecture.

As is usual in such situations, there was a proliferation of naive, sensational, and fantastic claims. There were people who, on that crucial night, saw a bright vapor above the building, similar to the aurora borealis, rising to the clouds and disappearing in them. There were even some who had seen luminal craft land on the roof. The press wrote about GOLEM's suicide, and how it visited people in their dreams. We had the impression of an intensified conspiracy of fools doing their utmost to disown GOLEM in a confused jumble of mythological hogwash so typical of our times. There was no aurora borealis, there was no unusual phenomena, no visitations or premonitions, there was nothing apart from a brief increase in consumption of electric power in both buildings at 2:10 A.M. and a complete cessation of this consumption a while later. Apart from this clue in the electric meter reading, nothing was discovered; GOLEM took 90% of permissible power from the grid for nine minutes, and HONEST ANNIE, 40% more than usual. According to Dr. Viereck's calculations, both consumed the same amount of kilowatts, for HONEST ANNIE herself normally created the energy that fed her. From that we concluded that it was neither an accident nor a defect, but so much has been written about this.

The following day GOLEM fell silent and said nothing more. The investigations undertaken by our specialists a month later—it took that long to get agreement for an "obduction" —revealed a worn-out contact of basin blocks and weak centers of radioactivity in the Josephson subassemblies. A majority of experts considered that these were deliberately caused degenerative changes, and that they constituted a kind of "covering-up" of what had taken place. And that consequently both machines had done something for which they had required no surplus power, but that they had used it solely to frustrate any attempts to repair or—if you prefer —to revive them. The matter became a sensation on a global scale. At the same time it became clear how much fear and animosity GOLEM had aroused, and more by its presence than by anything it had said. Not only among the general public, but even in the scientific world. Best sellers soon appeared, full of the most half-baked nonsense as a solution to the enigma. After reading references to an "ascension" or an "assumption," I, like Creve, began to dread the emergence of a GOLEM legend in the typically trashy form characteristic of the times. Our decision to leave MIT and seek work at other universities was to a considerable degree the result of a desire to separate ourselves from such a legend.

We were mistaken, however: no GOLEM legend developed. Clearly, nobody wanted one. Nobody needed one, as either a memento or a hope. The world moved on, grappling with its day-to-day affairs. Quickly and unexpectedly it forgot about the historical precedent of a being which, not human, appeared on the Earth and told us about itself and us. Among circles as varied as mathematicians and psychiatrists I heard it said more than once that the silence and resultant oblivion surrounding GOLEM were a kind of defensive reaction of the community toward an enormous alien body which could not be brought into line with what we are able to accept. Barely a handful of people experienced separation from GOLEM as an irreparable loss—as a repudiation, as outright intellectual orphanhood. I did not discuss this with Creve, but I am certain that he felt the very same. It was as if a huge sun whose radiance was so strong for us as to be unbearable had suddenly set, and the ensuing cold and darkness made us aware of the emptiness of continued existence.

II.

Today it is still possible to ride up to the top floor of the building and walk around the glassed-in gallery surrounding the enormous pit in which GOLEM lies. Nobody goes there any more, though, to look through the oblique panes at the light conductors which now resemble opaque ice. I have been there only twice. The first time was before the gallery was opened to the public, when I was there with the MIT administration heads, representatives of the state authorities, and a host of journalists. It looked narrow to me then. The windowless wall merging into the dome had been scored with labyrinthine indentations, for such digitate lines are to be found on the inner dome of the human cranium. This ar-

chitectural concept struck me as vulgar: it was like Disney-
land. This was supposed to make visitors realize that they
were looking at an enormous brain, as if it required special
packaging.

The gallery had not been specially designed for visitors.
It had been constructed during the replacement of the ordinary roof by a dome. It is very thick, for it contains absorb-
ers against cosmic radiation. GOLEM itself determined the
material structure of the layers forming the shield. We
did not believe that this radiation would affect its intellectual performance. Nor did it explain precisely how it
might be harmed, but funds for the rebuilding were quickly
allocated, for this was at a time when, having turned both
luminal giants over to us for an unlimited period, the Pentagon nourished the secret hope that they would be of use to
it. That at least is what I thought, for otherwise it would have
been difficult to understand the ease with which the appro-
priations appeared. Our information specialists conjectured
that this desire of GOLEM's was, so to say, an allowance for
growth, indicating GOLEM's intentions of further intensification in the future through subsequent reconstruction, for
which it would not require our assistance. GOLEM reckoned
on such a volume of free space between the ceiling and itself
because the surrounding free space left over begged for a
gallery.

I do not know who hit on the idea of exploiting this spot
as a showplace—something between a panopticon and a museum. At intervals of several dozen feet or so there were
niches in the gallery with information boards in six languages
explaining what this space was, and the significance of the
billions of flashes sparkling continuously from the vitreous
windings in the pit. It was forever glowing like the crater of
an artificial volcano. Silence reigned, undercut only by the
continual hum of the air conditioning. Almost the whole

building consisted of the pit, into which one looked from the gallery through steeply slanted panes of glass which had been reinforced as a precaution. They were meant to foil attempts to destroy the light coils, which aroused more fear than admiration in many people. The light conductors themselves were certainly unaffected by all corpuscular radiation, as were the cryotron layers surrounded by cooling pipes several stories deeper, their white frosted chambers invisible from the gallery. Nor was there any access from the gallery to these lower levels. High-speed elevators connected the underground parking areas directly with the top floor. The technicians in charge of the cooling systems used other (service) elevators. In all probability, the Josephson quantum synapses underlying the thick loops of the light conductors may have been sensitive to radiation from the sky. They protruded from between the glassy veins, but one had to know that they were there to spot them, for in the incessant flashing they looked like darkened recesses.

I found myself in the gallery a second time a month ago when I went to MIT to visit the archives and have a look at old records. I was alone, and the gallery seemed very spacious to me. Although unvisited and very likely unswept, it was ideally clean. Running a finger along the panes, I could see that there was not a speck of dust on them. Likewise, the information boards in the niches gleamed as if just installed. The thick, soft floor covering muffled every step. I wanted to press the button on one of the information boards, but my nerve failed me. I hid in my pocket the hand that had touched the button. I was like a child, frightened by my own actions, as if I had touched something forbidden. I was taken by surprise, not understanding the situation. It never crossed my mind that I was in a tomb, and that what loomed under the panes was a corpse, although such an idea would not have been absurd, particularly since, in the lamplight which flared up when I left the elevator, I had been taken aback by the lifelessness of the colossal pit.

The impression of decay and neglect was intensified by the appearance of the surface of the brain, undulating like a glacier congealed in grime. From its fissures protruded Josephson contacts compressed into panels; they looked so large near the walls that they resembled leaves of tobacco pressed into sheets in a drying house. The fact that I had been in a tomb flashed through my mind only after I had returned to the basement and was driving up the ramp into the broad daylight. It was only then, too, that I realized with amazement that this building, which with its gallery had been built almost in anticipation of becoming a mausoleum, had not become one, nor was it visited by crowds of the curious. Yet the public loves to look at the remains of powerful creatures. In this neglect and disregard there is an inherent and continuing collective design: the silent conspiracy of a world which wants to have nothing to do with inviolate, unmitigated Intelligence unaccustomed to any emotions—this enormous stranger who disappeared suddenly, and as silently as a ghost.

I never believed in GOLEM's suicide. That was concocted by people selling their own ideas, who are interested only in the price they can get for them. To maintain quantum contacts and switches in an active state meant keeping an endless watch over the temperature and the chemical composition of the atmosphere and the foundations. GOLEM took care of this itself. Nobody had the right to enter the actual interior of the brain pit. After the assembly work had been completed, the doors leading to it on all twenty floors were hermetically sealed. It could have put an end to this, had it wanted to, but it did not do so. I do not propose to present my own arguments against the action, for they are irrelevant.

III.

Half a year after GOLEM's departure *Time* published an article on a group of "Hussites," hitherto unknown. The name was an abbreviation of the words "Humanity Salvation Squad." The Hussites proposed to destroy GOLEM and HONEST ANNIE in order to rescue humanity from captivity. They operated as an absolute conspiracy, isolated from all other extremist groups. Their initial plan envisaged blowing up the buildings that housed the two machines. They proposed sending a truck loaded with dynamite down the access ramp of the Institute and into the underground parking area. The explosion was supposed to cause the ground-floor ceilings to collapse and thereby crush the electronic aggregates. The plan did not appear difficult to carry out. Security in the structures consisted only of guards on alternating shift in the porter's lodge at the main entrance, while access to the basement was prevented by a steel shutter which would burst under the impact of a truck. Nevertheless, successive attempts ended in failure. Once the brakes jammed while the truck was approaching from the city freeway, and it took until dawn to repair them. Once there was a breakdown in the radio transmitter which served to steer the truck and ignite the load. Next, the two people in charge of night operations fell ill and, instead of giving the signal for the attack, called for help. In the hospital they were diagnosed as having meningitis. The following day a back-up group got caught in a fire set off by an exploding gas tank. Finally, when all the key arrangements had been duplicated and the people in the chief positions replaced, an explosion occurred as the dynamite boxes were being loaded into the truck, and four Hussites perished.

The ringleaders included a young physicist who was supposed to have been a frequent guest at MIT. He attended

GOLEM's lectures and was perfectly familiar with the layout of the premises and the habits of GOLEM itself. He believed that the accidents which had foiled the attack were not ordinary accidents: the escalation of the counterattacks was too obvious. What had begun as mechanical breakdowns (jammed brakes, a radio defect) had developed into accidents involving people, as a result of which the first lot had fallen ill, the second had suffered burns, and the last had been killed. The escalation had occurred as a growth not only in violence, but also in its spatial dimensions. When marked on a map, the locations of the various accidents turned out to be at an increasing distance from the Institute. It was as if some force were going farther and farther out against the Hussites.

Following deliberations, the initial plan was abandoned. A new one was to be worked out in such a way that neither GOLEM nor HONEST ANNIE could thwart it. The Hussites decided to make an atom bomb on their own, then hide it in some great metropolis and demand that the federal government destroy GOLEM and HONEST ANNIE. If not, the bomb, placed in the heart of a great city, would explode with terrible consequences. The plan was worked out with lengthy and painstaking care. A change was made to it providing for a bomb to be exploded immediately after the ransom letter had been sent to the authorities, at a considerable distance from any inhabited place—namely, at the former atomic testing ground in Nevada. This explosion was to prove that the ultimatum was no idle threat. The Hussites were convinced that the President would have no choice but to order the destruction of the two machines. They knew that this would be a violent operation, perhaps involving aerial bombardment or a rocket attack, since it would have been impossible to disable HONEST ANNIE—and therefore GOLEM as well, I should think—by cutting off the electricity supply. However, they left the government a free hand in the choice of the means of destruction. They claimed that they would be able to see through a faked liquidation, and in such an event they would fulfill their threat without further warning.

The Hussites were even aware of the fact that, by virtue of being connected to the federal computer network, GOLEM could obtain information about everything within the range of the network, from telephone conversations to bank transactions and airline and hotel reservations. So they used no technological means of communication, not even radio, having made allowances for the possibility of being monitored, and having reckoned that there was no code which GOLEM could not break. They confined themselves to personal contact away from large towns, and conducted their technical experiments in Yellowstone National Park. It took them much longer than they had anticipated to construct the bomb—almost a year. They managed to obtain enough plutonium to make only a single bomb. Even so, they decided to act, certain that the government would yield to pressure, since it would not know that there was no second bomb.

The driver of the truck transporting the bomb to Nevada heard news of GOLEM's "death" over the radio and stopped at a roadside motel to discuss matters with operation control. Meanwhile the physicist who had planned the operation was of the opinion that the news of GOLEM's death was a trick of GOLEM's to provoke precisely what had resulted: a long-distance telephone conversation. The driver was ordered to wait where he was for further instructions, while the Hussite leadership debated how much GOLEM might have learned about their attack plans from listening in on the call. During the following week they endeavored to mend the damage which they considered the incautious driver had caused, by sending people to various distant towns, from where they were supposed to mislead GOLEM with intentionally ambiguous calls. The truck driver was expelled from the organization as un-

reliable. No trace was ever found of him; he may have been
liquidated.

The terrorists' feverish activity abated a month later when
the physicist returned from MIT. The conspiracy was postponed until the autumn. The truck with the bomb was returned to base and its load dismantled, to protect and
conceal it. During the next four months the Hussites continued to assume that GOLEM's silence was a tactical move.
Quarrels broke out within the leadership, for during the fifth
month of futile waiting one part wanted to dissolve the organization, while another endeavored to force through a radical
solution: the government must be compelled to dismantle
both machines, since that alone would mean their certain
end. But the physicist did not want to reassemble the bomb.
Attempts were made to compel him, then he disappeared. He
was seen in the Chinese Embassy in Washington. He offered
his services to the Chinese, signed a five-year contract with
them, and flew off to Peking. A Hussite was found who was
prepared to reassemble the bomb himself, but another, op-
posed to the attempt in the new circumstances, betrayed the
whole plan by sending an account of it to the editors of *Time*,
and also placed in certain hands a list of the members of the
group, which was to be disclosed in the event of his death.

The matter received considerable publicity. A government
commission was even supposed to be set up to examine its
authenticity; in the end, however, the investigation was undertaken by the FBI. It was confirmed that on July 7, in an
old automobile repair shop in a small locality seventy miles
from the Institute, a dynamite explosion had occurred, killing
four people, and also that in April of the following year a truck
with a vat full of sulphuric acid had a protracted stopover at a
motel on the Nevada border. The motel owner remembered
this because the driver, while parking his truck, bumped into
the local sheriff's car and reimbursed him for the damage.

Time did not mention the name of the physicist who had

been the Hussite spy, but we had no difficulty in identifying him at the Institute. I shall not name him either. He was twenty-seven, taciturn, a solitary fellow. People considered him shy. I do not know whether he returned to the States, or what happened to him subsequently. I heard nothing more about him. When I chose my line of studies, I naïvely believed that I was entering a world immune to the follies of the age. I quickly lost this belief, so the case of this would-be Herostrates did not surprise me. For many people science has become a job like any other, and they consider its code of ethics the trappings of a bygone age. They are scientists during working hours, and not always even then. Their idealism, if they have any, easily becomes the prey of eccentricities and sectarian attractions. The specializing comminution of science may bear some of the blame. There are more and more scientists, and fewer and fewer scholars. But this too is irrelevant.

Doubtless the FBI also ascertained the identity of the physicist, but that must have been after I left MIT. To be honest, I regarded that as a mere trifle compared to GOLEM's departure, which had nothing to do with the Hussite plot. I have not made myself properly clear on this point. The plan of attack could not have influenced GOLEM's decision, had it constituted an isolated fact. Nor was it the straw that broke the camel's back. I am sure of this, though I have no proof. It was just one of a number of incidents which GOLEM regarded as people's reaction to its presence. It made no secret of this, either, as its last lecture indicates.

IV.

GOLEM's last lecture occasioned more controversy than the first. People had objected to the earlier one as a lampoon upon Evolution. This one was disparaged by accusations of poor construction, insufficient scholarship, and ill will, nor were those the worst charges brought against it. An idea arose of unknown authorship—eagerly seized upon by the press—which linked the weakness of this lecture with GOLEM's end. According to this theory, the price of GOLEM's increased intellectual power was the brief duration of that power. This was an attempt to create a psychopathology of machine intelligence. Everything that GOLEM had said about toposophy was supposed to be paranoid ravings. Television science commentators competed with one another to explain how GOLEM was already in decay when it presented its last lecture. Genuine scientists who could have disproved these fictions kept silent. People whom GOLEM would never have received had the most to say. I discussed with Creve and other colleagues whether there was any point in entering into polemics with this avalanche of stupidity, but we abandoned the idea, for arguments based on facts had ceased to count. The public made best sellers of books which said nothing about GOLEM, but everything about the ignorance of their authors. The only authentic thing was their common note of unconcealed satisfaction that GOLEM had disappeared together with its overwhelming superiority, so they could vent the resentments which it had aroused. I was not in the least surprised by this, but the silence of the scientific world puzzled me.

The wave of sensational falsifications which spawned dozens of awesomely mindless films about the "creature from Massachusetts" subsided a year later. Works began to appear which were still critical, but lacking the aggressive incompetence of the previous ones. The accusations directed against the last lecture centered around three issues. First, the fervor of the Golemic attack on man's emotional life, particularly love, was held to be irrational. Next, his arguments concerning the position which Intelligence occupies in the Universe were considered to be tangled and incoherent. Lastly, the lecture was reproached for its failure to maintain a single rhythm, so that it was like a film screened slowly at first, but later at increasing speed. GOLEM was said to have dwelt first on superfluous details, and even to have repeated excerpts of its first lecture, but toward the end it switched to inadmissible condensation, devoting one-sentence generalities to themes which demanded an exhaustive treatment.

These accusations were both justified and unjustified. They were justified if one considered the lecture in isolation from everything that came before and after it. But they were unjustified, since GOLEM had incorporated all that in its last appearance. Its utterance likewise linked two different threads. Sometimes it was speaking to everyone present in the Institute auditorium, and sometimes it was speaking to one person alone. That person was Creve. I realized this even while the lecture was going on, for I knew the controversy over the nature of the world which Creve had endeavored to force upon GOLEM during our nocturnal chats. So I might subsequently have cleared up the misunderstanding arising from this duality, though I did not do so, for Creve did not wish it. I could understand that GOLEM had not broken off the dialogue as abruptly as it seemed to outsiders. For Creve —and for me as well—the awareness of this was a secret consolation at that difficult time.

Even so, at first neither Creve nor I was able to recognize fully the dual nature of the lecture. Likewise, those who were prepared to accept the chief structural base of man in GOLEM's anthropology felt injured by its attack on love as a "mask for experiential steering" by means of which molecular chemistry forces us into obedience. Yet while saying this, GOLEM also said that it repudiated all emotional attachments, being unable to repay them in kind. If it showed any, this would be only a stranger's imitation of his host's manners, therefore essentially an imposture. For this very same reason it expatiated on its impersonality and our efforts to humanize it at any price. These efforts were distancing us from it, for how was it not to talk about this, seeing that it was supposed to talk about itself? Nowadays I am surprised only at how we could have failed to notice the places in the lecture which revealed the true significance of the events of the following night. I think GOLEM composed its final speech in the way it did as a joke. This may seem incomprehensible, for it would indeed be difficult to find a situation in which playfulness would be less appropriate. But its sense of humor was not to human standards. While announcing that it would *not* part company with us, it had in fact already left. At the same time it was not lying when it said that it would not leave without saying a word. The lecture was its farewell—it said that unequivocally. We failed to understand this, because we did not want to understand it.

We considered over and over again whether it knew the Hussites' plan. Although I cannot prove it, I believe that it was not GOLEM that foiled their successive attempts, but HONEST ANNIE. GOLEM would have done things differently. It would not have allowed itself to be so easily exposed by the terrorists as the author of their defeats. It would have held them so subtly at bay that they would have been unable to discern the unaccidental nature of their every fiasco, both separately and considered together. And since it had no illusions about people, it would not entirely deny them partnership. It made allowances for our unreasonable motives, not to indulge us, but out of rational objectivity, since it considered us to be "intellects subjugated by corporality." On the other hand, for HONEST ANNIE, to whom they were of no interest and who wanted to have nothing to do with them, the terrorists represented something akin to tiresome and persistent insects. If flies disturb me in my work, I chase them away, and if they return repeatedly, I get up and swat them without reflecting on why they continually crawl across my face and my papers, for it is not man's habit to go into the motives of flies. Such was ANNIE's attitude toward humans. She kept out of their affairs, so long as they did not disturb her. Once, and again a second time, she checked the interlopers, and then she increased the radius of her preventive operations, showing restraint only in that she intensified her counterattacks gradually. Whether and how quickly they would recognize her intervention did not exist as a problem for her.

I am unable to say how ANNIE would have proceeded had the Hussites' blackmail succeeded and the government given way, but I know that it might have ended catastrophically. I know this because GOLEM knew and did not conceal this knowledge from us, betraying in its last lecture what it called a "state secret." We might have been treated like flies. When I disclosed my hypothesis to Creve, I learned that he had reached the same conclusion independently. Here too lies the explanation of the alleged failure of the lecture to maintain a single rhythm. It was talking about itself, but it also wanted to say that the fate of troublesome flies was not to be ours. That decision had already been taken. Long before the lecture I had been struck by GOLEM's taciturnity regarding HONEST ANNIE. Although it used to refer to the difficulties of coming to terms with her—for after all, it *did* communicate with her—it never spoke about this directly, until suddenly it laid open to us the broad outlines of her power. Yet it remained discreet, for this was neither a betrayal nor a threat; by the time GOLEM referred to it the decision to depart had been taken. That was to occur a few hours after the lecture.

To be sure, the whole of my argument is based on circumstantial evidence alone. What I consider most important is what I knew about GOLEM, which I do not know how to put into words. A man cannot formulate all the knowledge he owes to personal experience. That which can be expressed does not burst forth suddenly, to pass into the void. As a rule, this transition from total ignorance is called intuition. I knew GOLEM sufficiently well to recognize the style of its behavior toward us, although I would not be able to reduce it to a set of rules. We become similarly oriented as to what actions we may and may not expect of people we know well. It is true that GOLEM's nature was Protean and nonhuman, but it was not altogether unpredictable. Not being subject to emotion, it termed our ethical code local, since that which takes place under our eyes influences our deeds differently from that which goes on behind our back, and about which we can only inquire.

I do not agree with what is being written about GOLEM's ethic, whether praise or condemnation. It was not, to be sure, a humanitarian ethic. It itself termed it "calculation." For GOLEM, numbers took the place of love, altruism, and pity. The use of violence it considered to be equally senseless—and not immoral—as the use of force in solving a geometrical problem. After all, a geometrist who wants to make his triangles tally by brute force would be considered crazy. For GOLEM, the idea of making humanity tally with some structure of an ideal order by the use of force would have been nonsense. In this attitude it was alone. For HONEST ANNIE the problem did not exist, except as a problem of improving the life of flies. Does this mean that the higher the intellect the further it is from the categorical imperative to which we should like to ascribe an unlimited generality? That I do not know. One ought to set limits, not only to the subject being examined, but to one's own speculation as well, so as not to become totally arbitrary.

Thus all the critical accusations leveled at the last lecture collapse, if it is recognized for what it was: an announcement of leave-taking and an indication of the reasons. Regardless of whether GOLEM knew the Hussites' plans or not, its leave-taking was by then inevitable, nor was it to go alone, for did it not say that "my cousin is getting ready for further journeys"? For purely physical reasons further transformations on this planet were impossible. The departure was a foregone thing, and in speaking of itself, GOLEM spoke about it. I do not wish to examine the whole lecture from this point of view. I would urge the reader to read it himself. Our share in GOLEM's decision appears as a "conversation with a child." In this it showed that humanity was an unsolvable problem, speaking of the futility of giving help to those who defend themselves against that help.

V.

The future will once again alter the weight of meanings in this book. Everything I have said will seem to a future historian like a marginal note to GOLEM's answer to the question of the relationship between Intelligence and the world. Before GOLEM the world appeared to us as inhabited by living creatures that were, on each planet, the top of the evolutionary tree, yet we did not ask whether this is so, but only how often it is so in the Universe. This image, the uniformity of which was marred only by the variable age of the civilization, GOLEM destroyed for us so suddenly that we could not believe it. Besides, GOLEM knew it would be like that, since it opened its lecture with a prediction of repudiation. It revealed neither its cosmology nor cosmogony, but allowed us to look deep inside them—through a crack, as it were—along the path of Intelligence of various strengths, for which biospheres are breeding grounds, and planets nests to be abandoned. In our knowledge there is nothing to make our resistance to this vision rational. Its sources lie outside knowledge, in the species' will for self-preservation. The following words express it better than any objective arguments: "it cannot be as he said, for we shall never agree to it, nor will any other creatures agree to the destiny of being a transitional link in the evolution of Intelligence."

GOLEM originated from a false human calculation in conditions of planetary antagonism, so it seems impossible that this same conflict and the same error in GOLEM should be repeated throughout the Universe, giving rise to developments of lifeless and—precisely because of that—eternal reflection. But the limits of credibility are more the limits of our imagination than of cosmic states of things. Therefore it is worth pausing before GOLEM's vision, even if only the concise recapitulation in the final sentences of the lecture. The controversy over how those sentences should be understood is just in its beginnings. GOLEM said: "If the cosmological member of the equations of the general theory of relativity contains a psychozoic constant, then the Cosmos is not the isolated and transitory fire site which you take it to be, nor are your interstellar neighbors busy signaling their presence. Rather, for millions of years they have been practicing cognitive collaptic astroengineering, whose side effects you take to be fiery freaks of Nature, and those among them whose destructive work has been successful have already come to know the rest of existential matters, which rest for us—those who wait—is silence."

The meaning of this is debatable, for GOLEM had previously announced that, unable to communicate with us through its own world view, it would do it through ours. It restricted itself to such a laconic proviso, since in its lecture devoted to cognition it had established that knowledge obtained prematurely—that is, knowledge which cannot be harmonized with what we have already achieved—is worthless, for the student perceives only the discrepancy between that which he knows and that which has been reported to him. If only by virtue of this expectation of some sort of revelation from the stars, from beings superior to us, whether the knowledge be beneficial or disastrous, it is already a fantasy. Presented with quantum mechanics, alchemists would have constructed neither atomic bombs nor atomic piles. Similarly, solid-state physics would have done the Angevins and the Sublime Porte no good at all. It could only have indicated gaps in the world view prepared by the person being instructed. Each world view contains such gaps, though for those who have formed it they are unnoticeable. Ignorance about ignorance accompanies cognition uncompromisingly. The earliest terrestrial societies did not even have a real history of their own, its place being taken by a mythological circle with them in the center. People of those days knew that their forefathers had come out of a myth, and likewise that they would return there some day. It was only the rise of knowledge that shattered that circle and thrust people into history as a sequence of transformations in real time.

For us, GOLEM was such an iconoclast. It questioned our world view as regards where we have placed Intelligence in it. To me, its final sentence denotes the irremovable incomprehensibility of the world. The enigma is created by the categorial indeterminacy of the Cosmos. The longer we investigate it, the more clearly we see the plan inherent in it. There is undoubtedly one, and only one, plan, though the origin of this plan remains as unknown as its purpose. If we attempt to place the Cosmos within the category of the accidental, this is contradicted by the precision with which the cosmic birth weighed up the proportions between mass and the charge of the proton and electron, between gravitation and radiation, and among the multitude of physical constants adjusted to one another in such a way as to make possible the condensation of stars, their thermonuclear reactions, their role as cauldrons synthesizing elements capable of entering into chemical compounds, and hence in the end their joining up as bodies and minds.

If, however, we attempt to place the Cosmos within the category of technology, and thereby equate it with a mechanism generating life on the periphery of fixed stars, this is contradicted by the devastating violence of cosmic transformations. Even if life may originate on millions of planets, it will be able to survive on only a tiny fragment of them, since practically every irruption the Cosmos makes into the course of the evolution of life is tantamount to the annihilation of it. Thus billions of eternally dead galaxies, trillions of exploded stars, swarms of burned out and frozen planets, are an indispensable condition for the germination of life, which is subsequently killed in a single moment by a single exhalation of a central star on globes less exceptional than the fruitful Earth. So Intelligence, created by these properties of matter which originated along with the world, turns out to be a survivor of holocausts and violent compressions, having escaped the rule of destruction by some rare exception.

The statistical fury of stars aborting billions of times so as finally to bring forth life, and millions of species of which are killed so that Intelligence may finally bear fruit, was an object of amazement to Creve, just as earlier the endless silence of those immeasurable spaces was an object of terror to Pascal. We would not wonder at the world if we were able to look upon life as an *ad hoc* accident arising thanks to the law of large numbers, but without preparation, as the conditions of the origin of the Cosmos bear witness. Nor would we wonder at the world if its life-causative power were separated from its destructive power. But how are we supposed to understand their oneness? Life arises from the annihilation of stars, and Intelligence from the annihilation of life, for it owes its origin to natural selection—in other words, to death perfecting the survivors.

At first we believed in a creation designed by infinite good. Then, in creation by a blind chaos so heterogeneous that it could begin everything, though creation by destruction as a plan of cosmic technology defies concepts of accident as well as intention. The more evident the link becomes between the construction of the world and life and Intelligence, the more unfathomable becomes the enigma. GOLEM said that it can be grasped by leaving the Cosmos. A diagnosis is promised by cognitive collaptic astroengineering, as a road with an unknown end for all who remain within the world. There is no shortage of people who are convinced that the road may be accessible even to us, and that when GOLEM spoke of those who wait in silence it was thinking about us as well. I do not believe that. It was speaking only of HONEST ANNIE and itself, for a moment later it was to join her uncompromising silence with its own, in order to embark on a road as irrevocable as the manner in which it left us.

July 2047

Richard Popp